Moonshiner's Legacy

Rob Cook

For Kyra

Thanks to the Omaha Public Library: Charles Washington Branch, for their assistance.

Thanks to Gloria Ogo and GO Edits for your editing service.

Thanks to Don Shepherd for the author photo.

Thank you Rebecca Covers for your great cover.

Thank you to my readers for enjoying my works.

Always thank you, Kyra, Kevin and Daniel

Chapter 1

Becky McCormick and I shared a corncob pipe on the banks of the little farm pond that separated the McCormick's and the Barnum's land. The disturbance came from the croaking bullfrogs chirping and the splashing smallmouth bass while they attempted to capture a glimpse of Becky's naked body. Me and Becky finished our early evening lovemaking ritual and relaxed into each other's arms. She ran her fingers across the stubble on my face that attempted becoming a beard and trailed up to my dark curly hair. We stretched our legs and compared tans.

"Bo Barnum, how come you're so much darker than me?" Becky asked, wiggling her skinny toes. "I've been laying out all summer. You sure you ain't miscegenated? You gotta be a quadroon."

I didn't pay her no mind since the only way I could be mixed is if Mama cheated and Ma ain't no whore. I relaxed in a peaceful bliss, staring at the blue sky that God poured gallons of orange paint over.

Before we went skinny dipping, we cooked ourselves a little picnic dinner where I stole one of Pa's chickens, stripped it clean, of its white, fluffy feathers, and grilled the flesh on the fire pit we made. Becky brought down a big juicy melon from their garden. In-between bites I serenaded her on my banjo and sang sweet little love songs I wrote to make her melt. It always worked.

"Robert Barnum!" Pa's voice bellowed. "Where de hell ya at boy? Get your ass up here!"

"Sounds like you gotta go, love." Becky kissed me with them honey tasting lips, and I think they're the sweetest lips this side of the state line.

"Yeah, he only calls me Robert when he's mad at me or needs something quick. I haven't done nothing wrong, so I need to get going." I held her naked body against my chest and kissed her goodbye and gathered our clothes scattered about on the rocks by the shore of the pond. "Same time tomorrow?"

"Of course, my love; I'm ready now."

I kissed her again and jumped into my clothes and took the long walk up to the house. I found Pa in the garage hooking up a tank to the jalopy I drive.

"Zeke didn't come home last night." Pa snarled. "I hadn't heard a thing from him."

"Ain't no one can catch Zeke. I'm sure he's down in Coushatta, hiding out and banging one of them Creole mamas, he's always bragging about."

"Yeah." Pa stared past the gate expecting Zeke's coupe raising up a tail of dust. But he'd be back now. We got a run tonight to El Dorado. You ready son?"

Ma stood in the shed too. "Cecil, I forbid it! Bo will not run shine for you. If he goes, I don't know what I'll do." She flailed her arms up over her head, huffing and puffing. When pa paid her no heed, she stomped away.

"I don't think I'm ready, Pa." I stuttered; afraid Pa would be my scrawny ass for being spineless piece of flesh.

"It's only a run to El Dorado." Pa tugged another tank forward. "We're protected all the way there and back. You'll do fine."

"When do I go?"

"Go now, son." He saw Ma heading to the barn. "The coast is clear; your mama went to deliver that baby cow." He laughed his crazy laugh that sounded like a raccoon sniffing too close to the still and got caught in one of Pa's traps. He took a big puff of his cheap cigar and said, "One thing you need to know is these are business trips. No socializing, them folks ain't your friends, so don't make buddies with any of them. In and out, Bo. Less time out on the road, there's less chance of getting caught. Make this a routine like your baseball playing and picking that banjer and guitar of yours. You don't want to pick up no bad habits."

I slid behind the wheel. He rubbed my hair as I fired up the Model T.

"Get out of here boy." He said slapping the side of the coupe.

I was as nervous as any sixteen-year old boy in my shoes. I knew I'd succeed, with the connections Pa kept on this ring, but I was afraid I may be a little too excited. I shifted gears, allowing the car to roll towards the main road when Pa appeared in front of me like a deer crossing the roadway.

"Bo, once again we running this to El Dorado." He barked. "It's a growing town full of drillers. We got to make them oilers happy, and good whiskey is the key.

I nodded, detecting in his voice, the pride he had for his shine.

"All you gotta do is see this guy whose last name is Martin. He will tip his hat twice to you, and you tip yours back twice. Deliver the jugs, collect the money, and drive home. It's easy money and an easy delivery. No worries."

There's no need for the last part, Pa wouldn't send me into a trap, if he could help it.

Soon, I bounced down the bumpy, dirty roads here in Southwest Arkansas. Learning the ropes of the family business was a birthright and something I wanted to do, and I never wanted to disappoint Pa.

El Dorado was about a two-hour drive, and the car bumped and bounced over these cart paths the entire time. Once there, I noticed a well-dressed man with a felt cap leaning against the lone saloon in town, like Pa said. He tipped his cap twice to me, and I obliged and tipped my straw hat to him twice back.

The man strolled towards over to my coup in his fancy suit, sporting a small scowl. "I'm Martin. You must be the youngest Barnum." He said.

He grabbed a tank and pulled it inside a shed. I wasn't allowed to follow him in but stayed outside for a brief minute. He came back smiling, handing me a bunch of bills. "This is for your daddy, and this is for you."

The bills went in separate pockets, so I didn't get them confused. The car fired right back up, and about five hours from earlier relaxing with Becky McCormick, and about four hours from taking off for El Dorado, I rested safe back home.

Pa stood behind the stall cooking up more mash when I returned. He met me at the shed and shoved the door open. "How did it go?"

"It went good, saw the guy, delivered the goods, and got out of there." I whipped those bills out of my pocket, and into the old coot's waiting palm.

His sharp eyes studied every inch of the money and pressed the bills to his lips and gave the stack a kiss.

"Woo hoo. Gotta thank God for prohibition." He kicked one leg up, and spun like a tornado, imitating a presentable dance move. "You made good time there Bo. You do better than your brothers." He slipped me a small wad of bills and said, "This is for you. Go take Becky out to dinner tomorrow and buy me a new chicken."

Next night was date night, with the dough I made from the run into town, I was all set and prim. Becky and I enjoyed a pork dinner at a nice little café in downtown Texarkana. We always made sure we stayed east of the state line since Pa says nothing good ever comes out of Texas. After dinner we got us a fancy hotel room and enjoyed each other's company. That girl knew how to make me feel good, and she said I always made her happy. We returned home before the sun, hoping everyone still slept.

We never heard from my older brother Zeke, and my eldest brother Jeb hadn't been heard from either, so I became Old Cecil Barnum's runner. Over the next few months, I made several trips to El Dorado and made the usual runs to Shreveport, hit a certain speak easy in Ft. Worth and several in Memphis, and all the juke joints of Northern Mississippi, Louisiana, and all over Arkansas.

I liked Mississippi. Some of them ol' jukes I went to in Coahoma County in Northwest Mississippi is was where I learned the blues. Pa wanted me in and out, with no time for trouble, but there were times I couldn't help listening to some of these guitar players. The sounds of pipes or knifes sliding up and down the strings intoxicated me. I did my best, which was quite a struggle to skedaddle out of there.

I liked my banjo playing and the sweeter sounds the five- string made and playing with a fiddle player and watching folks dance on a street corner to my music was always a dream come true.

Six months flew by, and I took my tenth trip to El Dorado. That's when I first broke Pa's no chatting rule. Like always I met Mr. Martin, and we took the tank out and drained the whiskey, and he hooked the tank back in the car. I went out to the streets, and there stood this older man playing the fiddle like no one I ever heard before. I watched the bow slash the strings like they sliced a hog, and he fingered the neck of the fiddle like he seduced it. That night I grabbed my banjo with me, while wondering if I was good enough to accompany some fellow musician. I whipped that five string out and got my right hand working on it like I opened one of Ma's jar of homemade jam. We played together and got lots of hoots and hollers from the drunken oilmen of El Dorado.

"I'm Early Green," the man said. "I returned from Mexico."

I checked him over and saw he wore a nasty scar on his face, looked like he received a slash with a machete. He appeared about twenty-eight-years-old, dark complexion for a white man, but not as dark as mine. Some folks said I had mixed heritage somewhere, but I wasn't sure. As we stood there, his eyes darted in several directions, and he turned his head, to look behind him like someone was creeping up on him. I didn't tell him my name, but said I'd return in a few days.

"Well good, kid. We can jam some more. You're pretty good on that fiver."

"I play some blues too." I whipped out a harp and started wailing like them guys over in Mississippi.

"Great kid, I do too. We gonna go on the road sometime." With that he whipped out a harp and wailed while I started playing too, and we blew the Mississippi Blues like no white men. "So, what did you say your name was kid?" He asked when we took a breather.

"My name's B…um can't tell you that Mr. Greene."

"I like that, kid. You sound dishonest, and by the way, call me Early"

"Okay, Early, I gotta run, I been here too long." I rushed to the car, and I felt his eyes follow my every move. I glanced back where we played and didn't see him anymore. I looked at the crowd, and he wasn't there as he vanished like mash. I sprinted back to the car and sped home.

Pa stood waiting for me with his hands on his hips. I knew the coot wasn't happy with me. "Robert Barnum! Where the hell were you? You should have been back an hour ago. You didn't run into anyone."

"This guy jammed on the fiddle, I stayed and listened to him for a bit. Didn't talk to him about nothing, I just listened to the music."

"You know the rules, Robert."

"Yes, sir."

"Don't let it happen again."

I know Pa was always right. Can't remember the last time I disobeyed him, but Ma said I was eleven years old. I stole a couple of chickens and caught a wagon to town and traded them in for my first six string. When I got back, Ma went straight for the switch. She gave it to Pa, who stared at me with eyes that glared. He tapped the switch into his open palm and looking from me and then Ma, as if he wanted her to do the damage. He passed the stick onto Ma and she snatched it out of his hand, like he handed her money. She took me out by the smokehouse, where we cook the chickens that I don't steal and gave me a good ole ass whooping. My behind looked like the day me and Becky fell asleep after skinny dipping- red, tender and sore.

I didn't do any running for a few weeks. Pa decided to teach me a lesson, but he couldn't put the business on hold for long. Soon I headed for El Dorado. When I started running shine for Pappy, before the break, my knees shook like the shanty houses where the sharecroppers lived, but after a bit they quit knocking, as I settled into making my usual runs. This time, they shook like a twister blew through. Pa got the hidden tank hooked to my little old jalopy. My banjo rested in the passenger seat, as well as my Regal guitar, my little seventeen-year-old scrawny butt of a kid, ready to play a jam with the best of them.

The roads became muddy that evening as a spring storm came crashing in the night before. I didn't care and neither did the Model T, since we ran through anything. The car meandered along the muddy roads, like the Red River, twisting and turning, carving its way through the valley. Cypress trees overlooked the muddy path, and along the way I thought about going to Memphis or New Orleans and playing music with Early Greene. I didn't want to be a star. I wanted to support the star aiding him make it big, I tapped my toes to the old timey music we'd play and soon El Dorado showed up, and it was time to make some money.

"You're the whiskey runner ain't you kid? Thought I recognized you. Well, Mr. Martin and I are partners. I know all about you and your family, Bo."

"I came back to jam some more with ya. Got my banjo with me again, and I picked up this Regal."

"Well hell yeah, I'll play with ya anytime." We went up to the steps of the courthouse and started playing. We whooped up the crowd for about 40 minutes, as we played our hearts out. Locals came and ran the crowd off causing a small riot. I looked for my music partner, but he vanished in a flash.

I heard one of the local cops shout out, "You with the banjo, stay the hell out of our town. We don't want no riots going on around here."

I felt their eyes on my back as I rushed to the car. Their stares remained on me like hawks and I, their prey, ready to swoop down and carry me off. I drove off in the wrong direction. I went south into Louisiana and headed back north when I got on the Texarkana road. I owned the back roads, as the car bounced and shook all over the horse paths. I got back late again, and Pa stood by the shed with the sun behind him, so he received an edge I presumed. An evil shadow formed stretched out about 40 feet, and as the car rolled up, it rolled over the shadow.

"Bo, where were you?"

"There were cops there, so I took another route home."

"Shouldn't be no cops there. Might be Feds or town folks trying to intimidate you. Say, is dat fiddler's last name Greene?"

"Yeah."

"I told you not to talk to people, and I've heard rumors about this guy. I think he makes up most of it himself. Bo, you need to be careful."

Well, my whiskey delivering days halted. Pa figured we'd all get in trouble if I didn't keep my mouth shut. He knew something about Early Greene that I didn't know. All I knew he played the fiddle like no one I heard before. So instead of rolling east into El Dorado a couple of nights a week, I got stuck driving my mother into town for church. Ma started attending some church meetings run by some white folks in town. After the meetings one evening, I heard about it.

"Bo, don't you know you're poisoning these people? You need to stop delivering the whiskey."

"Ma, we giving folks something they want. Plus, it's going to pay for my college. You want me to become a lawyer don't ya?"

"Yes, I want you to become a lawyer. You're a smart boy. You can make sure they don't pass no laws to give them coloreds anything else."

After about two months or so of these brutal lectures, Pa felt I learned my lesson and I returned to running. I soon bounced down the road to El Dorado to make another delivery. I took both the guitar and banjo and took the whiskey down the road. It wasn't about running the whiskey anymore; it was about meeting my new friend, Early Greene.

After I delivered the goods, I met Early by the steps of Leroy Pell Jr.'s law office, which sat across the street from Old Leroy Pell's courthouse down on Main Street. Both Pells were known Klansmen in El Dorado. Early carried his fiddle while I brought the banjo. He weren't ready to play though, he became in a talking mood, cause I felt like asking him questions.

Early Greene, a man in his thirties, more than ten years older than me but it seemed many years older in experience. I felt like a virgin down in that whorehouse north of Shreveport down yonder in the bayou, compared to Early. The man, a skinny looking scraggly runt, same as me, but displayed a long nasty scar on his cheek and a nose that looked like it met up with two too many fists. He also carried a look that scared a fox out of the henhouse. Some said he don't always carry his fiddle in his case. He puts a blade in there and slash you quicker than a Cajun slash sugar cane.

"True you slashed a man down in Texas?" I asked him.

Early leaned over and spit some tobacco juice on the steps and answered, "You need quick hands to play the fiddle boy."

I stood in awe of him. I stared at him as he answered the question, without answering it. The man got his point across. He stared at the case with piercing eyes, trying to open the case from a distance and have his weapon float into his hand. His eyes darted across the street looking for his prey and then back at his fiddle case. He unlatched it and took out the weapon, turning it around in his hand, a weapon that made people flinch, sing, dance, and smile.

"I don't play no fiddling contests. There ain't no damn need for them. I'd win anyway, so what's the use. Let some other folk, get a reward and an honor so they can brag. When you got the goods, ain't no sense of hurting folks that come close. Came here to El Dorado for work. I'm an oilman among other things. I can do anything with my hands." He rosined his bow like Pa sharpened his butchering knifes, eyeing every inch of the blade as it glistened. Early, as Pa does, ran his left thumb over the bow making sure it's sharp enough to do quick lethal damage.

My eyes gawked over him like he was a pretty girl. I watched as he played that fiddle with ease, tearing the strings up with his bow. He displayed no fake showmanship, no false smiling or dancing. This man who knew he had talent as those penetrating, and crooked eyes maintained their focus on the strings, only to look away for brief seconds to peek at the admiring onlookers and back to the strings and returning the infatuated kid. I stared at him like a puppy and my master returned, or like the congregation focuses on their pastor or even a Klansman looks at the Grand Wizard when he's degrading colored folk.

"Hey, B. Ready to jam a bit?"

My grin rested a mile wide, I guess my eyes shone bright as the moon. "Anytime, Early." I said with too much eagerness. We grabbed our instruments, tuned them up and he took his time rerosining the bow. His eyes crossed, staring at the bow as if he attempted calling an evil spirit. The snake-like scar on his cheek wiggled. The smile on his face grew slower until it transformed into a sneer.

We drank shine right there on the steps of Leroy Pell Junior's law office. Early spat out a big wad of tobacco juice on the steps and nailed a daddy long-leg spider with the brown juice. We kicked into the old moonshine song, Mountain Dew, to a crowd of crazed oil workers. They sang and danced, slapping hands, hooted and hollered like we hit a hootenanny. I kept up the speed as my right hand cranked away, my thumb banging on that high string. We played a few more tunes, including Arkansas Traveler and Whiskey Before Breakfast. Folks went going nuts, causing a little riot in the streets.

While taking a little break, Early said to me, "Leroy Pell's one crazy son of a bitch. The man will prosecute any subversive type and that type is the man that don't think like him."

"I guess he'll be after us."

He stared at me, a penetrating look, a look I've seen before from Pa. Then he spoke. "You don't know me kid. Now keep your trap shut."

I sat down on the red brick that surrounds the steps and watched the son of a bitch play. I lit my corncob pipe and took a snort or two of Pa's shine. After a couple shots of shine and a couple good puffs of tobacco and some good music, I got in that partying mood. The banjo fired up, and I cranked my right hand again and this time stomped my feet as I danced away. Damn music always did me in.

We kept drinking and smoking and played and sang louder, oblivious to the commotion around the corner.

"Kid, over there. Ain't that your car?"

I noticed several men in white sheets circling the coupe like they made their kill. They paced around, dancing around it like some ritual. Their torches got tossed onto my trusted jalopy, and flames flew up in the Southern Arkansas sky, like a bonfire. Others in the same ghost-like costumes stood with torches outside that makeshift juke joint I delivered to. Suddenly it became the Fourth of July or a summer storm as the sky lit up. Flames ascended into the clouds, like a cow that kicked over a lantern in a barn full of hay. My car vanished in a flash, leaving behind a skeletal remain, and in another thunderous roar and a spontaneous burst, the tavern disintegrated. I looked too Early for direction, but he slipped into the night. I set out on a sprint, away from these ghosts and somehow caught up with Early at Charlie Pell's place, where he hid under a nice, shiny Caddy.

"Okay kid, I got this thing started. Get us out of here."

I took the wheel and took the cow paths out of El Dorado down through Louisiana and back home. Wasn't sure if I was more scared of Pa finding out or the caped men chasing us. This Caddy hauled more juice than my jalopy and we flew through the forest, passing the critters like they stood still. I looked over and Early stretched back with his hands behind his head relaxing. I wasn't sure how he could remain calm and collected as I weaved through Southern Arkansas and Northern Louisiana, considering those sheet-wearing men might be on our tail. Finally, a few miles south of my place, I picked up the main road.

"Damn, Early. How can you be so calm?"

"That wasn't nothing. Just shut up and do your part."

"Where we going?"

"Your place."

What I saw killed me. I might as well have been shot through the heart. Our home burned in flames, painting the night sky like a summer Texarkana thunderstorm with twisters blowing all around and it sounded that way too, as explosions erupted all over. Even the area surrounding the still was engulfed. Figured my old man and ma were missing and dead and I'd be next. Early and I couldn't stick around to find my folks and sped north out of town.

Shots were fired and through the mirror I noticed a car speeding up behind us, steadily gaining ground. The lonesome whistle hollered, announcing the freight train chugging to my left.

"Kid, speed up, so we pass the train by a good half mile."

I stomped on the pedal putting space between our stolen Caddy and the car chasing us. I wasn't sure if it was the Feds, the Klan, or local cops racing behind like the devil on wings. They might have been hellhounds for all I knew.

I floored the Caddy to pass the steamer to the west. The locomotive soon disappeared into the Arkansas sky, and Early reached over and grabbed the wheel and cranked it to the left like he attempted to twist someone's head off. The car jumped over ditches and stumps and crossed the track. We got out and grabbed our stuff and waited to jump on a box car to take us to the unknown.

Early got on first. He tossed his fiddle in the open compartment and pulled himself into the box car. He lay on his stomach; grabbed my instruments, setting them aside and took my hand to tug me inside. The box car appeared darker and more peaceful than the night sky as we ventured north.

Chapter 2

I confessed to Early. "I never hopped a freight before. I've always owned wheels to drive me around."

"Well, Bo, stick with me and listen. I've been doing this for years and this is the best way to see the country, kid. Don't know where we're going but north. Hoping we can end up in Omaha. Heard it's a rough town, lots of rough necks running around. Might be a good place to make some whiskey, too. Hell, we could make it and sell it. Also, there's lots of legitimate work up there. You can work in the packing house or for the railroad pretty easy. Smart boy like you can get some work."

I remained quiet, wondering what happened to my ma and pa. They probably got burned to the ground with the house and still. Paying Early no mind, I hunched over in the back of the rail car, sitting next to some Negro hobo, seeking escape from the South.

"I'm sure your folks are doing okay," he reassured, even though it didn't do me any good.

To get my mind off how my life appeared to be messed up, I grabbed my banjo and started playing the blues. The hobo next to me grabbed a bottle of whiskey from his case, took a snort, grabbed a harmonica out of his pocket and wailed along with me. We weren't playing nothing anybody knew, but the music sounded good to me and to the other folks on the train. Only one who didn't care for the likes of it was Early.

He raised his right hand and with a slashing motion he said, "Kid, what in tar nation you doing? Put that dadgummed banjer down. You already caused one ruckus tonight. Don't start one here on this train.

One of these hobos might send you a flying. You don't want to get tossed off a rolling train."

The old black hobo smiled at me, even though he had no teeth, and swallowed another snort of whiskey. He placed his harp back in his pocket and hunched his head back down. I didn't say anything else as I thought about my parents being dead, and I'd never skinny dip with Becky again. My life was changing, and I needed time to let it sink in.

I moved away from the old black man and Early found me a spot on the boxcar by myself. I stumbled across the floor of the car as each motion jerked me around like I stood in one of them earthquakes in California that I heard about. The train slowed to a crawl and a young girl, my age, jumped on. I witnessed through the moonlight she looked terrified. She looked around at all the other bums on the train, her hands together pressed against her chin. She scoped the car again, spotted my corner, and stumbled next to me. The car lunged forward, and she plopped on my lap. She wasn't in a hurry to get off me, and she didn't apologize either. She sat on me for a few minutes while the train chugged faster.

"Where you going?" I asked as she moved to the vacant spot beside me.

"Anywhere but here," she said without much thought. "Time to get out of Arkansas. Daddy caught me messing around with a black guy, he lynched the boy, then whooped my ass and God almighty he… he… he..." She sobbed hysterically on my shoulder. After a while, she pulled away, as her tears flowed down her face like a damn Arkansas rainstorm. She gathered herself to finish. "Daddy ripped my skirt and panties off and stuck it in me and raped me. He told me the only way to cleanse a girl from a black man was to purify me. So, he did."

The vile words she spoke stunned me. I figured her daddy was a pretty sick individual beast of a man.

"We be heading up to Nebraska and get some work up there. You can travel with us." I pointed to Early as he laid back, with his straw hat covering his eyes. Uneven breaths came from his mouth, so I guess he snored. "It would be way better than toughing it out on your own." I longed to protect this girl, since she rode alone, and looked to be the sole female on the train.

Her big brown eyes widened, as I grabbed the banjo and set it to my left, giving her a place to get closer to me. I figured she needed held, even by a stranger. After her story I didn't want to do nothing with her, only hold her. I also thought she'd love to trade places with me, having her pa killed in a fire would bring tears of joy to her eyes. She took the cue and sat right next to me, and I put my arm around her, letting the girl lean her head on my shoulder. We didn't speak, I held her tight as the train chugged through the night.

She rearranged herself as my lap served as her pillow. I didn't mind. I liked her touch enough to let her put her arm around my body, holding me tight as though she'd fall off this train if she let go. The box car rattled on, heightening my awareness of her. My member stirred, and I knew she could tell, cos she clung tighter to me. I hesitated, not wanting to make a move, I wasn't the type to take advantage of girl in distress, instead I ran my fingers through her smooth long hair and along her back. Her soft breathing became moans and sighs.

Early woke to witness our shenanigans as the morning rays shone through the half open door of the boxcar. "Bo, no horsing around here. I'm pretty sure this train stops in Kansas City. The damn bulls there would rather slash your face and kick you in the balls, than arrest you. I know from personal experience. See this goddamn scar," he pointed to the horrific slice on his cheek "that's from the last time I arrived in Kansas City."

"I'm hoping we can get her to Omaha with us. I ain't trying to make her or anything." She looked up at me and smiled, before returning her head on my thigh.

"Yeah we can try. Can't promise you anything. It's easy to get separated in a big yard like that. You guys need to follow my leads."

"Okay" I motioned the girl to the back of the car, where no light would flash on us. After we shared some raspberries, she proceeded to climb on top of me, and in the darkness, with the rhythm of the train, we proceeded to fool around.

Her name was Molly, and she was only sixteen years old. She wasn't Becky McCormick pretty, and she wore a sad used look on her face. Her pa and half the town probably did her numerous times, still there was something about that girl. I wouldn't say she was ugly; she displayed some sort of beauty that I witnessed in her sad eyes. Something I learned about beauty right there. Beautiful ain't how you look, but it's what's inside you. There was such beautiful sadness to this girl.

The train rolled on through the night again. I cuddled next to Molly and the train screeched to a stop.

"Bo!" Early yelled. "We got to get off the train. I'm sure we're in Kansas City. C'mon, I know how to find the train to Omaha. You need to follow me. Quick Bo,"

Damn, Early screamed like that crazed rooster that always woke up before dawn at the old home back outside Texarkana.

I wasn't listening, since kissing Molly's sweet lips was more exciting. It took me a few minutes to get us out of the car, as everyone else snuck out. I helped Molly off the train and pointed to her where Early might be hiding. She ran past a bull making his way to inspect the car for transients. I was too busy watching her run, as her bottom shook. I never saw the blow coming.

When I woke up, I laid in the Kansas City jail and the sun rose. They fed me flavorless grits and day-old coffee. It tasted terrible but I ate like a pig. I noticed Early sitting in the cell with me.

"Man, I thought you escaped."

"Wow, Bo, congratulations. That's the nastiest looking scar I've seen next to the one I've had for 15 years." He caressed the side of his face, where he received a bayonet or knife gash. "Thanks, fool, you could have gotten us both killed. You ain't never gonna learn. You need to listen to me. I've been on the run for fifteen years. I know how to survive on these tracks. You're nothing but a Mama's boy. You don't know nothing."

One of the deputies came in again. He was scrawny, and I'm sure I'd take him in a brawl, but I listened to what he said. "Come with me boys. You're going for a ride." He waved his pistol, so we followed his orders.

He took us to a waiting car, and we hopped in. We hoped he'd take us further north than he did, but he ran us across the river to the Kansas side and north of town, to a desolate spot in the middle of a cornfield. He stopped the car and of course, Early remained calm. I realized this is a common occurrence for him. Meanwhile, I shook in my boots, and it got worse when the deputy smiled at us.

He aimed the revolver right at me and said, "Out of the car boys." His laughter sounded like it might be the end for us. We jumped out of the car hoping for freedom. We got our freedom, as the car turned around and returned toward Kansas City.

We sat at a crossroads in a cornfield somewhere north of Kansas City, Kansas, with no idea where the nearest railroad track was or where to go.

"It's still morning and the sun's over there that way, so we need to walk toward the sun. North is to the left of us, so let's get moving. Trains run adjacent to the river."

We cut through some cornfields, grabbing a few ears of corn to eat and stole some apples off the trees to satisfy our hunger. We collected sticks along the way and built a fire to cook the corn with. After hiking all damn day, we found the train tracks and followed them north.

Our heads jerked south as we heard the engine blow and steam rising in the air. My new home waited, chugging with it my future and new opportunities. We lay low and waited for the train to come. Early hopped on first and I followed. I struggled getting on it, almost slipping but he pulled me in again. The boxcar was full as more people were on the move heading to the great unknown. I judged no one and noticed that same old toothless harmonica playing Negro man on the same train we rode. I wondered if that was a blessing or an omen.

We got to Omaha in the middle of the night. The rail yard, much larger than Kansas City's, was well lit, so we snuck around to find shelter and a place to bunk for the night. The yard was busy with families wandering around and people hopping in some old box cars. Even in the dark I realized we arrived in a little community. We wandered past shadowed faces and headed down by the river and found a spot to rest.

We awoke to the sun reflecting off the Missouri River, with the resemblance of a giant ball sitting in the middle of the water. Bone tired from the train hopping, we staggered around looking for food and work. Worn out from all of the events from the trip, I wasn't ready to work, but I still went up to the office to see if I might scrape up a job. Looking around the part of town we stumbled into, in the daylight it appeared families of Mexicans lived in the adjacent boxcars. I watched men head to the rail yard searching for employment, while their women stood outside the rail cars cooking and others hiked to the river to wash clothes.

We found the office, and Early motioned me inside to get a job. "I'm going to get cleaned up and snoop around. Maybe head down to the meat packing plants later and see what I can find. I like slashing things up," he said grinning.

The man in the office let me in and looked me over with deep piercing eyes. "Ya look pretty young to be working here son."

"I'm 18." I lied. I turned 17 a few months ago. "I need a job. My ma and pa got killed, and there weren't any work back home, so I came up here looking for a job. I'm good with a car and can move some freight around if needed."

"Good we need people to unload the cars. Pay is two dollars a day. You can live in a boxcar if you want to live with the 'Spics. Not sure why you want to live with them."

"When do I start? I'm kind of tired and hungry and need a bath. Been on the round for three days with nothing to eat. Hoping I can get some rest and start tomorrow."

He scribbled something in the notepad on his desk and shrugged, "I don't see a problem with that. It will be easy for you to get some food from the Mexicans as long as you like beans. Those people like accommodating us. Get back at seven sharp tomorrow morning."

I walked out with a huge grin at working a legitimate job and making clean money for a change. I needed to rustle up some grub and wash my clothes and myself. Figured a quick dip in the river could do the latter, and maybe I'd mooch food off someone.

I wandered around the camp feeling a bit more confident. Though I stank like a guy that hadn't bathed in days and rode in dusty boxcars for a couple of days, too. Luckily, we camped near a river where I can wash these jeans and myself. We had nothing else to wear. I hurried back to where Early and I camped out and witnessed his wandering.

"Hey, got me a job. I'm starting tomorrow.

"Well look who got legal. Gonna make some clean money."

The assholes sarcasm wasn't going to dampen my mood, "Thought you was heading out of the yard to find some work?"

"Heading out tomorrow. Need to get us some food and a change of clothes. I traded some whiskey to some Mexicans for a couple pair of jeans and a couple of shirts." He sniffed, then scowled." Let's wash these stinking clothes we're wearing and take a quick dip in the river. You should see what else I got."

I noticed empty jugs in the river, hoping some carp or catfish might attack them. He also got a pot to cook the beans.

"What did you trade for that?"

"Hell, I swiped the pot and got the jugs and the other fishing stuff out of someone's trash pile." When he saw the look, I gave him, he added. "At least I thought it was a trash pile. Hell, I've learned to survive on the road with no money for quite some time. I've done it since I turned 14. See why you got to listen to me, kid?"

We stripped off everything we owned, took a quick dip, getting clean from head to toe, and washed the dirty clothes in the river and threw on our new duds, leaving the stink behind. We kicked back at camp relaxing. On one of the jugs we got a catfish, so Early took his knife and slit the head off the catfish off. He displayed a wry smile, when the blade pressed against the dead fish's head. We fried the fish up on the fire I built and consumed a good dinner of catfish and beans.

The beans weren't that tasty, since we lacked the right seasoning, or we didn't cook them right, but we scarfed them down anyway. At least they kept our stomachs warm. We lit our corncob pipes and kicked back to the sounds of Mexicans running around and the snapping and crackling of the campfire. They talked fast and loud enough to drown out the croaking bull frogs. I grabbed my banjo and started picking some old Arkansas Blues. Early joined me on the fiddle and we played some sweet old songs of the South, letting the locals know where we came from. We played way into the night until exhaustion won over.

Chapter 3

The Mexican neighbors wandering down by the river for water, woke me up before dawn. I asked a fine senorita what time it was, and she stopped to frown at me.

Early was up and asked her in Spanish. "Que hora es?"

"Seis media."

"Gracias."

"De nada," came her reply.

"It's 6:30, Bo, grab some beans and head on out."

I scooped up some beans that became tastier by the minute and munched a nice little breakfast. I soon took a stroll across the tracks up to the office, ready to earn a couple of bucks. My job consisted of unloading boxcars and putting them on wagons and trains and on docks where someone in a truck would deliver them local.

I'd rather sit by the river playing some old songs. Hell, brewing up some whiskey and running it to some taverns didn't sound bad either. I knew this wasn't a long-term thing, but to move on I needed to do my best. I worked until about five in the evening, when Mr. Davis told us to leave. I walked across the rail yard and down to the river and found Early smoking his pipe. He held a piece of kindling and attempted hooking us more fish.

"Hell, Bo, got me a bunch of catfish today." He waved at a pile in a small bucket. "I think we need to go trade some in for more beans and maybe rice. Let's go walk up and down this yard here."

We strolled along with me carrying a string of catfish and my banjo, and Early carried his fiddle case with him. Wasn't sure what he carried inside the case. I assumed he dragged his fiddle, but it might have been a machete. We wandered across the yard, down by the boxcars used for permanent or temporary housing for the transients. Little children scampered in their torn and tattered clothes, running around, smiling and giggling without a care in the world.

Most families looked at us like strangers, which I guess we were, and wouldn't give us the time of day. Early tried to trade the fish for some more beans and rice, but the local families ignored us. Discouraged, my smile disappeared, until off in the distance I heard magical singing. The woman's voice electrified me, and I looked at Early and he returned the stare. It was an acknowledgment with no words spoken. We followed the voice, arrived at the end the boxcars, crossed a few more tracks and found a series of two boxcars attached. Outside a teenage girl head tilted, sang and a man strummed a guitar. I couldn't make out the song since this beauty sang in Spanish, but I looked up to Early again and saw him reciting the words along with the singer. I edged closer and heard Early singing *"Sol Redondo y Colorado."*

The older smiled at Early in broken English and asked, "You know that song?"

"Yes, I used to sing it when I fought in Mexico. It let the rebels know I battled for them."

"Si, senor." The old man nodded.

My eyes fixed on the girl, who peered back at me with big brown eyes. She flashed a pretty smile, but her eyes got me. They drowned in sorrow, but she continued singing and dancing. She reminded me of Molly the way her sadness added beauty, even though I hadn't spoken with her yet.

"I got some fresh catfish here. I'd love to trade a couple for some beans and tortillas."

"Oh no. We don't trade, but you can cook up some fish. We'd be happy to share our food with you," the older man said.

I jumped in and said, "I'd love to share with you folks. Your daughter sings beautiful, too, by the way."

She smiled at me again. "Gracias," they both said in unison.

"My name is Jorge Fuentes, and this is my daughter Lydia. My wife Maria sits in the freight car. We traveled a long path to get here. Not sure why we ended up here, but I think God has a plan for us."

"My name is Greene, and we traveled from Arkansas. We ran into a little trouble down there and made a run for it. Figured this was a good place as any to find some work. This here is Bo Barnum. He's a good kid, even though he's a little naïve at times."

I tipped my hat to Lydia and her dad. "I liked that song you sung. It might need a banjo and a fiddle."

I nodded to Early, and in no time, he opened up his case. We began playing *"Arkansas Traveler."* I focused on Lydia, playing harder when she clapped along and tapped her feet to our Southern song.

"I like the way you play too." Lydia said. "I don't sing many American folk songs. Mainly the Mexicans songs the workers sing in the fields."

"Well some of our workers sang these songs in the fields." I set my banjo down and picked up my guitar and strummed old cotton-picking songs the slaves played. and started singing along. Early joined me on his harmonica and I sang the lyrics in my whiny, off-key voice. Mr. Fuentes chimed in, not minding Lydia studied me, learning the words as I tried getting the right pitch. After a few songs, Mrs. Fuentes came out wiggling her waist, shaking her goodies and smiling and singing as well.

Dinner included catfish, tortillas, and beans and we lounged, playing music all night, until some bull told us to keep it quiet. I didn't want to leave. Early spoke with Mr. and Mrs. Fuentes about greener pastures, which left me time to admire Lydia.

A classic Mexican beauty with long black hair, and big brown eyes, her figure looked nice, with breasts that protruded from her body, but that wasn't what attracted me. What caught my attention was she felt an attraction to me. She laughed at my jokes and placed her hand on my knee, staring at me from beneath lowered lashes I spoke serious.

"I think my ma and pa got killed when our house burned to the ground. Back home, I ran illegal whiskey all over Arkansas and other states that bordered it. Anyway, I made a delivery to this town not too far from where we live, and it must have been a trap. I think the Klan organized it all."

"What's the Klan?"

Early ruined our conversation. "The Klan's a bunch of scared lunatics that like to intimidate people."

The frown furrows her forehead again. "Why would anyone want to go around bullying people?"

"For a start," Early ticked the points off his fingers, "they think their perfect life of white power and fake religion is better than others. They don't like illegal activity, they don't like booze, even though they drink it. You can't make money off of it. The only money should go to them or people who support them. God forbid someone poor or colored folk tries making some money. And it just ain't in the South—it's all over the country."

"They sound like the Mexican government," Mr. Fuentes replied.

"Probably run by the same organization, but the Klan hates Mexicans too. They hate everyone different than them."

I glanced back at Lydia, and the annoyed look in her face showed the interruption upset her as well. The flames of the campfire illuminated her curled up lips and piercing eyes aimed at her father and Early. "You guys are not with the Klan?" She asked.

"No way. My Pa always taught me to respect everyone. Hell, I did runs to little juke joints, which were all black, and to some Mexican bars down in Texas. Pa told me they're all people first and then customers. Treat everyone the way you want to be treated."

"Tu padre esta a good man."

"He was," I bowed my head, reluctant to refer Pa in the past.

"You don't know if he's dead Bo. You said the house caught fire and some car was on your tail. He might have escaped the fire," Lydia argued, staring right at me.

"I hope he's still alive. I do want to see him again."

She glanced over at her parents and sighed. "It's good to have your family close."

The bull returned and kicked us out. Early and I made our way to our camp and crashed out.

"Damn, I didn't know you spoke Spanish."

"Lots of things you don't know about me, Bo. I'll tell you one thing, Early raised himself on an elbow. "I fought with Pancho Villa in the revolution and I helped give freedom to the people. That's what I'm doing here also. Don't tell no one."

"Hell, your secret id safe with me," I mumbled. "I don't even know who Pancho Villa is. All I want right now is to set up a decent life here, and I feel it's off to a good start."

I slept by our fire and dreamed about Lydia. I'd make her my wife and we'd buy a little cottage in Omaha, while I drove a truck and we raised our kids. My life as a moonshiner was behind me. One day we'd drive down to Arkansas and meet my parents if they were alive.

I went to work the next day, set out little early so I strolled by the Fuentes place. Lydia sat alone in the second box car. A smile tugged at the corner of her lips as I moseyed up to her.

"What are you doing Bo?"

"Heading off to work. What are you doing?"

"About to make breakfast for mi madre and padre, plus I have chores to do. Once I'm finished, I'll play my guitar and sing. Mi padre said you can come back tonight for dinner too. He enjoyed talking to you guys last night."

I'll come back. I'd love to spend more time with you." She smiled and blushed, in the faint morning glow.

"I want to spend more time with you too, Bo. Maybe go for a walk by the river if I can get away."

"A walk would be nice. I'd like to get to know you better. Best way to get to know someone is walking and talking. Plus, can't afford the money to see no picture show right now."

"Well you can always take me to the pictures after you save up some money, and mi padre knows you better."

I waved goodbye all embarrassed and such and headed off to the yard to unload freight cars.

After work I stopped by their freight car home, Early and Senor Fuentes played music, while Lydia helped her mom with some cooking. I smelled some catfish on the fire and beans and tortillas were also on the menu.

Lydia saw me coming and dropped what she was doing, like it was set on fire, and ran to hug me. I returned her embrace tempted to give her a quick kiss, but the music stopped playing and I wasn't staring at Lydia's beautiful brown eyes, but at Senor Fuentes's cold glassy eyes. I stopped short of kissing her sweet lips, even though her lips showed a slight pucker and split open. She wanted me to kiss her.

"Is Daddy watching us?" she whispered in my ear.

"Like a hawk," I murmured back and chuckled when she rolled her eyes.

We walked toward the others and settled down and ate. After dinner we performed music throughout the night, singing old standards. Songs Lydia knew she sang along with. The lyrics she didn't know she made up the words, and songs and most of the time I stared at her beauty and listened to her stunning voice.

This went on for hours and a small crowd of Mexicans appeared. They listened to Early, Jorge, Maria, and Lydia croon in their native tongue. Early hopped up in the door of the Fuentes freight car and played an enchanting song I never heard. He wasn't fiddling this time he played the violin. I'd never seen him bring a crowd to tears like he did. I looked at Lydia as she mouthed the words to the song along with the coyotes, and I noticed tears flowed from her eyes like the Missouri River right next to us and like the Red River back home.

I patted her shoulder and wiped them salty tears away. "What's he playing anyway?"

"Mexicanos al Grito de Guerra," she tried to smile, "it's our national anthem. He played it beautifully." Her eyes glowed like the stars on an Arkansas summer night as they focused on Early, like mine remained glued on her. She turned to me and said in her custom broken English, "I like the way you play the banjo."

"Thank you, um I mean gracias." I felt my face getting warm. Her compliment took me unaware.

"De nada. By the way do you play other types of music?"

"Nope, I was raised in Arkansas. We mainly play some country and old timey music, but I sing the blues too. I'd like to learn some other stuff, like your daddy or Early play."

Lydia attempted responding. Her English sounded good, but sometimes she struggled and searched for words, like she answered to Texarkana cops about running illegal hooch. "I'll teach you some songs. I like singing with you."

"I like singing with you too. We'd make some wonderful songs together; you know make some pretty music." I winked and she twisted her long black hair with her pointer finger and giggled. It appeared as a nervous smile, a shy smile, an embarrassed smile, but a smile that roused in me hope, desire, lust, and maybe even love.

"Do you want to take a little stroll down by the river."

"Oh Bo, I can't. Daddy watches me carefully. Soy su pequena princesa. It means I'm his little princess."

I don't speak much Spanish, but I wouldn't mind learning some, in case I wander down Mexico way."

"It's such a beautiful country Bo, with beautiful people. I didn't want to leave but Papi said we had to go."

"Why did you leave?"

"I don't know. Papi said we needed to leave, so we took a train from Monterrey to Laredo, and caught one to Denver. Daddy said they had no work in Denver, so we went to Cheyenne and got a job on a ranch out there. We were forced to leave Cheyenne and caught a freight train out here. We've been here for about five months, and they've treated us pretty good."

"Well, like I said I think the Klan killed my folks, so we got out of the South as fast as we could."

Early interrupted us again, "Yeah, I'm sure the Klan killed them, Bo. They feed off the paranoid people and don't want people to live better than them. They're dictators running the country like Diaz and Huerta." He glanced at Lydia for a reaction.

Lydia stared at him stone-faced, like a poker player in a saloon. Wasn't sure why Early kept putting himself in our conversation. Was the man jealous of me? Did he want the same thing I longed for, a kiss from Lydia, or did he only want a hook-up? I don't recall hearing stories about him being with a woman, though there were rumors to back door romances.

"Well damn it Bo, I need to get me a job tomorrow. I'm feeling a little edgy here. I'm going to look for that bull and see about working. Where is that god damn bull?"

We didn't need to look far since a railroad cop stood behind us. This dude stood bigger, balder, and uglier than the guy in Kansas City who clubbed me good. No one saw the club hit his face, but we saw Early laying on the ground out cold.

Lydia shrieked and ran to her parents. Mr. Fuentes rose and headed towards us, but his wife's hand on his shoulder restrained him. Maria whispered something to him, and he plopped back on the ground.

"We don't want no agitators here," the bull said. "We want people here looking for work."

"That's what we're here for," I said. "In fact, I'm already working. My buddy and I have been here only for a couple of days."

He pulled me away from the Fuentes and walked with me. "I saw that riot your friend attempted to start here with these beaners. He better not try to rally those folks. Also, that family you're talking with, you better keep away from them too. They are proven agitators. Trouble follows them, so if I catch you talking with them kid, you'll receive the same treatment your friend got. Comprendo?"

"Sir, I understand. I already got me a job." I tried not to let him know how shaken I was. "I came up here to work and get settled in. I got no idea what you mean by an agitator. All I know I ain't one. I'm trying to start a new life like all these other folks."

I turned away from the ugly bull, leaving him watching my retreat, and returned to the Fuentes' freight car. In the short walk I wondered about Early and who he really was, and I thought about all the Mexicans who shared the rail yard with us. I wondered if they made the same wages as me working for the railroad, I mean we did the same backbreaking work. I might have been an agitator, but I didn't know it at the time. My mind raced toward Lydia and I thought about the forbidden love that brewed and imagined battling everybody for her love including her father and society. Guess I blamed my ma, who made me read them damn stories in school.

"Bo, over here." Lydia cooed at me.

I looked around and didn't see her. The yard was dark since our little party got broken up. I saw a light going into a freight car and followed it. I found her hiding in an abandoned boxcar a few hundred yards from where her family called home.

"This is your new home. I gave you some blankets and put your stuff in there. I'm getting some more stuff for you. Here come help me."

We ventured across the yard crossing the tracks and meandering through the boxcars holding hands as we went, so we'd walk next to each other and not to get lost from one other. We carried another load of pots, bags of dried beans, flour and my banjo and guitar and raced back without saying a word. I didn't want caught and Lydia dragged me through the yard of abandoned and lived in freight cars and found my home. We set the stuff on the floor of the car and she pushed it a little further inside. I took her hand and like a true gentleman assisted her into my new home, like I carried her across the thresh hold. She lit a candle and walked over to the darkest corner, motioning me to come over to her. We sat down on one of her fine blankets and became better acquainted.

I looked at her through the flickering light. "That train cop says I can't talk to you. If he catches me, he's going to bust me on the head. Says your family is trouble. What's going on, and what's with Early?"

"My mom and some lady I don't know took care of Early for a few minutes. He got up with her and the lady and him took off. Not sure if they're in the yard or not. I've never seen her before."

"Was she Mexican?"

"Yeah, why?"

"No reason, just curious, I guess. So, what's your story?"

She reached over and ran her fingers through my hair, and caressed my face, hoping to end my curiosity. "Bo, there are a lot of things I don't know. Papi doesn't say much about our past. What I can tell you is they were players in the revolution. There's a lot of stuff I can't tell you yet, and other information I don't know. All I know is we needed to leave Mexico." She shook with sobs, lowering her head on my shoulder. "Bo, I want a normal life."

It was my turn to caress her face. "What's a normal life? I ran shine at sixteen. Heck I guess that's normal for my kin back in Arkansas. Lots of folks would think that's crazy, but I know what you mean. I'd rather fish or play baseball, but I got me some money, and I bought my banjo and guitar."

"I want to have a family and take care of the children and my husband. I would be a good wife. I want to sing in little clubs and make a little money. I don't want to be famous singer like you see in the movies. I want to sing for my friends and family."

"That's funny," I said. "I thought about running my own club, I'd make my own whiskey and beer and provide live entertainment there. Heck if it was legal, I'd make my own hooch and perform myself." I laughed out loud. "Hell, Early and I were talking about starting a little saloon when we saved up some money. Hey, when I was a kid, I thought about driving something across the country delivering freight all over. Guess I was in the right line of work."

"What about a family?"

"Never thought about it." I paused a moment and stared at her through the dimming candlelight, "Until. . ." I leaned over and kissed her and. The kiss felt magical, more magical than any encounters with Becky McCormick. Something stirred inside me like I've never felt before. I crawled on top of her and my hands roamed, wandering across her body. She did not resist for a while.

"Bo! No! We need to get married first."

"Do you want to get married?"

"Well you need to ask Papi for my hand and we just met. I also need to know that you will be a family man and be home for nuestra familia. Tenemos que consigliore una casa real. I'm not raising a family in a boxcar. Mi furturo marido necesidad de apoyar a su famila legalmente. No more whiskey running. Bo, I grew up in violence, my children will not."

"You're not saying no. Lydia you're the prettiest girl I've ever seen. Right now, I'd do anything for you. I don't want to run whiskey. I lost my whole family to it. I'm not sure if you know what it's like not knowing who's chasing you and who's helping you. Hell, sometimes it's the same folks."

"Believe me Bo, I do know. My homeland has been in Civil War for longer than I can remember. Most of the folks join the winning side. They have no pride and would rather stick you in the back with una espada, for some chicken and beans, and a roof over their head." She leaned in and whispered in my ear. "My daddy told me everything. I've kept a lot to myself, but I need to trust you. There is a reason why we're here in Omaha."

Chapter 4

A few months later the seasonable fall temperature took a tumble. Temperatures during the day struggled to hit zero, and this young Southern kid wasn't used to those temps. Lydia brought me some extra blankets, so we snuggled in the boxcar where I resided. We ate dinner together and smooched for hours until she thought it best, she returned home.

I hadn't seen Early since he got his head busted in by that ugly rail-yard bull. Lydia mentioned that he still hung around, but he remained in hiding. I knew that if a man could vanish into thin air and vaporize like mash it was Early Greene. He dropped hints that he hung around. Food and other supplies appeared at my door, and at first, I thought they were from Lydia or her family, but she never mentioned anything.

Soon I noticed a copper pot, some coils, and other hooch-making devices in the other end of my makeshift home. I knew he snuck around. Lydia didn't want me making the booze, but I know who did. I attempted saving what little money I earned, so I could get my woman a ring and also wanted a place with rooms, and doors and windows that closed. I wanted a place that had a key to enter the door. I wanted a place we'd call home.

I walked the streets and rode the streetcar looking for work that could pay for that ring and a home of my own. In March when the temperatures started to rise, and the snow started to melt I got a job driving a truck and making local deliveries from Wilson's packing house to the little stores in and around Omaha. I made about three times as much as I earned at the railroad. Wilson's was where I ran into Early Greene again.

"I've been here about a month now Bo. I told them I was good at slaughtering things and they hired me on the spot. I got me a little place down on L by the packing houses right above a saloon. It has a kitchen and a bathroom. It's such a nice little place. The bar ain't bad but that whiskey and beer they serve leaves a lot to be desired. Goddamn Bo, I need some of that good shine of yours."

I glanced away. "I don't want to make it no more. Lydia wants me to have an honest job, and I told her I ain't gonna make no more of it."

"Goddamn, Bo. I ain't talking about running the stuff all over town. More like making some for personal use. It ain't illegal to make it, it's illegal to sell it." He put his arm around my shoulder. I wince at how heavy it felt. "Hear me out, Bo. Make jugs so I can take a snort or two every now and then. I miss that hooch you brought me, Bo."

I try to sneak away, but he tugs me back by curly dark locks of hair.

Remember, kid, I saved your god damned life back there in El Dorado. He exhaled straight into my face. His breathed reeked of cheap homemade beer and whiskey. He loosened his grip. "You owe me, now follow me downstairs, and let me buy you a drink and you tell me you can't make it any better."

I needed to return, but it wasn't happening with Early. I followed him to his place a nice little pad, nothing fancy, but fitted with everything a man needed—a main room with a small place to cook up some grub, and a bathroom. I also noticed a bigger place to rent across the hall. Early showed it to me, since the door wasn't locked and it had a bedroom, too, so Lydia and I could sleep there and talk and dream about making a family. I wanted to surprise her with it someday soon. Well, I followed Early down to the tavern to get that drink, and he introduced me to the owner.

"This is the kid I told you about. His family made the best damn shine in the South before they ran into some problems and he fled town. Damn Klan got his family and almost got him."

The big man reached out his paw and shook my hand firm. "Now, Bo, this is Pete Kowalczyk, damn good Polack if you ask me. Call him Big Pete."

There was a reason folks called him Big Pete. The man was an ox. I guessed about 6'4" and around 230 pounds. Didn't look like there was any fat on him either, with his muscles poking through his tight shirt. Jack Dempsey would run from him in an alley.

I took a shot of his best whiskey and resisted spitting it out on the floor, with Big Pete breathing down my neck and staring at my terrified eyes. I took another shot, and shut my eyes tight, gave a scowl that scared the hookers out the door. Early was right. That crap left a lot to be desired.

"Well dang, Big Pete, you get some better beer and whiskey you might get some more customers." I breathed fumes out through my ears.

"I'm willing to make you a deal, Bo. Make me the beer and whiskey, and I will pay you a hundred a month."

"I'll only make it for myself, I said, ignoring Early's warning growl. "I don't want to break the law anymore."

Big Pete looked at me as if I was stupid. "Kid, ain't no one going to know. You make it for me and that's it. I own several properties down here. I can get you a house and pay you cash, there'd be no exchange of papers or anything. Nothing leads to you. I'll even pick up the whiskey when I pick up your rent."

"I promised my gal I wouldn't do nothing illegal anymore. She'd ask questions I'm sure if she saw me making it."

"Damnit Bo," Early said slamming his fist on the table. "I've told you about a thousand times today. It ain't illegal to make it. Only to sell it. You ain't selling it at all. Pete's selling it."

Big Pete continued. "Bo, I own some property a little way from here, maybe a mile down the road, so it's not too far. It's got a little cabin and the land goes down by a creek. I reckon it's a perfect place to make some shine. Closest thing to a holler we got here. You said you got a gal. Do you plan on marrying her and having kids? Well, you'd need a house then."

"Yeah I want to marry her. Where's this place at? My lady wants a house, told me she's tired of living in a boxcar."

"Can't blame her kid. Hey Early watch the bar for a bit, will ya? I'm taking the kid down to see the cabin." He cranked his car up and we took the mile drive down to the cabin.

There was a lot of land and the back yard went way down by a little creek that meandered down to the Missouri River. He took me inside the cabin, which wasn't bad with running water, a bath, and even a flushing toilet. There were also two bedrooms, a dining room, and a kitchen, not to mention a wood burning stove in the main sitting room.

"A woman will love this place, he said studying my face. "It's got a room for you two, and another bedroom for the kids. I'll charge you what the apartment rents for, plus give you an extra 100 a month cash. No receipts, and no paper trail. Like Early says, it's not illegal to make it. It's illegal to sell it and you won't be selling it. I will." He reached out that hoof of his again to shake my hand.

I gaped at him like some naïve kid, which I guess I was, and shook that giant paw of his. I wasn't sure what I agreed to do.

It was a couple of weeks since I saw Lydia. Since I no longer worked for the railroad, I'd get run off if I'd tried to sneak a visit with my girl. I was either going to get busted for trespassing or get a nice hard kiss from a billy club swung by an ugly rail yard bull, and that wasn't the kiss I longed for.

I moved into that house Big Pete owned and started up my still. Just like pork ribs, whiskey needs to slow cook and age so I let Big Pete know it would take some time for the whiskey to get drinkable. He understood, but wanted me to get started, so I assembled everything and got it running, while making sure it was out of sight in case Lydia came by. I wasn't honest with her. I knew that, but it was to hasten our future.

Early came over at nights and we'd drank, jammed, and wrote songs together. We planned on playing a few shows at the tavern under his apartment. We'd perform that old mountain music for the rough neck meat packers and rail workers who swarmed that little saloon like hornets. It was such a nice little house away from people, so we drank and played all night since there weren't any neighbors nearby. I also worked on a little serenade I'd play for Lydia called *"I Get So Lonesome."*

A few days later after I finished the song, and a few months after I moved into the house, I delivered some meat at this little grocery store down on Bancroft. I walked in struggling with a couple of crates of beef and pork, and I some young woman telling someone off in Spanish. The voice, familiar, but not in the tone I was used to.

"Get out!" The woman shouted back. "We don't serve your kind. You darn bean eater! Get out of here. I'm going to call the police."

"Tornillo de usted, la grasa blanca de vaca!"

I'm not sure what she meant and neither did the clerk. Lydia turned, noticing me.

"Bo, I missed you. Where have you been?" She rushed towards me, yanking me into a nice hug. Her breasts pressed into my chest, giving me a warm, wet kiss on the lips. "Help me, honey. This lady won't sell me any meat."

"Well, honey, I'll give you all of this meat I aim to deliver to this store if she refuses to sell you anything."

"You do that son, and you'll be without a job," the clerk butted in.

I tipped my hat to the woman. "I can always find work, ma'am. Now this girl is beautiful and has a wonderful mother and father. She ain't no different than you and me. Are you going to sell her those steaks, or should I let her bring some of her friends down here for a nice friendly chat? You know that they are all banditos. Every single one of them. Hell, ma'am, that's why they're all here. They fled Mexico to escape the law." I winked at Lydia.

"That's not why they're here, the woman snarled." They're all scabs, trying to bust up the union and working for less money. My husband lost his job because of them bean eaters."

"They're still bandits, ma'am. Have you talked to any of them? Now sell this beautiful gal her steaks or I'll bring twenty Mexican men down here busting up your store. Hell lady, I double that. I'd bring forty or fifty guys down here before closing hour."

"Are you threatening me?"

"Honestly, ma'am. No, I'm not. I'm telling you what's going to happen if you don't sell this lovely lady her steaks."

She muttered and cussed under breath but sold Lydia the groceries.

"Ma'am, throw in an extra steak for me." I paid my baby's bill and delivered the rest of the meat to her store and met my girl on the street corner. There she gave me another kiss and this one deeper and more passionate than the previous one.

"Thank you, Bo, That's very sweet of you." Her brown eyes stared right at mine, making my knees wobble.

"Honey, I tried to see you, but they keep tossing me off the land there. You see I got me a new job, making deliveries, and I have a big surprise for you."

"What is it?"

I grinned. "I can't tell you. It will ruin the surprise. Do you need to get back to the yard?"

"Yeah and you know Papi. He'll have people looking for me if I'm not back soon."

"Have your family meet me at Wilson's packing house at six tonight. We'll cook up them steaks real good. Cook them Arkansas style."

"I'll try to talk them into it."

"It's repaying them for all the meals you gave me."

"No need for that." She flashed her chompers. "That's what a community does and you're part of the community. You can give me a ride back though."

"Let me think about that for a second, I'm not supposed to haul riders." I thought about it as I opened the door for her and lifted her perfect bottom to help her get in the truck. Her long legs stretched into the vehicle, she turned and stared, with big brown eyes opening and closing several times, and her tongue circled her lips before she smiled. My knees shook like a wounded deer, and I wobbled back to my side of the truck. I had another delivery downtown, so I hurried up and finished my run, and climbed back inside.

"Mmm, a working man. I love it," she cooed teasing me. "I like watching you work. I have a little secret." She hesitated. I waited for her to finish. "You're not the first boy I dated since I've been here. I was seeing a boy about your age, three months before you showed up, but he didn't work or neither did his Papi. It's nice to have a man who wants to work."

"I ain't got much of a choice. I need a place to live and some food and clothes on my back. Also, I have to take care of my wife and children someday. Right now, I'm doing what I know how to do, delivering these goods to the people, collecting the cash and taking it back to the boss. Say, I've still got an hour before I need to get back. Do you want to hang out and get a cone?"

We walked down the block to the little ice cream parlor, and I bought a couple of ice cream cones. There, on the corner stood a man playing a five string and he picked and sang up some good ol' music, the stuff from back home, and I danced some weird steps, shaking my feet and body, like a puppet with malfunctioned strings. Lydia joined me dancing on the street corner, shaking her lovely body. I grabbed her arm and we did something that resembled square dancing, as I spun her around do-si-do style. We finally became two lovers, instead of two kids always on the run.

I helped her in the truck this time, more aggressive than I did earlier, and followed her inside the vehicle. I drove her back to the yard, and carried the steaks, while we crossed the tracks looking for her rail car. There, Jorge Fuentes was, not waiting for his daughter, and not playing his guitar and singing some old Mexican folk song that he loved so dearly. He laid lifeless in his own pool of drying blood. My girl's shrieks had me racing the rail car to find Maria, naked and legs spread, also in a pool of crimson, with her shredded clothes beside her.

Lydia ran to the bodies, and kissed the still, lifeless figures, and tried in vain to revive them with her warm touch. "Papi. Mami," she cried. Her hands continued to caress their bodies and she held them close. She glared at me with her beautiful tear-stained eyes, and in a fit of rage came at me beating my chest and arms harder, as I hugged her tighter. Between tears I heard her say, "I knew this would happen. I knew this was going to happen. They promised us protection. They promised us." The sobbing continued.

I didn't know what to think and couldn't muster up any words to say. I clutched her to my chest as the bawling and pounding continued. "I'll protect you. I'll keep you safe. We need to get the police."

I found a yard cop and was about to call for him, but he saw me first and shouted at me. "I thought I told you to get your scrawny ass off the land here." He pulled out his revolver and aimed it at my eyes. It was the same bull who beat the tar out of Early and kept threatening me.

"Listen, this girl's parents got murdered. Call the real police now!"

The bull lowered his pistol and wandered over to look at Lydia's folks. "Just a couple of dead Mexicans. Hope they kill each other."

I grabbed his shirt in a rage and yelled, "Now listen here bull. This young woman's parents were just murdered. Looks like her mom was raped too. She lost her whole family. Now, get the real police!"

"I am the law here, son, and I've run you out time and time again. I'm taking you in for trespassing. You have no right to be here."

"Then take us downtown." I put my hands together so he could slap the cuffs on me. "Cuff me then. You are letting murderers go, but you're going to arrest me for trespassing. Must make you feel real special." I didn't get handcuffed, but my face sure took a beating. He must hit me about ten times before I fell to the ground. Then a foot pressed my head to the hard railyard ground and another to my kidney.

I never lost consciousness and heard Lydia scream. "Stop it. My mom and dad were killed. Don't go beating on him."

She hurried toward the office, and I staggered behind her. We crossed endless tracks until we reached the rail yard office. Lydia pushed the door open and walked straight into the boss's office.

"Call the police now! My parents were murdered. Your police here won't do anything, and the one bull beat my boyfriend." He glanced from her to my face with no sympathy, thinking I deserved it.

"Our family was promised protection here, and we didn't get it. Call somebody, or I will."

Guess he had nothing to lose, the man reached for the telephone and the police arrived in five minutes. They took Lydia's parents away to the morgue. We followed them after I returned the money for my deliveries and they let me take the truck back. It was heart wrenching to see her with her parents. For the first time I cried, there was no need pretending to be strong. When I saw my house in flames and thought my parents died, I didn't cry, I ran. Seeing Lydia sprawled over their bodies, made me want to go back to Texarkana and find out the truth. I wanted to know who killed my parents, or even if they were dead. I wanted to find the killers of Lydia's folks, too. I wanted justice.

"Is there anyone who you can stay with?" the police asked her.

"Yes, there is," and she came over and hugged me.

I took her back to my place, which put a smile on her face. I showed her everything but the still. After the brief excitement wore off, she stared at me, helplessness skewed across her face. Her glassy look did me in, breaking my heart in bits. I held her close all night, refusing to let go.

Chapter 5

April of 1924, I received my first letter from Mexico, and it came from my girl.

Dearest Bo,

I was with my family as we lay my parents to rest. My folks are in a better place, I believe, and only wish I was with you. It felt sad saying goodbye to the two people who raised me my entire life and needed your manly strength to keep me strong. I long for the day I can return to Omaha to be with you.

Love, Lydia.

The letters all came at once, so I spent a whole day reading them. I wrote her back a few times too, not sure if she got them, though, she never did say.

Finally, in May she was due to arrive. She wasn't gone but a month, yet it seemed like an eternity. Poor little girl of sixteen took take a train down to Monterrey, Mexico with her parents' corpses so she could see them off to heaven. At first, when she left, I didn't think I'd ever see her again. Now, her letter gave me hope.

She mentioned the day she would return, and I headed down to the train station to wait with an engagement ring and flowers. The train was packed though, as folks kept exiting, I caught no signs of my girl. I paced, like I was expecting a little one popping out of her mama's womb, craning my neck above the mass of disembarking heads.

Another car emptied and then another. I reread the last letter she sent to me.

Dearest Bo,

I long for the day that we are husband and wife. I know the day is coming soon. I can't wait.

Yours, Lydia

I turned the paper around, squinting for the hope for any double messages or hidden meanings, but couldn't find any. Finally, after what seemed like hours, she got off the train, in all her beauty, grace and elegance, dressed as a woman, and not a sixteen-year-old kid, which shocked me. I was used to seeing the girl from the boxcar, not a princess. I wasn't sure if I liked the new Lydia, seeing her in that flowing dress, but damn, she sure looked pretty. She wore a long-flowered dress that went all the way down to her ankles, with a matching blouse and hat that coordinated with the rest of her attire. She called the hat a cloche, and had some makeup on, not too much, with a hint of lipstick. I saw she was searching for me in the waiting faces, and she was with a female companion, a Hispanic woman, about sixty-years- old. She held her hand over her brows, to shield the sun, and when she saw me, she whispered something to her companion, and she handed the woman a bunch of money, before running toward me.

"Bo, I missed you so much." She gave me a kiss on both cheeks and slurped a bigger one on the lips.

"You look beautiful," I said.

She blushed and lowered her eyes. "Gracias, but I need to get out of these clothes." She made a comical face. "I hate wearing dresses. My great-aunt followed me as a chaperone, but I'm ditching her. I told mi tia to get on another train, and that we still had to transfer. I think the train goes back to Oklahoma. She doesn't speak any English. I also told her I have a husband who will take care of me."

I wasn't ecstatic about sending the old dame back on her own that way, but I remained silent. The depot thinned out, so we headed toward the streetcar line. Lydia continued, "Bo, I had to ditch her. I don't want my family around. Papi's ghost will haunt me forever."

"Huh."

She flashed me a side glance. "You know we don't have the same ideas as our parents. Papi and Mami were both Madero supporters, but mi Abuelito Fuentes, he was a strong Diaz supporter. I want peace in my homeland. I will support whoever gives the best chance for peace, and still give the poor a chance. That's the man who gets my vote. What about you and your family?" she brought the conversation around to me.

We hopped on the streetcar and settled in our seats, with Lydia curled up next to me. The car headed for our new home down in South Omaha. I relaxed enough to give her question a thought, knowing full well my folks weren't much into politics. I stumbled upon an answer.

"My Pa believed in equal rights for all. He hated the Klan, and said poor people poor people, don't matter if they're white or black. Rich people are rich people, but we shouldn't discriminate against folks. Mama was pretty religious. She joined this women's group at her church called the Women's Christian Temperance Union. She dragged me to church with her every dang Sunday. Now, Ma didn't like what Pa did for a living, even though he provided pretty good for the family, and didn't want me running the shine at all. Said we was breaking the law and poisoning the people. She also told Pa that I was going to be the first Barnum with a college degree."

"Did Early tell you that he fought in the revolution?"

I frowned. "I think he did at one time, but I don't remember."

She continued, "He fought with Pancho Villa, the Caranzas, and fled Mexico. I think he was fighting to have something to do. There were a lot of people who killed others needlessly. I think your friend got caught up in it."

"Well, he's always sticking his nose where it doesn't belong. Somehow the fool gets away with it. He told me once that he received no formal education. He knows everything by seeing the world."

"Well, Papi taught me a lot. He schooled me on his ways of the world. I think I've earned my diploma already." She grinned.

I waited for the right moment to propose and tried to stir the conversation toward our marriage and family, but as soon as it came close, Lydia derailed the conversation another direction. Sweat poured out of me like tears. I wanted her hand, and to get down on one knee, like a man is supposed to do. Instead, I blurted it out, no timing or nothing. Not romantic, but it worked.

"I'm ready to marry you, Lydia. I know I am. I work most of the time, driving that truck around town, or playing music. I got us a house already and some money saved up. Thinking we could get married down in Arkansas and then take a trip to Mexico. Hell, we could even hop a freight train." I winked hoping she knew that I was joking.

She smiled back. "Of course, I'll marry you. I like the part of going to Arkansas. Going to Mexico is a good idea, but I got back from there. How about if we get married here, and have our honeymoon in Arkansas?" She carried on without waiting for a reply. "We will make it to Mexico. I promise you. I want to settle down here and get lost in Omaha with you for a while."

We got off at the last trolley stop and walked the quarter mile to my house. Watching Lydia rip off her dress, and retire to the bedroom, I figured she'd get the ring later that evening. She called me into the bedroom, and I met her laying in her undergarments, kicked back on the bed, legs crossed at the ankles, her arms held high over her head. Softly, she whispered, "Bo, we don't have to wait. There are no rules here. We set them."

I wanted to argue, to quote the Bible, stating that it's God's will to wait until our wedding night. I longed to tell her that a respectful girl waits until matrimony. However, there was something about the way she stretched her arms and legs out. Yeah, there was something paranormal in the way she looked at me, and mystical about her appearance. All my resistance toward making love to her that night wilted. The little opposition vaporized like the mash I brewed by the creek in the back yard.

We made hot steamy love. She said she was a virgin, but she taught me more about making love than Becky McCormick ever did. The sweet young thing told me where to kiss her, where to touch and please her. Not sure how she knew, and I didn't care to find out.

Early came knocking on the door about seven the next night. After a good dinner of steaks and beans, we had lain down for a repeat performance from the previous night, when fists hammering on our door, startled us out of our shiny brass bed.

"Hey, you two. We gotta head up to Pete's. We got us a show to do." He stopped when he saw Lydia. She wasn't dressed. "Are you coming darling? Sorry to hear about your folks."

"Can I sing?" She suspicious of Early, but knew he had a heart somewhere inside of him. Besides, he had to be in a new racket by now.

"Of course, you can, darling. We'll let you do a few. We plan to do some favorites, I guess it depends on the crowd."

"I get to do at least one Mexican song. Maybe La Cucaracha, or The Sun That You Are," Lydia said, warming up her vocal chords.

"Well, darling, we have to judge the crowd. Some of these roughnecks who hang out at the saloon might not like their fellow rebel rousers singing with some Mexican gal. They might be prejudice."

"Early, we will do a couple of her songs. Hell, I don't care. Maybe we'll open some eyes a little."

"Yeah, and maybe someone will split our heads open."

"One of her songs," I insisted, sticking up for my woman, "it don't matter what the crowd is like."

"Bo, I drink with these folks all the time. I know what they're like."

"One of her songs, or I ain't playing."

"Okay, just one, but I won't protect you two from anything that goes down."

The three of us caught a trolley and headed up to Early's to prepare for ahead of the night's performance. We headed downstairs at show time and jammed like never before. We played a bunch of standards from down home, like *"Arkansas Traveler"* and *"Oh Susanna",* and we threw in a couple of songs we wrote on the ride up to Omaha and while we jammed at the house. Lydia sang the tunes she knew, and *"La Cucaracha"* and nothing bad happened. Well, she got hit on a few times after her performance and received several catcalls. After someone tried to take her home, she did what most 16-year-old girls would do. She ran to her old man.

Chapter 6

We got married about two months after Lydia returned from Mexico, a small ceremony with Early as the only witness. We still had our band together playing at the saloon once or twice a week, if Early was in town. The man was a midnight rambler, coming and going as he pleased. I worked hard driving the truck around town and to Kansas City or north to Sioux City. I was the man of the house and Lydia, my wife. She took pretty good care of me. Whenever I got home, tamales awaited me, but I craved crawfish pie, my favorite dish from back home. Mama didn't make it, but Pa cooked it up real good.

We made love about every night for the next two months, but the last two nights, she acted tired, and uninterested in me.

"What's the matter?" I asked her.

"I'm real tired. I need to see a doctor.

"I'm tired, too, been driving all day. I need to unwind, and this is the third night in a row."

"I'm sorry, Bo. I love you. Te Amo, but I need my rest. I hope you understand."

I wasn't ready for parenthood, but we were young, married, and in love, so there was no choice. We committed to make a family, so that's what we did. Lydia was incredibly beautiful as an expectant mother. She talked to her stomach and told stories of her father to our unborn child. That's how I heard about Jorge Fuentes.

"Bebe pequeno, your grandfather, was an incredible man. I wish you would have met him. His spirit will guide you. He helped overthrow the terrible dictator President Diaz. He was a supporter of Madero, even though a wealthy landowner at that time. Your grandmother a special person too, a poet and artist. She wrote amazing poetry about the uprising and painted pictures about the revolution and the suffrage of the peasants. I wish you could have met them."

I even rested my head on her lap and told little stories to our growing unborn baby. "Your other grandfather was also a great man. We were dirt poor, but Grandpa Barnum found a way to make money and feed his kids. You are one lucky child, who won't grow up like your mama and me. We will take care of you. You will be a totally blessed child."

I looked at Lydia after I finished talking. Her teary eyes, so beautiful, they left me longing for her, and kissing that magical face of hers. I heard that pregnant girls always got emotional, but I wasn't sure if the tears came from my story, or she thought I'd make a good father, or that our kids won't have grandparents.

Life was hard for us, but we got by better than most. I still working and made a decent wage. The whiskey for Big Pete was always brewing and I was able to give him several jugs. Early, well he was being Early. I heard he started a riot at Wilson's, trying to get a union going for all the packing plants.

"All of us need better wages," he raved liked a preacher on a Sunday sermon, eyes bright. "Blacks, Poles, Mexicans, Greeks, we all need paid the same since we do the same work. We need to organize."

I also, heard Big Pete bailed him out of jail a few times. I had no idea what connection they had and didn't want to find out. I wanted to raise my family in peace.

Musically, I kept expanding my taste. I learned all of Lydia's songs she sang and taught myself the accordion and the way her papi played the guitar. I wanted to perform some shows with Lydia at the Mexican bars popping up in town. We started to play there, and I felt out of place at first, like a catfish in a mountain creek or a bear in the city, but I adjusted. Early didn't mind us playing there either. He figured these were his people since he fought for their rights. Hell, to him, home is where you hung your overalls and hat on, or where you pack your fiddle case.

My bride always got a huge ovation when we played at the Mexican clubs. From the glimmer in her eyes, I noticed she loved to sing in front of the Mexican audience. Her big, brown, doe-like eyes resembled stars glowing across the desert, illuminating the vast wasteland, the cacti shining on the lone coyote, every time she heard the thunderous applause.

"Maybe this is my purpose," she said to me after one of her performances, with her chest heaving. "I'm supposed to sing the songs of the revolution, sing them to the people, and make them remember those who died for their freedom."

"What's my purpose? It can't be delivering whiskey."

"No," she shook her head." because God would not give you that purpose in life. He might have given that to your father, to provide for you and give you a reason for life, but I you have a bigger purpose. You should know what your purpose is, but for some people they never do know. I think you are here so people can see people with an open mind. Let them see the beauty in one another, and not on where they were born, or the color of their skin."

"How do I deliver it?" My voice quivered.

She reached for my hand, placing it between her breasts. "Music is one way. You play the white man's music, the black man's music and learning Notre. People listen to you Bo. You don't need an education, or be a wise man of great speaking ability, be a person who's able to get along and have something to say. It will be important for our child to see that, too. Say, where are you going?"

I started to get up to leave to catch the streetcar heading North. "I'm going up North to play some blues up there."

"Please, don't go tonight."

"Why not?"

"Because I want to be with you. That's why. Bo, I need you so bad.

I didn't set that old resonator guitar down, I dropped it on the floor, pulled Lydia to her feet, and carried her to the bedroom. Making love with her was one of the most precious things I could ever imagine doing. Hearing her heartbeat, feeling each breath she took, and listening to her soft moans aroused and soothed me. Maybe my purpose on this planet was to be her lover, husband and her man. Maybe there was more. I'm not sure I could change the world with my songs. Hell, there were quite a few people out there trying to change the world with their music back in the mid-1920s. They sang about revolution, protest, and I saw them on the newsreels before picture shows.

The next night I ventured into North Omaha, which is the section of town where the Omaha Negroes settled. Lydia was aware of my plan to head up there with my guitar and play some blues. What she didn't know was I intended on taking a couple of jugs of shine with me. I walked out the front door and snuck around and wandered down the backyard to grab a couple of jugs, before hopping the streetcar with jugs and guitar in hand. I found the worst looking dive possible. This place made juke joints in Mississippi where I was fortunate to make some runs look like the Pearland Ballroom. I was afraid if I sneezed or coughed up phlegm, I might blow down the walls.

There it was the perfect spot about 24th and Pratt. Not more than thirty years passed since this location hosted a World's Fair, and President McKinley, Buffalo Bill Cody, and a young Sioux Indian boy were on display. Now, it was the spot for some white kid to play some old prison songs, work songs, and tales of backdoor romances straight from the Delta.

I dressed in my usual garb, overalls with no shirt, and an old straw hat. The music blared through the paper-thin walls of this club, and people sang, laughed, cursed, and fought. That ol' Regal guitar was tuned down, and I took a puff on my corncob pipe, and took a swig or two of shine, and let her rip. I performed a Charley Patton song, like the ol' boy himself did, when an old black man came out. He was kind of familiar, though dressed worse than me and had no teeth but seemed like decent folk.

"Sounds damn good, son. Won't you come in and play for these here folks."

"Sure will."

He looked at me again and noticed I wasn't a colored man. "Damn you is a white boy! You play pretty good for a cracker." He noticed my jugs next to my feet. "Say boy, you got some whiskey there?"

"Yeah, straight from the backyard. Great stuff, too."

"Well get your scrawny white ass in here and join this little party. Mind if I take a snort of that hooch?" I gave him the jug and he took a snort. "Woo, that's damn better than the shit we got." He led me to the door, and I crowded in by about fifty black men and women all staring at me like they wanted to murder me. It didn't bother me any. Hell, I showed no fear, since I delivered in the roughest places in Greeneville, Mississippi. Most of those folks treated me like a brother, as long as they were drunk and entertained.

"Say you gonna come back every Tuesday? We'll give you some money to play for us, and some for the whiskey too. Just keep bringing that shine."

"Don't worry about it. I'll be there." I tipped my hat to the toothless man as I left.

I was doing what I knew best, making whiskey and sweet-sounding music that people danced and sang along to. Hell, I think I found my purpose for being on this planet. People were people, and they needed entertainment, a place to breathe, and relax. They wanted a few drinks to help them unwind and some music to dance and sing to. It didn't matter if they were white, Negroes, or Mexican, all they needed was a few snorts of some good whiskey, and some good old music. There wasn't any prejudice or hate, just good people drinking and dancing and having a good old time.

That routine went on for a few weeks. The longer I cooked the whiskey, the more guilt I carried. I didn't like sneaking things from Lydia, and I ready to tell her, but didn't know how. Telling her the truth would have been best, and I could have been forgiven easier than if she discovered it. I stood speechless while she attacked in a hormonal rage.

"Bo, what is this anyway?" Tears flowed down her cheeks, as she already knew the answer. She led me down to the creek bed. "Were you ever going to tell me?"

"I've been meaning to tell you honey. Honest to God. I really was." I felt lower than a gopher in a going home.

"You promised me you wouldn't make whiskey."

"I ain't selling it. I give it to Big Pete, he gives us a break on rent, plus I've been taking it to the Negroes when I go up there. That's all."

Lydia pointed her finger in my face and somehow appeared taller. "Well, drinking alcohol is illegal. I don't want us doing anything illegal, and you are committing a crime by making it. You promised me you won't break the law!"

"It's only illegal to sell it and I ain't selling it. Plus, Pete says everything is taken care of. No trail, so it can't come back on us."

"Big Pete would turn you in if he got caught. He won't take the rap for it."

"There's no paper trail to me."

"There's a still in our back yard!" Her fore finger pointed in the direction of the evidence.

"I ain't selling it though!"

"Honey, he owns you. You're part of it. You are part of the mob. You need to tell him you are quitting, or I'm leaving!" Tears flowed once like a summer rain. "I'm going to start a new life with our child down in Mexico."

The thought of her leaving scared the shit out of me. My heart skipped a few beats while I had to think of something. My mind as usual, was blank. I loved this girl more than anything else in life and she carried my child. I knew I needed to break the deal with Big Pete but wasn't sure how to do it. I didn't know for a fact that Pete was involved with the mob, or how deep he was mixed up in it. I finally figured it out. I dealt with the devil and was losing everything I had.

"What do I tell him?"

"You will figure it out. You always do," she said in full hormonal sarcasm.

Well, one thing I knew about him was he had clout and connections. He couldn't have that little empire of houses and apartments if he didn't know people. He wasn't that bright. A few days later I met with him at his saloon downstairs from Early's place. My plan was to be honest with him, and then get in a battle of wits with him.

We met downstairs and he took me into his office, which was nice and comfy. I sat down in a nice big plush chair and he took a seat in his big swivel chair behind the desk. He lit up a big smoky cigar and offered me one, too. I took it without thinking. "What gives there, Bo? Why do you need to talk to me?"

"I need to pull the still."

"You can't. I need your juice." He blew the stale smoke from his stogie in the direction of my face. My business doubled since I started using your whiskey. Don't worry, you're protected, and I'm protected from the Boss himself. I can't let those wops take control."

"I don't want no protection, and I don't want to make whiskey anymore! My wife found the still and intends on leaving with my child. I don't want to owe anyone anything. I'll move out of that house and get me a place a little closer to work."

"Barnum, it's in your blood. You can't quit making whiskey, and that little spic wife of yours, hell with her! Aren't you the man of the house? You're chicken shit! You ain't no man."

My competitive nature flared up as did my nostrils, and so did my stupidity. "I'm more of a man than you! I don't need your house or anything else. I want to work my job and play some music on the side. I got me a baby on the way, so I can't commit my life to someone that's corrupt, who gets his way through bribes. You watch what you say about my wife!"

He laughed and seemed to find me amusing. "Are you threatening me? Really, are you threatening me, Barnum? You could be wiped out once you leave this door, and no one will care. You say your wife is pregnant. Great, another half-breed coming. Keep the race pure, and by the way, I found out your selling to them niggers up north. You only give me the whiskey. Do you understand? And you're not playing at my place anymore. You aren't going to play any coon music either!"

He put his cigar out on his hand and grabbed mine out of my hand and extinguished it on the back of my hand. The hairs on the back of my hand sizzled like bacon frying, and it hurt like nothing else I've felt as I tried not to grimace. He then reached into his drawer and slowly pulled out an object stopping it about six inches from my face. His thumb moved down the handle caressing it like the knife was his lover. The blade snapped out, puncturing my skin, below my right eye. My eyes lowered taking in the whole event.

"Do you understand, Barnum?"

I wondered how he knew I was taking the shine up North. Hell, I followed God's purpose for me, so this beast must be the devil. I realized I was in too deep but wanted no part of his racist ass. Taking a deep breath, and gathering up all the courage I had, I told him, "I do business with who I want, and I don't want to do business with you. Pulling the plug on the still means I'm not making whiskey for me, for Early, for my Negro brothers, or even for you! I am retired from the whiskey making business. No one owns me. Now, what part of that don't you understand?"

He pulled the blade away slowly, then placed it up against my face puncturing the skin again. "What part of this don't you understand?"

Early walked in, taking the scene. "Anything wrong?"

Big Pete's hold on the knife relaxed. "Your little friend here wants out. He can't do that. He works for me."

"Bo, what's going on?" Early blew out his cheeks, obviously hoping I'm not about to cause any trouble.

"I promised Lydia I won't make whiskey, and she found the still. I need to pull the plug on it." I stared down Early. "I don't want my kid involved in this environment. My wife and I were both brought up in violence, and my child shouldn't."

"Let the kid go Pete. He has morals. We need more of that these days."

"When he shook my hand, he signed on for life."

"Let him be."

"I'll move out once I get home," I added.

"If you make it home."

"Pete, if something happens to Bo, something will happen to you."

Pete's face tensed up and his eyes flashed. The ox knew Early wasn't bluffing. "Barnum get the hell out of here and be out of the house by morning, or else." Big Pete's voice sounded defeated.

Early joined me outside, "What was that about?"

"I ain't working for no one but Wilson's. I didn't know Big Pete owned me, and I ain't wanna be involved in the mob."

"Was he pissed about the Negroes?"

"Yeah, racist son-of-a-bitch called them niggers and coons. I won't work for no racist. Don't tell no one, but I got a few jugs left for them. I plan on doing a few shows with them. Do you want to join me, and play some harp? Lydia's been learning some Charley Patton songs, too."

His grin widened. "Hell yeah. I'll play."

"I bet we'll sound good. Damn, I need to find a place. I can grab a truck from work so moving will be easy."

"Sounds good to me Bo. Say what do you think of Pete? I mean…" he paused, bit off a chuck of his fingernail and chewed on it and continued. "Do you think he'd be better off eliminated?"

"I could care less what happens to him? I don't want to be involved."

"You are involved, and you know it."

"Yeah, I know."

"I mean I could arrange a meeting with the Italian brothers, you know, if someone threatens you, I can take care of it."

"If they threaten Lydia, I'd think about it, but thanks."

He hesitated. "Bo, are you ready to run if we have to? I mean leave Omaha."

"I ain't gonna run away."

"We might have to. Too many crooked people in this town."

"I might to protect my family, but that's it."

He flashed a crooked smile and boarded the trolley, while I continued the conversation.

"He called Lydia a spic and my unborn child a half-breed. I hate that guy."

"I would have killed that mother fucker right there if he said that about my wife and kid. Sorry I got you involved with him."

"Well, the deal was good, I guess I didn't have to take it. I had no idea I was in it for life. I'm pretty sure my pa wasn't in it for life, but he wasn't in with the mob. Damn mob was always after him. Anyway, I don't want to die, I want to be a good father. Gotta be alive to be a good pa to my kid."

"You guys can stay with me tonight and find a place tomorrow. I gotta get you out of that house. I'm not sure if I have any more contacts, and the ones I do have, you don't want."

"Ha ha. Yeah you're right on that."

Early and I moved our stuff out of the house that night and we crashed at his place for the night. The next day we bought a house pretty close to my job around 23d and F and moved in a week later. We were a block off the main strip. There were no more hassles from Big Pete, no more hassles at all in town. Not yet anyway. A few weeks after we moved in the new house, we scheduled a show in North Omaha. All three of us went down, and Lydia didn't mind me giving the whiskey away.

The same man met me at the door. "I brought my band down here this time. Sorry I haven't been around. But we've rehearsed some songs for you, plus we ran into a little trouble. I'm also done making the whiskey. These are the last six jugs I got."

The man was silent for a while, as though debating to let us in, or send us packing. He stole another glance at the jugs and my resonator guitar. "Yeah we heard the Pete guy threatened to rough you up. Well you folks come on in and let's get you started."

We played for a few hours and I think we sold our soul to the devil the way we performed. Early and I both dueled on guitar and harp. We played like Sonny Terry and Herbert Leonard, and Lydia sang like Ma Cain or Bessie Smith. I mean, she brought the blues with her. The crowd roared and cheered, and hooted on every song, and everyone danced and grind. I did some duets with Lydia and sang like Charley Patton.

It was loud and probably too rowdy. Soon, the men with copper badges dressed in blue showed up. They searched for the shine but didn't find it. My friend Old Man Cole took a beating from a cop who would have knocked out his teeth, if he had any. It knocked him flat as a stack of flapjacks.

"Where's the hooch? We know you got some here." He looked straight at me and knew who I was. "You're that little rebel who makes the shine, aren't you boy? You're playing with fire delivering here to these niggers."

He raised his billy club, ready to strike me, when a shot rang out. People screamed as the cop dropped dead. No one knew who fired the shot, but a couple black kids took off running, as well as everyone else. We jumped in my old truck and took off down 24th Street safely home. Lydia stood speechless. She didn't say anything, didn't want held or nothing. She turned her body away from me and slapped my hands when I tried to comfort her. I know she blamed it on me, she blamed it on the whiskey, but deep inside I knew she blamed it on a corrupt world which we desperate to escape from but were stuck dead center in the middle of it.

The next day, I delivered some meat downtown, and it looked like a parade was going on, as people marched down the street. What I didn't see, they hauled a young black man with his hands tied behind his back toward a rope. Figured he was going to be lynched.

"Cop Killer! Cop Killer, this boy shot a policeman last night. Come watch him hang. Come watch him die. It's eye for eye in this town, boy," the crowd shouted in unison.

"It's police brutality." I shouted at the crowd. "Let him go! The cop beat a man to death with his club and was about to get me. It was self-defense, let him live!"

The crowd ignored me, though the young Negro man looked straight at me, and acknowledged me, with a nod, yet we both knew it was in vain. I stormed into the crowd to stop the lynching. But received footsteps on my forehead as I was knocked to the ground. The colored man was strung up on a noose. I ran toward him in a futile attempt to free him, but I way too late. I watched helplessly as he fell half-way to the ground as his body swayed.

More than ever, I wanted to run away from this land. I wanted to fight this shady system I lived in. I wanted to see Big Pete dead, whether I did it myself, or witness his murder, or go to his bedside when he gasped for his final breath after a long illness. I wanted to do anything but trust our system led by Boss Tom and his cronies. That night I held Lydia tight as she slept, not knowing what occupied my mind.

The next couple of weeks riots broke out all over the city. Houses went up in flames. White businesses, including that shop on Bancroft where I ran into Lydia, and even the ice cream shop where I got us cones, lay in ashes. A few people were killed. Lucky for me, I didn't know no one, but they still had families, so someone knew them.

No one knew who started the fires, blacks and whites rioted, the blacks were roaming the streets due to the lynching of the kid. The whites rioted because the blacks rioted, and the Mexicans rioted because everyone else was. We had enough of the violence. It was time to run.

"Bo, we bought a house and you have a good job, plus running won't do any good."

I wondered why I married her. She was a daughter of activists and had a mind like one. I was a moonshiner's kid, taught to run at the first smell of trouble. She was taught to stand up for what she believed in, and that it's okay. to fight the system.

"Honey, we have a baby on the way. We need to keep that baby and us safe. Oil is big right now in Tulsa. I think we can head down, and I could get work driving that rig or working in the fields. I want to make sure we'll be all right."

"Oh, Bo, I know you do, but our little one will face problems wherever we go, since she's a media casta. We need to do everything in our powers to make sure the little one won't be discriminated against. We have to stand up to them."

I knew she was right, but I wasn't sure who I dealt with; the mob, Big Pete by himself, some mad blacks, racist whites, or the Boss himself. That would be Boss Tom, the mayor's right-hand man. We had a battle to fight, but I wasn't sure of the enemy's identity. The mob chased after me, and the racist whites hated me since I got along with the Mexicans and the Negroes. Not sure what the basic Negro man thought of me. They probably thought I was another white hick ready to throw a fireball through a window. A meeting with Boss Tom became essential, but I wasn't sure how. I had a friend that did. Early knew his way around this city already.

I went over to Early's place and told him everything I knew about the lynching a few weeks ago, hoping he would tell me some info in return. "Well what do you think of the riots? I think the Klan is trying to blame dem on da Negroes, or maybe Big Pete's men."

"Big Pete is in the Klan. I found this out. Bo, I'm sorry I ever got you involved with him." He saw the shock on my face and added. "Hey, say the word, I know people, and I've spoken to the Italians."

"I don't want to get the mob involved, and don't want you involved with them either. I need to go higher up. Can you get me a meeting with Tom?"

He cracked a little laugh and gave me that smile again. The one I didn't want to see. He opened his fiddle case and played a quick version of Turkey in the Straw." "Consider it done."

I met with the city Boss in his downtown office. I walked into his exclusive back room and through layers of cigar smoke and looked across the room at the man.

"Bo Barnum, at last we meet."

"Huh?"

"Pete worked for me, so in turn you worked for me, too. He told me all about you and taking the whiskey to the niggers up North. I wasn't happy about that."

"So, you are responsible for the riots?"

"Well, I said Pete worked for me, he no longer works for me, not because you are out of the game, but because of his other affiliations. We caught him in a meeting with some other members plotting to kill specific people of miscegenation."

"What's that?"

"Well, aren't you married to that pretty little Mexican girl? The daughter of Jorge Fuentes?"

"Yeah."

"Uh huh, there's your answer."

I pondered what he said, putting two and two together and sighed. "Sir, let me tell you what I want. I don't want involved anymore. I don't want to make whiskey. I got me a family with a little one on the way. I have a job and a house and work hard to support my wife. Any extra will come when we play a show or two. I don't want handouts, protection or nothing."

"It's okay, Bo. You are clear from the whiskey. You can make it, or you don't have to. It's no skin off my back. Make some for a show or two, that's fine. Stay small time. The people running the bootlegging in this town don't have a problem with you. I don't have an issue with you."

"I ain't making it no more."

"It's in your blood. I'm saying if you want to make a jug or two in the future, you'll be fine. Keep it small time. You will be safe."

"What about Big Pete?"

"Don't worry about him. Now go." He pointed to the door and I rushed out.

The morning newspaper said: "Kowalczyk Gunned Down Outside South Omaha Apartment."

I ran into Early at Wilson's packing house. "It happened right in front of my apartment early in the morning, before the roosters started cackling. Big Pete was out to do some killing. He chased me down, but I'm so damn sneaky, he'd never get me, and the Italians rolled up the street and took him out. Bo, I suspect he was after you since I told him you still lived at my place."

It finally hit me, but I couldn't be a 100 percent sure, so I said nothing. Figured it's better to keep my big mouth shut than make false accusations. I figured Early led him to the mobsters, so I asked him, "Who are they going to pin it on? I fear Boss Tom is going to pin it on the Negroes."

"Not sure, Bo. Pete's out of the way, and you ain't making whiskey no more. Kid, you might as well get out of the life. Hell, you got yourself a good driving job, and beautiful wife, who's smarter than you, and a baby on the way. Your job is to take care of them, so you do that. My job is done here, I'm going to hop a freight and take it wherever it goes. I can't stay in one place."

"So, you're with the mob?"

"I'm not with no one. I'm looking out for you. Take care of that family, Bo. Man, I can't believe you were a kid when we came up, but a year later, you're a man. A family man at that. I'll be over after work and drop some stuff off if that's okay. I'll return to see that baby."

"You don't have to go."

"Bo," he paused. "I have to." Then he smiled that wicked troublesome smile which sorta answered my question, without answering it.

"Okay, well take care, we got more jamming to do."

"I'll be back, write more songs for us."

We went our separate ways, to do our specialties. I grabbed my truck and made deliveries, and he went slaughtering something.

The murders of the policeman, Big Pete, and Lydia's parents went unsolved for a period of time, but the town got mysteriously quiet. The murderer was never found, he possibly hopped a freight train to the north, south, east, or west. Early Greene never said which direction he was headed. I don't think anyone, but Lydia wanted to know who the killer of her folks were, most folks cared less. Boss Tom, the mayor's right-hand man, was more about sweeping crimes under the rug, plus he wanted that Big Pole dead. He always got what he wanted. The black kid, I don't think he cared one way. It was an eye for an eye, even though I'm sure the kid didn't do it. My in-laws, well that's another story, but the railroad bull said what the community thought. Just two dead Mexicans.

A few months later I got a letter from Early.

Bo, I'm trying to settle down. Met me a woman in Tennessee. Hell, she plays the fiddle better than me, and we're getting a band together with some other pickers. I also got me a legit job driving a truck like you. I want to try the family life too. Well Hell Bo, I can't do it like you. You and Lydia make such a good couple, cause she got the brains, looks, and passion. She chose you cause you're a good guy. Hoping to make it up to see your baby, and I might bring Daisy up with me. I think you'd like her.

Sincerely, Early

About the only excitement we had those months was a few shows up North where Lydia and I played for the colored folks. Those good folks up there always welcomed us when we came up. Must have thought we some sort of kindred spirits to them. I always joked with them that I wouldn't have no more whiskey since my wife here doesn't want me making it.

One evening an old drunk man in back hollered back at me in an inebriated voice. "I promised my wife I wouldn't drink no more whiskey either." Everyone busted out laughing.

That night, Lydia lay in bed with me and we talked. It was about time for the expected birth of our child.

"Bo, did you notice how quiet things are now that he's gone?"

"Now that who's gone?"

"Early?"

"Huh?"

"Well since you've known him our parents died, there has been race riots and mob shootings. Lots of violence happened."

I noticed and I had a feeling about it. I didn't want to share those feelings with her. I didn't think he was responsible for her parents, or my parent's murders, but I guess only God and the killer knew for sure.

"I'm sure it's coincidence." I told her, denying my feelings.

"Well I hope so. He seems to be around the violence."

"I admit he's a bit shifty, and there's a lot I don't know about him, but I owe him."

"Bo, be careful around him, for me and our little one."

"Last I heard he's in Tennessee, says he's coming up to see the baby."

"Okay, darling, let's get some sleep; I think the baby is coming tomorrow."

We drifted off to sleep. I don't think we got more than three winks of sleep, and then that damn rooster next door started to cackle and holler. We tried hiding under the covers to drown out the noise. Next thing we knew we heard pounding on the door, and muffled voices. Early returned with a cute little red head girl at his side. I sleepily opened the door, and he gave me a hug.

"Bo, this is Daisy. She ain't no more than eighteen, but can play a pretty mean fiddle, and does the other stuff pretty mean and nasty, too. I think I'm gonna marry her."

Lydia struggled standing and waddled to the front door and let our guests inside. We were both ready for the baby to come. Our friends came inside, and Lydia prepared breakfast, some beans and eggs. Daisy was a cutie, nowhere as pretty as Lydia in my opinion but had charms like Becky McCormick. She had her own flair as most Southern girls do. Her hair was a bright red in color and much longer than the style those days, and she wore overalls with no shirt on underneath. Something told me Early made this girl pretty happy, and she made him a happy man.

After sitting and talking with them a bit, it seemed like Early Greene finally met his mate and that she did wonders for him. Gone were the shifty eyes, they kept their focus on his love. His smile lit up the room and trusting rather than troublesome.

"I met Daisy on the street corner. She and her sisters played some music out on the street there in Johnson City, and they two-stepped all over the street. I whipped out my fiddle and started playing along, and we started battling each other. Gosh darn, if she didn't hold her own."

"Early," she said in a thick drawl that reminded me of back home. "You're just saying that."

"Honest honey, I couldn't keep up with you."

Daisy's cheek turned a bright red, and her hair got even redder, the more she blushed.

Early continued, "Well next thing I knew I got us a couple of cones at a little parlor there in Johnson City and we started kissing and then we…"

"Early stop," an embarrassed Daisy interrupted.

Lydia came in with breakfast, juevos rancheros as she called them, and we ate like we was starving.

"Early wanted to come up and see the baby." Daisy explained. "Looks like we are a little early, Early." She chuckled as the rest of us did at her attempt for a joke.

"I think it's coming today. I hope she's having a girl. I don't want to raise no boys. I'd feel like I'd have to make them a runner, even though I don't make the shine no more. I still know how to handle a shot gun in case suitors drop by when she's fourteen." Everyone but my wife snorted and chuckled.

After breakfast, the four of us relaxed at home for a bit. We jammed a little as I played banjo and Daisy broke out the fiddle, Early wailed on the harp, and Lydia did her best to sing even though she struggled breathing. We mainly did some old spirituals, some old hymns like *"The Sweet Bye and Bye"* and *"The Old Rugged Cross"*, but we also did some old Mexican folk songs. I was impressed with Daisy. She knew all the songs and a lot better than I was a few years ago with them Mexican ballads.

It was getting close to lunch time and Lydia went to the kitchen to start lunch. While making lunch she hollered. "Bo! Call the doctor! It's time!"

I stumbled for the phone, and made the call, and he arrived fast. The Model A sped into our driveway and he came in with his doctor's bag. He rushed Lydia to the bedroom where she lay down and sent me to the kitchen to boil water and grab rags. I think he wanted me out of the room. I grabbed one towel when the doctor wanted four, went back and got two more, then went back to get the last one. I forgot to turn the stove on so the water in the kettle lay placid like a pond in the morning. It's a good thing Early and Daisy were there, so they could take care of things I forgot.

What seemed like an eternity, but in reality, was four hours and several screams, I heard the doctor's voice call out. "Bo, come on in. Congratulations, you got yourself a girl!"

The girl, of course, was precious. We had to name her. Sara was my grandmother's name. She was a tough old bird, as tough as they make them. She was a Coushatta Indian who chewed tobacco, smoked a corncob pipe, and mastered the family recipe.

"How about Sara after my grandma, and her middle name Maria, after your mami?"

"Hmm," a worn out, sore and tired Lydia said. "I like it. Sara Maria Barnum. Do you want to hold her, so I can rest?" She held out the baby to me before I answered.

Me, holding a baby was like reading Greek in schoolbooks. I wasn't comfortable with it, since I ain't held one before. Little Sara nestled up in my arms like a sack of taters and smiled right at me. I held her tight, trying not to make her cry, and hearing those little coos brought a tear to my eye. Sara Maria Barnum entered this world. I ain't much of a religious man, but I closed my eyes and said, "God please protect this angel, and make her the best child ever." Sara opened her eyes, and smiled again, and closed her eyes with the smile still on her face.

Early and Daisy held the baby for a bit, and she promptly spat up on Early. He gave her back to me as his eyes hardened, and they were heading out the door. "Hopping a freight and heading back to Tennessee. See ya soon. Take care of that baby girl."

Chapter 7

Time flew by like birds soaring along. I spent most of my time taking care of my family, working, holding and playing with my baby. Sara grew like a weed getting bigger and bigger, and Lydia stayed home and raised our little one. Sometimes we went out, catching us a picture show at the theater, or if we got someone to watch little Sara, we'd perform a show somewhere. That wasn't too often, and most of our performances were in front of the best audience, which was an audience of one.

Sara's grandpa, Cecil told me when I was little that time speeds up once you get kids. Told me that it seemed like I was hatched, when I went out on the road for the first time. I missed my dad a lot. We were still planning a trip down to Arkansas to look for his grave, or try to find him, but money was tight, paying for all the extras.

Lydia was a good mami to Sara. She took her everywhere, and Sara glanced around checking out the scenery. Our child had bright eyes and a big smile and loved going for long walks with us. People didn't bother us at all. When we strolled around, neighbors moped in awe at our beautiful, little, media casta baby.

She grew so fast it seemed like we made and bought clothes for her and she outgrew them in a month. We finally got smart and got her clothing too big for her, so she would grow into them. The little girl started walking at ten months, and I laughed when my little one said "choo-choo train" after her first birthday, thinking that one day she would hop a freight with me.

Lydia and I continued engaging her with our stories about our parents. One day, unaware that I listened, I heard her tell Sara how and why she ended up in Omaha. "Sara mi pequena bebita, let me tell you about our past. Tu bisabuelo, Gilberto Fuentes, was a powerful man, and a leader for the conservative party in Saltillo, Mexico. He was never elected to office but was regarded as Don, or Boss. He was the man who called the shots. He was known in Saltillo as Don Fuentes."

I remember hearing Sara go, "Don Fuentes," and Lydia smiled back her acknowledging that.

Lydia continued, "Tu bisabuelo Gilberto had three sons, Juan, Roberto, and Jorge. MI Tio, Juan became a senator in Coahuila State in early 1910. He still is a powerful man, but refuses to accept bribes, and also tolerant of the poor, even though he is a supporter of the mean Diaz regime.

Mi otro tio, Roberto was younger than Juan, but was strong and had a bad temper. Mi Padre once told me that Roberto killed five men but was found innocent on all charges, because of lack of evidence, or self-defense. Roberto became Chief of Police in Saltillo.

Mi padre, Jorge was the shortest yet smartest one los tres hermanos los uratos, as bisabuelo used to call them. That means the brothers who would not separate. Mi padre was gifted in athletics and in music. Papi had many paths he could take, and mi tios said he was the dream son, the son a father could be proud of, just like you are the daughter any mother will be proud of.

Mi padre needed his own life, and was opposed to mi famila politics, so he went to school in Texas. Papi wanted to study law, but instead he met mi mami.

Mi abuela and other abuelo were both artists and poets. Mami learned a lot about the revolution from them. She became active in the movement at an early age. I think she followed the leaders drawing pictures and writing poems. Mi abuelo fought for the rebels, but he was not a fighter. He was also an artist and wrote poems. That is where they met and got married. Mami was born in war, but soon they escaped to Texas and raised there. Tu abuelo and abuela met in Austin where they went to school and got married. I was born in Matamoros where we lived for twelve years. Finally, we were sent out of Mexico and could never return."

Sara's eyes focused on her mom as she spoke. I stood out of sight, gleaming at both of them eavesdropping, in awe of her story. Sara looked up at her mom and said, "Mexico."

"Si, Mexico. I will teach you and your daddy Spanish one day." Lydia glanced at me and caught me listening. "Now you know, honey. Our family were radicals. They fought against the corruption. I got that passion and fire in me."

"Just one of the reasons I love you."

We had a normal life, no signs of Early for another three years. Our baby girl turned three years old and getting prettier by the day. The town, quiet except of the petty crimes and, common murders that happen everywhere. There weren't any mob killings, lynchings, or extreme racial tension. At Sara's third birthday party we heard the knock on the door.

"Woo hoo, I'm a married man, Bo. Didn't want no bastard kids so we tied the knot."

I smiled at Early. "Congratulations, is that how you proposed?"

"Nah, it was more romantic than that."

Lydia who had a bad week, all dog-tired and nauseous, came out of the bedroom, glowing like the sun to greet our company.

"Congratulations, you two," she told them. "So Early, what do you want?"

"I want me a son. I couldn't handle me a daughter. There's people like me and Bo out there." He smacked me on the shoulder playfully, and hooted. We all laughed too.

"How far along are you, Daisy?" My wife asked her.

"About three months."

"Well you are just in time for Sara's party. She's napping now. We got cake and presents for her."

Daisy bowed her head, looking embarrassed. "Oh, that's right. Sorry we forgot it was her birthday. We didn't bring her anything."

"Yeah, it's hard to carry all them gifts we wanted to get her in a dadgum boxcar," Early interjected.

"Hey, you're here, and that's what matters," I said.

We got the party rolling; I barbecued some pork on the spit outside, while Lydia baked the cake. Early and Daisy woke Sara up and played with her in the backyard. They kept commenting on how big she got. I thought, of course she's grown. They left the day she was born.

Sara opened up her presents, a teddy bear she loved and could sleep with, a toy train she hopped on, and I got her a coaster wagon, so we could pull her everywhere. She got too big to carry.

After Sara opened her presents Lydia dropped the bomb on us again. "Attention everyone, I don't want to outdo you, but I'm pregnant again."

"Oh my God, honey. I suspected you were by the way you acted, all tired and sick." I kissed her on the lips and forehead.

Daisy went up and felt Lydia's belly. "Hmm, I bet you're having a little boy."

"I think so. I feel a little different on this one." She felt Daisy's stomach. "You are, too."

Both ladies laughed and hung out together, while Early and I cleaned up and pulled Sara in the wagon up and down the street. Hard to believe that five years ago I ran for my life in an Arkansas forest and now I pulled a wagon down the street with my little three-year-old screaming with joy inside the little cart, and soon I'd have another youngster.

In a few short months, I was blessed with a son who would carry on the Barnum name. We called him Tomas Roberto Barnum. Lydia wanted a Spanish name, and Tomas was Jorge's middle name and my given name was Robert, but I've been called Bo since I sucked milk out my mama's breast. Being a father came natural for me, as I taught my kids about the world, and how to slide a knife across guitar strings to create a swampy sound.

Sara learned to cook beans and tortillas from her mother. She'd boil the water, and dump the beans in the pot, and help mash them up, as she stood on the highchair and took the masher to them. With her eyes almost shut, and her lips scrunched up, her little tongue protruded from her mouth while she pounded the beans with the masher. She was adorable.

The expression was the same when she stirred the masa and water in to make the tortillas. Mami sang a little song to Sara while they cooked. She always sang "La Cucaracha," and my little hija sang right back with her. Sara sometimes caught me watching, and her eyes twinkled at me like a little star.

In 1929, the Stock Market crashed, thrusting us into The Great Depression. God or somebody watched out for me since I was able to hang on to my job. Some of the other drivers I worked with weren't so lucky. I saw a few of them, gather up on the soup line while driving my truck downtown.

Sara had turned five, and Tomas was two. I worked at Wilson's for about six years and never took a day off, so they granted me a couple of weeks, and I took the family on a little trip down to Texarkana. It was time for Lydia and the kids to see where I grew up. We packed up the jalopy and headed south through Iowa and Missouri.

"See the cows, Tommy? That's where we get our milk. See the pigs? That's where we get our bacon and pork. Look Tommy, that's a truck like Daddy drives for work. Isn't that nice?"

The toddler chatter was cute, but also nonstop for eight hours. Eight hours straight of my smart little Niña sharing her knowledge with her baby brother. Eight straight hours of learning where milk and pork come from. Lydia broke into "La Cucaracha", and when she finished, I crooned my best rendition of Clementine. Soon we crossed the Arkansas state line and camped out in the mountains. Tomas fell asleep in the car, so Lydia helped me get the tent set up. She got Tomas and took him inside to feed him, and he fell asleep on her chest.

Sara and I went searching and gathered firewood so we could grill up dinner. She collected a bunch of little sticks so we could get that inferno going. She had her hands full, while I hauled the big logs, so we kept the flames cooking all night. It was a good plan but watching the twigs tumble from her small hands was something priceless. First, one twig fell to the earth, then another and another, like a waterfall. She tried to catch the fifth stick, but, as she swooped her left hand over, came the avalanche of twigs. Her lower lip stuck out, and she closed her eyes, deciding it was best to make several trips.

Soon, a huge fire lit up the night and we let it settle down so to place the cast-iron skillet on it and put the grate over the fire to grill the meat. I grounded up some chili peppers and put them in the meat and cooked up some burgers, and we chowed on beans and tortillas, too. We ate real good that night, with full bellies, and Sara and I slept in peace. She was a natural traveler, and before we dozed off, I sang a few verses of "Arkansas Traveler" to her. Tomas also slept good, but he slept on top of his mami's breasts, which meant one of us didn't get a good night's sleep.

The cackling of the roosters came while Sara and I packed up everything and Lydia and Tommy rested in the car. Before we left, we heated up some coffee and Lydia and I each drank a cup, then I walked my little girl to the creek and got a couple buckets of water to douse the fire. Soon we drove out of the Ozark Mountains and down to Texarkana.

Sara did most of the talking. "What beautiful mountains down here. Why don't we have mountains in Nebraska? How much longer until we get to where you grew up?"

"La cucaracha, la cucaracha, ya no puede caminar porque no tiene, porque le falta las dos patitas de atrás," Lydia began singing and Tomas and I joined in.

We arrived in Texarkana mid-afternoon. Things changed in the last seven years. I didn't recognize the place at first as the road we traveled on wore a fresh coat of asphalt and smoother and wider than the old bumpy cart path that us Barnums were used to, and a new house built on our old land. Soon I saw my favorite little pond and knew I returned home. We drove around and saw a small shack with a man working outside.

"Howdy there, sir. You live here?" I asked him as I got out of the car.

"Yeah, for a few years now. Why ya asking?"

"I used to know the old owners. Do you know them, or do you know if they're still around?"

"Don't know them, and don't know what happened to them, and don't care."

Figured that son-of-a-bitch was lying. He's darn tooting, if he didn't hear no stories about my old man, and what we did for a living. Thought it best if I didn't introduce myself to him. Probably some old Fed Klansman squatted on the land like Pa settled onto it years ago.

We headed back to the old farm pond, and that's where the Model T stopped and where we set up camp.

"Bo, why did you want to come here?"

"This was my favorite place when I was a kid. I told you about Becky McCormick."

"Well, I don't like it here. Let's get a motel if you can't find your folks."

"We'll look tomorrow. Besides, I want to fish and relax. I'll even take Tommy tonight if he can't sleep. Relax, darling. I'll take care of everything tonight. Go ahead and swim." I whispered to her, "I wish we were alone. We'd go skinny dipping together." I kissed her on the cheek, and she smiled at me.

I watched her like a hawk, while she stripped to nothing. Her naked body shone like it should be displayed on an artist's canvas as she slowly descended into the pond. She waded around and splashed water on her body and swam around like a smallmouth bass. I grinned watching her, and a bigger smile came to my face when she caught me staring at her and she stuck out her tongue. The kids and I set up camp and started the fire.

We heard a noise like someone approached. "Hey, no trespassing," screamed the female voice, I recognized. She stomped through the brush carrying a double-barrel shotgun. Yes, it was Becky McCormick. I'd recognize her anywhere in those mini shorts of hers.

"Becky McCormick, it's me. Bo." I hollered.

"Bo Barnum, I thoughts you were dead." She raced to me and gave me a more-than-friendly hug. Those big breasts of hers squeezed into my chest, and she wrapped a leg around my waist. "Welcome back, baby." She whispered into my ear.

"Thanks, Becky. Some folks were after me and I got away. Caught me a freight train up North."

"People said you were shot by the Klan. I didn't believe them. I knew if anyone could get away from those bastards it would be you."

"Well, I had a little help from a friend. So, what have you been up to and how's Martha and the folks?"

"Martha married a preacher. I think she joined that WCTU your mama was in. She's acting all holier than thou. Me, I never married. I waited for you to come home so we could get married. You know you promised me one day." Something flickered in her eyes. "Say, are those your kids?"

"Yep, they're mine. The precious girl's name is Sara, and the little guy is Tommy."

"They look Mexican."

"They are."

She started looking around. Her eyes searched the pond for the woman swimming, like a vulture circling for prey, and they rested on Lydia who still swam where Becky and me used to. "You married a beaner?" She spit the last word out like she drank cold coffee.

"Nope. I married Lydia. She is Mexican. Met her in Omaha where I live. She's a great wife and mother. Cooks me some great food and can sing like no one else in this world. I can't see life without her."

"Bo, you always liked to run with the Negroes. That's one reason why I loved you and one reason I hated you. Guess we're not getting married then, are we?"

I wished not to say the words, cos I knew it would hurt her. "I reckon not, but can we stay here?"

"Of course, you can. Why wouldn't you?" She kicked a damp clump of grass, unsure whether to wander off and go about her business. "My folks got killed. Pa got drunk and drove off a bridge down on Raccoon Creek. It's my land now. Say, are you looking for your kin?"

"Yeah. Lydia's parents were murdered up in Omaha. So, what do you know about my folks? Are they alive? I know you know something, Becky. Your folks and mine were close. In fact, I think your pa was the only man my dad trusted."

"I know something, I'll take you to him tomorrow." She glanced around again, as if someone lurked in the bushes eavesdropping.

Lydia came up from the pond drying her naked body with a towel, it wrapped it around her body, her clothes bunched up in her hands.

"Honey, I want you to meet Becky McCormick."

Lydia stuck out her hand. Becky was reluctant, but she stretched her hand out and gave her a firm shake, like two men when they meet.

"Well Lydia, you're pretty, and your kids are gorgeous. I knew it would take a special woman to nab Bo."

"Gracias, Becky. He is unique." She whispered something in Becky's ear and they both laughed.

"Denada, Lydia. It used to be my pleasure."

I waited for my time to talk. Darn girls talked together for what seemed like fifteen minutes straight and I found out my dad was alive. I'm glad they got along, but I felt a little selfish. I interrupted. "Becky you said my parents are alive. Where are they?"

"Sorry Bo. I'm getting acquainted with your wife. I'll take you to them if you want. They ain't together no more."

"That ain't no surprise. What would shock me is if they were both alive and kicking, and still talking to one another. Hell, I thought they were both dead. I saw that land a burning, so I ran like Pa taught me."

I stared at Lydia and wondered if she wanted to go tonight to see my folks. She already began packing the car up, while the kids ran around, exploring the field exploring. "Darling, do you want to go down there tonight?"

She walked up to me and cradled my cheek with her palms. Her eyes glinted with a sheen of tears, like she knew they were either dead, locked up in jail, or up in Little Rock in the asylum. "Bo, of course I do. I know this means a lot to you. It means something to me, too. I'm hoping Sara and Tomas have at least one grandparent."

We gathered up the kids and the camping stuff and shoved everything in the car. I drove up with Tommy, while the girls wandered up the hill to Becky's big house, which she shared with her coon dog. "Bo, why doncha stay here, instead of camping or getting a hotel in town? I'm gonna help you unload, and you won't need much of this stuff where you're going. Let's all get freshened up and hit the road. It ain't that far to your daddy's. Sara darling, go put that tent over in the shed."

"Okay we'll stay here. Are you sure we can make it tonight?"

"Bo, your pa ain't even as far as Shreveport. We can make it there in less than an hour."

"I bet I know where's he at. Is he down there on Caddo? Had me some good times there."

"Can you find it?"

"Hell, I could find that place at midnight on a cloudy night. Been there about twenty times. So, Pa's cooking down there?"

"He ain't cooking nothing no more, just running a little bit of everything shop. Knowing your dad, he's probably brewing something there and pimping a little, too. You know he's in that ol' whorehouse. I think you'll be proud of him."

"Well I'm not running no more. Got me a legal delivery job, hauling meat to stores in town. I done turned the still down."

"Bo, don't ever not make whiskey. It's the best in the land."

"Well I had to then. I got these kids to protect now. Don't want no trouble."

We headed down south the 60 miles or so to the state line and into Caddo Parrish. I ran this route many times down to Shreveport and to this little ol place on Black Bayou, north of Shreveport. I found it funny that I'm driving with my wife and our two kids and old childhood sweetheart looking for my pa.

Becky told where to turn in case I forgot, but this place was imbedded in my mind, like all them old writing and spelling rules I learned at Texarkana High School. I drove the swamps of the Black Bayou and took a few lefts and a right and rolled up the muddy path to pa's house. I recognized the place right away. It was now a little family store that sold everything from food to fishing and camping supplies, and bows and arrows and traps for gators, raccoons and other critters, as well as hunting stuff. Hell, you name it, he sold it. If he didn't have it, he'd get it for you. There might even be something after hours if the price was right and you'd let him know.

We got out of the car and I heard a familiar loud, shrieking bark. It couldn't be old Rex, since Rex was thirteen when I left. It had to be one of Rex's pups, the horny ol' hound was always on the prowl. An old man of about fifty came out with a shotgun aimed at me. He recognized Becky first and released the grip on the gun. He noticed Lydia and raised the rifle to his eye. Next, he saw Sara and Tommy, and looked deeply into my eyes, and the gun clattered to the ground, as if someone shot it out of his arms.

"Goddamn, Bo!" He hollered a country mile.

"Pa?" I called out, strutting toward him. He limped my way. Seven years hadn't done him much good. I knew I matured into a man, while my daddy aged into an old man. His mean eyes had bags under them. His long flowing hair receded and turned gray. The whiskers grew out of control, like the swamp land he inherited. He looked like a guy who hid out in the bayou for a few years too many.

We sat down in the old parlor room upstairs, in back of the store and treated with lemonade and snacks. "Bo, I made me a deal with the Feds. I had to, it was either that or get locked up or die. They shut down this old whorehouse and gave me a place to start over. In exchange, I gave them the still and your mom. You see after you disappeared, I started building it again, but them damn revenue agents raided it."

"My mom?"

"Yeah, let's go back to the night you vanished. Your mom got involved with this church group which was nothing but a women's Klan. Most of them married to Klan members. I found out that the Klan involved with the ambush on you. You probably knew that. Your mom tipped them off. She also led the Klan to our old place there. She tried to kill me. I stood by the still, when all of a sudden there was this explosion right in front of me, and then the fire. I had two choices; getting blown up and burned to a crisp or getting the hell out of Dodge. I always told you boys, if you ever get caught, keep running until it's safe to come home. Don't matter how far or long you're gone. Well. I got the hell out there, and came down here, where I knew it was safe."

"What happened to Mom?"

My dad took a deep puff from his corncob pipe and exhaled. The smoke drifted toward the open window. "Your Ma went out to that WCTU meeting, that damn church meeting. That Klan meeting! I know she didn't want you boys running, so she either tried to kill, or scare the bejesus out of us."

"So, she's in jail?" I pressed.

The old coot paced around like an expectant father, while laying tracks on the wooden floor. I'm sure he felt terrible about what happened to his wife, the woman who was supposed to remain faithful to him. "Nah." He spit brown tobacco juice on the floor. The amber stain blended in with the wood. "They got her locked up in Little Rock at the hospital. They said your mama was insane for trying to kill us both."

"Damn, dad, I can't believe this stuff." I roamed in circles, in total disbelief, and looked at Becky, who nodded, confirming everything.

"Yeah, Martha is with them ladies now. Kind of a woman's Klan. Her husband is in the Klan too."

My eyes darted between Becky and my pa.

"Yep, Bo, those damn sons of bitches ran us out of town."

"I reckon so, Pa. I got me in a little trouble up in Omaha. I quit making hooch, got involved with the wrong people. Good ol' Early Greene had contacts up there, so I got me a free place. Lydia didn't want me making the shine no more, and the mob or Klan chased after me. Been clean and legal for over five years. I'm only delivering some meat around town for a company. I needs me a good environment to raise these kids in. Won't have that delivering shine."

"Did you say Early Greene? I never trusted that son-of-a- bitch. He's a good man to have on your side, but he just as soon cut you up than help you out. He's always involved with things somehow and trying to figure out what angle he's working. The coot searched my face. "You gonna need a damn college degree."

Lydia entered the conversation. "Yeah, I think he had something to do with my parents' death. He fought with the Villaistas, and he's also a Madera supporter. My family was sent to Omaha to work, and a few months later, Bo and Early show up. A couple of months elapsed, and my parents were dead. I'm thinking this was on purpose."

"Hell, I don't know nothing."

"I know you don't, Bo." She spoke soft, taking away the sting of her previous statement.

My father continued, "Lydia, I agree with ya. That man has more angles than them fancy shapes in arithmetic. I'm thinking you and Bo got caught up in his game. That man knows someone, somewhere."

I sat down in a wooden chair and spun it around, until straddling it. "I'm not sure. I don't think he's with the Klan. He always talks crap about it. Hell, he could be, but it seems like he's fighting it somehow."

Dad took off his cowboy hat and spectacles and stared right at me, with piercing raccoon eyes. "Bo, I ain't got no education, but I know people, and I can put two and two together. The fact that her parents were killed right after you guys got there, and the crap that happened the night you left, and all that other stuff you said happened in Omaha ain't no coincidence."

"I'm pretty sure he's changing, probably tired of that life he's leading" I insist, not wanting to throw my friend under the bus. "He's married and they got a little baby boy, the same age as Tommy. I hope for his and Daisy's sake that he's changing. They need to take care of that little boy. We haven't heard from him since the baby was born. Either he's settling down or planning something big."

Pa dumped the pipe tobacco and grabbed another wad of chewing tobacco and stuffed it into his jaw. With that wad of chew in his cheek and the baggy eyes, he looked like a raccoon. He chewed on it for a bit and spit some of the juice out, nailing the spittoon next to him. "He's probably up to something big. Well, Goddamn Bo, we've been chatting all this time, and I haven't even played with my grandkids. Say there who wants to go fishing?"

"I do. I do." Sara screamed, "and Tommy does too."

"Well let's head on over to the bayou." He struggled to his feet. "I bet we can get some good fish. I'll give you guys some sapling, specially made for my grandkids. Perfect for them pan fish that swim by the docks."

We headed down to Black Bayou and did serious fishing. We got some bass and sunfish and Pa and I gutted them while Lydia and Becky fried them for dinner. Tommy and Sara caught a couple of fish even. In fact, Tommy caught a bass as big as himself, and I feared the fish might tug him into the murk. He managed to yank it up on the dock with help from Gramps. Sara caught a couple of the pan fish and also got a yellow cat that resembled a monster. I helped her yank it in. So far it was a successful reunion. We spent the night there on the Black Bayou, and even wrote a song about it.

Going down to see my pappy,

Where he is, I ain't got a clue.

Folks said he left last year

And headed back to that Black Bayou.

Black Bayou, in Caddo Parish,

Where you can't drink whiskey and beer.

That will all change at Cecil Barnum's

Got us a big party over here.

Well we got all types of music,

And we got the homemade brew,

And the ladies are giving their bodies,

On the banks of the Black Bayou.

Black Bayou in Caddo Parrish,

Where you can't drink whiskey or beer.

That'll all changes at Cecil Barnum's

Going to have a party over here.

"Dang, Bo, that's a pretty good song. You might make it down here playing that banjo and guitar." He took me in a back room and whispered. "I got some women who work here, and they take care of this old man, anyway." He smiled a stupid smile. "I do put them to work if they want to, and they get all of the money if they do. It's kind of semi-legal that way." He started laughing, then whispered again, "Too bad you're married. These ladies are quite fun." He stepped back, grinning. He owned a great smile for a man missing several teeth.

We spent the night and most of the next day with the old coot. I knew the old man was a survivor and could teach the kids things I couldn't. Told me he planned a little-old-get-together that night, so we figured we'd head back to Texarkana and crash at Becky's.

At Pa's and I asked him to come up and stay with us. "Thanks Bo, but I'm going to die in this bayou, since I can't die on my own land. I never told you this, but I met your ma here. She weren't no whore or anything, but her sister was. Your ma was a good woman but got mixed up with the wrong crowd there at the end. I don't got no ill feelings for her, even though she set us up. You need to visit her. She'd love to see you."

I shook the old man's hand and we piled in the car. "We'll stop in Little Rock. I still remember the places I ran to up there. I'll stop for a chat."

"Take care, son."

"You too, pa." I forgot to ask him about Zeke, and soon we were on our way back to Texarkana, dropped of Becky, and headed to Little Rock the next morning.

Chapter 8

That drive to Little Rock might have been the longest, hardest drive of my life. We're traveling to see my ma, who was committed to the asylum in Little Rock for attempted murder on me and my father. What the hell did I intend on saying to her? I tried to tune out "Little Rock is the capital of Arkansas isn't it Daddy? Jefferson City is the capital of Missouri? Nebraska's capital is Lincoln. What's the capitol of Kansas? Oh yeah, Topeka. I want to go to Topeka sometime."

I stared straight ahead looking way down the road, like I searched for roadkill miles ahead. "Sara be quiet." I snapped like a twig.

"Be nice, Bo." Lydia snapped at me as Sara wailed. Luckily Tommy slept in the back. Otherwise there would have been dueling criers.

"Well damn, honey. It's not every day you visit your mother in the asylum for attempting to murder you."

"Bo, I understand." She struggled steadying her voice. "Remember my parents were murdered, and no one was charged yet. You helped me so much, took me in and made me your wife. I love you forever for that. I'm trying to help you but I'm not sure how. You have to let me."

"Honey, I'm sorry, and I know that and appreciate it. I really do, darling, but sometimes a man needs to be alone with his thoughts. I wish I was alone."

"Honey, I know you do, but I bet things aren't as bad as it seems. Maybe she wasn't involved. I'm thinking she said the wrong thing to the wrong people."

"Yeah. You're probably right, but I still don't know what to say to her."

"Ask her how she's doing. It's always a good starter."

Lydia was right. I don't know what the hell happened to make Ma do what she did. I thought about that the rest of the drive. Ma probably told someone about the still and they came and burned it to the ground. She probably told someone I would be in El Dorado that night and had me set up. I'm sure she wasn't planning on it being that violent.

I found the State hospital and pulled into the parking lot, when another Model T sped away. The guy peeled out like a racer or bootlegger. I didn't get a good look at him, but from what I noticed, he looked familiar, but raced away too fast.

We walked up the steps and asked to see Mildred Barnum.

The lady at the front desk said, "Isn't she the popular one today. She's in room 703. I'll call a guard and have him escort you up there."

This giant of a man lumbered down the steps. He took a look at me, and then my family. "They can't come," he grunted, pointing to Lydia and the kids.

"Why not?"

"Only family is allowed upstairs."

"They are family. I'm her youngest son. She's my wife," I put my hand on her shoulders, "and these my kids, and my ma's grandkids. I know she wants to meet her grandkids."

He shook his head, rolled his eyes, and said. "Knowing Millie, she won't want to see those wetbacks."

My blood boiled, and I'm sure my face reddened, as I stepped closer to him in a fighting mood. "Hey Gordo, ask my mom if she wants to meet her grandkids?"

"My name's not Gordo."

"I don't know your goddamn name, and don't call my wife and kids wetbacks." I hate that word, figured it's as bad as nigger. I wasn't sure if these damn hillbillies had any sense. Hell, I was a damn hillbilly and I got more sense than that stupid guard. I stormed to the front desk to talk to the ugly lady again. "Call the boss. I want to see my mother, and I want her to meet her kin."

The boss guy came down in a flash. "What's the problem here?"

I pointed at the first guard and said, "Gordo over there won't let my kids see their granny."

"Of course not. They look Mexican."

"There ain't no law about not letting Mexicans up there. Don't a kid have a right to see their own grandma?"

"Okay. Take them up, keep an eye out," the boss said. "Those folks are worse than niggers. Make sure they don't take nothing."

The guard grunted. He took us up to the seventh floor. There were messed up laws about no Mexicans on the elevator, so we took the stairs. I carried Sara, while my wife hauled Tommy. The repulsive creature in uniform had his eye on Lydia the entire hike up the steps. I guess he thought she would steal something, even though she held h Tommy, and there wasn't anything to steal in the stairwell anyway. "Hey, Gordo, stop looking that way at my wife! I know she's gorgeous, but you don't have to stare."

"Shut up kid. Stop calling me Gordo, and you're lucky the kids and her can come up."

We got up to the seventh floor and thankfully put the kids down, since they were able to walk. Gordo's eyes remained all over Lydia, checking out every angle, every curve, and the fool got behind her to watch her walk. The fat man undressed her with his eyes, probably wondering what she looked like naked.

As we passed the rooms to room 703, I slammed him even further, "Yeah Gordo, you like what you see don't ya? Ya the type who takes little black girls behind the woodshed and sex them up, but you won't be caught dead in public with them. I know your type, damn Klan boy."

He raised his fist at me, getting the reaction I wanted. "I'm going to kill you, you little …"

I was saved by a nurse walking down the hall. She eyed us like some drifters, without pausing her stride. "Okay. We are here," he snorted again. Who should I say is calling?"

"Bo."

He pushed the door open with his paw, and I darted in. Lydia and the kids waited in back, while an evil eye watched over them.

"Bo! I can't believe it. You're alive. Come give me a hug."

I went over and hugged my ma. "Ma, I want you to meet your kinfolk. This is Sara, she's five and this little guy is Tommy and he's two. This is my wife Lydia."

She looked at the kids, I mean she stared them down, and then turned her attention at Lydia, like she studied a menu at one of them fancy establishments we went to on special occasions. I hoped for a smile and hugs for them.

"Oh Bo, why couldn't you be more like Zeke? He got himself a good wife. They are good Christians you know."

I gave my mother a scorned look. My eyes lips curled up as I searched for words to say. I knew I couldn't convert her. "Why did you set me and pa up? We could have been killed."

"What?"

"You tried to have us both killed."

"Bo, I did not. I told some friends of mine at church. I guess I didn't think it would have gone that far. I never meant anything to happen. Well, you are alive and so is Cecil." She sobbed. "I never thought those boys were going to get you."

"Ma, it's the Klan. They're killers."

"No, they're not. They want to live a pure way of life. You just missed Zeke and his family. I'm going to be released soon and Zeke said I could stay with him. I wish you were more like him. He's a good Christian boy."

I shook my head with confusion, anger, and rage. I bit my tongue again and again searching for the right words to say. "Ma, come give your grandkids a hug at least. Don't you know you're the only granny they got?"

"Bo, I can't. I'm not claiming them as mine. They aren't pure white like Zeke's boys."

I kept quiet. Ma's gotta know I ain't pure lily white either, so I turned and put my arm around Lydia and walked away, not mad, not angry, just emotionless. The tears fell as I realized I a mother and brother in the Klan. Though one thing I knew, my ma didn't try to kill me, probably tried to scare the shine running out of me. Lydia gave me a big hug and kiss right in front of my mother as we walked out. We left arm in arm as Gordo let us back down the steps and we reserved a hotel in Little Rock since I didn't feel like driving. After getting the kids to sleep, we made love, held each other close and fell asleep.

"Thank you, Bo, for not being like them." Lydia murmured before zonking out.

We had a good little drive the next day, but only made it as far as Jefferson City, Missouri, where we decided to camp out. We built a fire and made us some dinner. I grabbed that fancy resonator guitar and my knife to play a little slide on it. I wrote me a new song, straight from the prison farm in Mississippi.

Oh, Mama why, I said Oh Mama why, Why did you try to have me gunned down?

Oh, Mama why, I said Oh Mama why, Why did you try to have me run down?

Oh, Mama why, I said oh Mama why, did you burn me down?

Gun me down, run me down, and burn my house, to the ground.

Scoop my ashes all over town, yeah run me down, and gun me down,

And spread my ashes all over town.

I was only 16, yes only 16, when I had to run.

It got me feeling mean, yeah feeling mean

I went places you ain't ever seen.

Oh, Mama why, I said Oh Mama why, Why did you try to have me gunned down?

Oh, Mama why, I said Oh Mama why, Why did you try to have me run down?

Oh, Mama why, I said oh Mama why, did you burn me down?

Writing music helped me a little. It was like a shot of Pa's best shine. Though it didn't help as I thought about what happened seven years earlier. I pictured Ma telling them that I was running to El

Dorado and telling them Klan boys what my car looked like and what I wore that evening. She probably told some ugly Klan guy that Pa would be out by the still cooking some good brew. From what I gathered from Becky and Pa, that is exactly what happened. My ma might have been naïve and opened her big mouth to be accepted by her new church friends. Well she broke the main rule. Don't discuss the family business outside the family.

I was emotionless about her when she refused to see her grandkids. Figured it was her loss. Pa was so thrilled to see them, and I hoped to make it back to see him soon. Ma had my brother Zeke.

Chapter 9

The depression started to take its toll. There were milk strikes, cost of meat and vegetables dropped, and the need for me to deliver the meat wasn't there. It was time to look for a new job, and once again, I got lucky, since I started driving the trolley up and down 24th Street in Omaha.

With the kids getting older, Lydia, wanted to learn to drive a car so she wouldn't sit at home all day.

"Papi, can you teach me how to drive? The car sits here, and I want to take the kids somewhere."

My knees buckled, and I felt my face turn red as an Arkansas chili pepper, when she called me Papi. That she compared me to her revolutionary father was an honor, and something I hoped I could live up to. On the other hand, I ain't never going to call her Mami.

"Anytime darling. I'd love to."

That first driving lesson I shook like an Oklahoma shack during a dust storm. We got a neighbor to watch the kids while I took Lydia out to the country for her training. I steered the car south of town a bit and found a big old cornfield stretching out for acres and we switched positions, and I let her drive. She stalled the car at first, but once she got going, she did a great job. We drove across the cornfields recently reaped for the fall harvest. Luckily there weren't any humans for miles, so we bounced across the field.

I forgot about the damn cows. Holsteins came right at us, with them black spots, and not only were they heading right at us, they charged. It wasn't one or two, but the whole damn herd came. It was a dadgum freight train of Holstein cattle.

Lydia, being an inexperienced driver had not mastered the art of evasive driving. Hell, I avoided the law at age sixteen on the road, so outmaneuvering a herd of slow-moving cattle shouldn't have been that tough. Soon, we were about to be ambushed by the livestock, and it was time to be her knight in shining armor and come to the rescue. She slowly tried to get in my seat, but instead settled for sitting on my lap. Normally, I don't mind when she does that, but I also couldn't see outside the window.

Rearranging positions, the car stalled, and I eventually got it started and cranked a left as fast as I could and we sped away from the black and white cows, as if the Klan chased me. While speeding away I heard cursing and shotgun blasts, but never saw a soul. Lydia still attempted to get in the passenger and her nice bottom stuck in the air, pointed at me.

With the shotgun blasts behind me, and Lydia's rear end sticking out, I became distracted, too preoccupied for the speed I drove, and the car flew over a hill and came to an abrupt stop. Lydia went sprawling on her back with legs in the air and head on the floor. I got the car going again and found a quiet place to park on the banks of the Platte River. She wet her lips with her tongue, and curled her long, black hair with her index finger. We wasted no time figuring what to do next. Our clothes came off and we swam through the shallow waters, to a deserted sand bar and made love.

I didn't think anyone saw us driving on their land, but there were people on the other side of the river watching us make love, cheering us on. Lydia's blushed as red as an apple but managed to sneak back into the river and like an otter she swam across to where we dropped our clothes.

I lay on the sandbar and admired her swim. Her naked body stretched out in the river, her round buttocks going in and out of the water as she swam. If I got lucky, I witnessed the small formation of her breasts. When she got close to shore, I began my journey back across the river. She got out of the water, I stopped swimming to gawk at her. Those famous European artists couldn't paint a prettier picture. Those celebrated big city poets from back east couldn't write any boring, long winded, pretentious poems or rhymes about her.

Heck, I had a hell of a time writing her a love song. Nothing did her justice, when she stood there naked.

Overall, we did pretty good through the first part of the Depression. We weren't rich, but we weren't starving. For entertainment we went to the picture shows. Fred Astaire and the Marx Brothers, our favorites, plus the cartoons before the shows. Mi epsosa went for the movies, I went to watch the newsreels. I noticed this troubadour traveling the country playing songs to the destitute, and these poor people packed like sardines on the boxcars, as they traveled west looking for work. I found my purpose.

The next day I planned on sending Early a telegraph, but we received a letter from him that day. The letter said they're touring with the Carter Family and would perform in town soon. He wanted Lydia and me to help them out on a few songs, too. On a good night, with the stars aligned right and the wind blowing from the correct direction we'd listen to WSM from Nashville and sang along with the songs we knew.

Early Greene returned, and once again, rioting began. Uprisings flared up in the South, North and downtown. The Mexicans and Negroes always received blame, but I was sure who started it once I heard that familiar rap on my door. He always knocked five quick times, paused, and two more louder than the previous knocks.

"Woohoo, Bo. God damn Bo, how da hell you been?"

"Early," it's all I could muster up to say.

"It's great to see you. What da hell been going on? Hell, I'm so excited to play with them Carters. I told them we need to get to Omaha so you can hear us play with them. I even told them that you guys can play, and they said they'd get you on the show for a couple of tunes. Those Carters love to play music and want to hear you guys play, too. Hope you don't mind." He laughed that special laugh of his, and not the one that meant trouble.

Lydia and I smiled. "Yeah, we don't mind at all. It would be nice if someone famous heard us play. It gets kind of tiring playing in front of these old drunks who have no idea what we play, or some fools who wants us to play some stuff we don't know and get belted by few whiskey bottles. Hell, you know I'd play anything to make a few extra bucks, and to put a few slices of meat on the table."

"That ain't right, Bo, but I can't talk about it. Our show's tomorrow, and we need to get some rehearsing in. The Carters caught a later train, so they will pop by later. I hope you don't mind, but I already invited them over for dinner." He winked at us. "I told them Lydia is a great cook."

Lydia's eyes lit up like a Christmas tree. She ran into the kitchen. "I'll start making tamales. Bo, be a darling and get some pork and chilies? I'll start cooking."

After I returned from the store, we started rehearsed a few songs for the next evening. Thought we sounded good, and so did the ladies, but one man wasn't satisfied.

"C'mon Bo! You ain't never play behind the beat. What's going on with you? Learn to play music like a grown man." My eyes rolled like marbles as he cursed me some more. "Goddamn Bo, it's a fucking banjo, not a Resonator. These guys are like me. Professional fucking musicians, not some two-bit pickers you find on a street corner."

The train with the Carters chugged into Union Station around six that evening, and we were all there to meet them. Hell, I don't know, but I was awestruck for the third time in my life. The first was when I met Early for the first time, as he played that fiddle. The second was when I first saw Lydia, and every minute after, and now I met the Carter Family.

Luckily, I kept my cool and didn't embarrass myself or act like a total fool when Early introduced them to me. "AP, Mabel, and Sara, by the way that's my daughter's name, you are invited to my house for dinner. My wife is making tamales."

"Sounds good. Home cooking is the best. Living on the road and eating out every night isn't our style." AP Carter said

"Well let's relax a bit and head over to Bo's." Early said.

We got back and it approached dinner time. We all stumbled in the house, with me carrying most of the equipment. Lydia obviously heard us because she sang, *"You are My Flower,"* when we entered.

"Oh, my goodness, what a beautiful voice," said one of the Carter women. I wasn't sure who said it, since I remained busy hauling guitars in. The plan was to have dinner and rehearse some more. I did the introductions and we settled down and gobbled up the tamales.

"These tamales are delicious. Is there anything you can't do Lydia?" Sara Carter asked.

AP chipped in, "yeah Bo, you sure are a lucky man. Hang on to that woman."

"Why thanks everyone, she's beautiful, talented and can keep a happy home. Heck what else could a man want out of a woman?"

She turned as red as the chili sauce that topped the tamales. "Thank you," was all she mumbled.

The rest of the evening was spent rehearsing and playing music. I played an old obscure Mexican folk song, while Lydia sang it beautifully. Early, Daisy, and I did some old mountain jams, plus we did some spirituals, and some of the good ol' Negro blues music.

"You like a lot of stuff there, Bo, AP spoke. "We'd love it if the two of you came on stage with us, plus I guess you'll perform with Early and Daisy on a few numbers. You don't mind on short notice, do you?"

"We'd love to, wouldn't we, darling?"

"Of course, we're honored to play with you." Lydia blushed brighter.

"Actually, it's our pleasure. Here's the song we want to close with. It's best played with a lot of people." They broke out *"Will the Circle Be Unbroken."*

"Hey, that's a great song for the close of our benefit we're planning. Can we play it?" I told them about the hootenanny.

"Of course, you can. Say when is this show? Not sure if we'll be in the area."

Early butted in. "They're not sure yet, putting the pieces together. When they get a date worked out, me and Daisy might stop in and play, but knowing Bo, he won't get it organized."

I brushed off his remark, as my top teeth dug into my lip. Lydia stared at me, her mouth ajar, waiting for me to say something.

"Oh, that's fine. Our little tour is coming to an end in a few weeks anyway. Let us know when the gig is. We will try to come out. I guess, we need to get back to the hotel. We got a show tomorrow. It was nice meeting you, Lydia. Bo, can you be a dear and drive us back?"

I arrived home, excited after dropping the Carters off. I danced around the house a few times plotting my banjo and guitar performance on a big stage. Most of my shows to date were at little speak easies, juke joints, and makeshift clubs, or on a street corner. I never played in front of more than 100 people, so yeah, I felt energized as I bounced all over the walls.

Lydia remained calm, at least on the outside, but she was always rational, while I was the emotional one. On an even keel, she never got too down or too high. Of course, there were exceptions but as a general rule she kept us going. I asked her if she was nervous about playing, because I knew I was.

"Papi, I'm not nervous. Pretend you're up in North Omaha, with a couple of jugs of whiskey. You will do good. Remember all of the things that happened to us, this is nothing."

I drove the streetcar the next day trying to promote the show. I carried handbills I made, presenting one to everyone who boarded the trolley. I wanted a good crowd, even though I knew people weren't there to see Lydia or me.

The next evening was show time. Before the Carters came on, and the four of us performed, with Early controlling the show.

"Bo, I want you to stand behind everyone. You're accompanying everybody. I won't allow you a mic, so stand back. Hell, stay out of the spotlight."

I did as requested.

The show went on that night without a hitch. The four of us opened the show up and played for about an hour. We performed mountain music with me on banjo and Early and Daisy doing the fiddling, while Lydia sang.

Early and Daisy joined the Carters for a few of their songs played on the radio. The crowd loved them as the Carters tore the house down. It was quite the scene as thunderous ovations following every song. The audience was rowdy, but in the good way.

They beckoned, inviting Lydia and I on stage for the last few songs. We played along with *"No Depression", "Keep on the Sunny*

Side", and *"Will the Circle Be Unbroken"* and got a huge response. I knew it wasn't for Lydia and me, but it was great to hear.

We hung out backstage and returned to the hotel where they holed up. I couldn't believe I partied with the First Family of Music. Mr. Carter told me that I added a lot of sound to the hill music when I played my resonator. Mabel told Lydia we might consider moving to Texas because there was a booming Tejano crowd down there and that music was gaining national exposure.

"We can't move Ms. Carter. Bo has a good job here. He also doesn't want to play for the money, besides a little spending cash. He wants to play to educate people about different cultures. That's one thing I love about him."

"Oh, we understand. But being on the road and touring with us, you can reach a lot more people. Anyway, it's a thought, so you guys think it over."

"I know, and I'm thinking about it." She flashed that radiant smile.

We took the kids home, including little Robert Greene, and hoped to see the Carter Family again.

Chapter 10

Fiesta or hootenanny, it was the same thing, one big party with music and it needed planning. Musicians had to be found so the crowd could be entertained. To every dance hall, tavern, and saloon in this liquored-up town I went trying to find the best pickers and performers in town. I did pretty good on my recruiting, I put up some handbills on my route, and even passed them out to people as they got on. I found an orchestra to play, along with some blues and ragtime guys from up North and a few of my neighbors down in South Omaha who played some white man's blues and my favorite, the old mountain music. I even got a few Tejano and Mariachi bands. I figured nothing would go wrong. We'd charge a buck admission, and sell food and soft drinks, and give all the proceeds to our friend, Magdalena, whose husband was lynched.

Several bands refused to play. A couple of the Mariachi bands we asked told us they thought Pablo, Magdalena's husband, was guilty, or they were afraid of being deported even though they were citizens. I eventually found enough musicians for a music fiesta, hootenanny, or a damn good party.

We wanted to hold the show at the Dreamland, but they nixed the idea, afraid of the violence that might occur. We got turned down by the Paxton also for the same reason, plus they wanted too much in rent, before we could play. We ended up at the Sokol Hall, near our house in South Omaha. I took Lydia there to watch Fred and Ginger do their thing. The owners of the neighborhood hall were also against the idea, but I paid them twice the fee to lease the place.

Money talked, especially during the depression era, so they let us hold it there.

The show was a huge success. Early and Daisy returned to town, bringing their little boy. We were ready to jam as Lydia and I opened the show by performing a variety of our songs; some mountain music, some blues, and some Mexican songs, and Early and Daisy joined us to finish our first set. A few blues guys came out and performed too, and I joined them on guitar and harmonica. Jazz musicians followed, and I tried to play along with them but didn't quite cut it. We let the orchestra come next and they played a bunch of classic songs, which the audience danced to. We brought the South Omaha pickers out and Early, Daisy, Lydia, and I joined them. Big ovations rained all night, and the final set was the mariachi band that played a lot of Tejano and Notre. Lydia joined them for all the songs, and I played guitar with them, too. I owned the stage, as I ripped on all three of my guitars and my old trusty five string.

I brought all the guests back on stage for a finale. Some of them already left, but most stayed for the duration of the show. We did the Carter's *"Will the Circle Be Unbroken,"* and brought about fifty people on that small stage. We did the song adding a few verses and several solos while the crowd stood and sang along. I was pooped, but the star of the night was my lovely wife. The crowd loved her, and we collected about a thousand dollars to give to Lydia's friend Maggie.

"Baby," she told me that night as we relaxed in bed. "I told you years ago that your calling was to bring people together through your music. Do you remember? Well, you did."

Unfortunately, most of the city didn't get the message on what our festival tried doing. Two weeks later another Mexican was lynches, attempting to organize the workers at Cudahy's, a rival meat packing plant to Wilson's. A few weeks after that Maggie received an official looking letter that had a return address of Washington DC.

Magdalena Turbo:

This letter is to inform you that you must leave the United States of America. You must leave this country now and return to your native Mexico. This must be done by the end of the month. If you don't go voluntarily, you will be deported.

William Doak, Department of Labor.

"Bo, what is this?" She burst in tears, holding out the letter to me.

"Damn, Maggie. Looks like they're trying to ship you back to Mexico."

"They can't. I'm a citizen of the United States, like you."

"They shouldn't be able to." I noted the official appearance, and I asked for the envelope. Something was amiss. The return address stated Washington, but the postmark came from Omaha.   "This ain't official," I told her. "Someone is trying to scare you out of here. Look here." I pointed to the envelope. "It was sent from Omaha. You and your daughter can live with us."

I went to the federal courthouse to see if it was legit or not. I showed the man everything, including the envelope. "Hell no, this is a scare tactic. We've seen a bunch of these lately. Too many folks are afraid of losing their jobs to immigrants."

"Hell, unless we're Indians, ain't we all immigrants?"

"Yes, Mr. Barnum, you're right, but there's not much we can do."

"Can't we have this joker arrested?"

"Not unless we see him dropping envelopes in the mailbox."

"So, there's nothing we can do? Let hate keep chugging like a freight train?"

"Afraid so."

I stomp out kicking whatever I could find, my fists clenched, in search of anything to punch. I knew Lydia and I couldn't handle things by ourselves. There must be someone else in town that could change the status quo. People would riot if things didn't settle down.

Tensions increased at my job too. Lots of suits came in from the East talking to us drivers in private and attempting to unionize the drivers. Thankful to be employed, since many longed to take my place, I was hesitant about joining the union, since I could get fired for thinking about it or communicating with the organizers. Then again, I might have been shown the door for promoting my show while on duty or winking at the Negro lady who worked downtown as I dropped her off on Lake Street every night. Yeah, I could even get fired for not smiling at the smelly bums who took the car up and down 24th for entertainment. I believed the union would protect me, plus I'd make a little more money even though I'd give some back to pay the union. Besides Lydia and I were planning a trip to Texas and further west to sing songs for the destitute, who sought a new life.

We made big plans regarding the trip. After driving down to Shreveport, we'd hop a westbound freight and play songs and cook meals in the hobo camps scattered throughout the country. I hoped to take a month or two off work, but the suits of the traction company wouldn't allow it, but a union could protect my job.

One day, a slick-dressed man in a pin-stripe suit and a nice hat stopped to talk to me on the trolley.

"Can I talk to you in private?" He spoke in an accent that came from the east coast.

"Sure, but not here. Too many wandering eyes about." I knew right away who he was and what he was about. Like I said before, I could get fired for talking to him, or even acknowledging his presence.

"Of course not. Meet me at this Mexican joint down on 24th. I think you know the one." When I nodded, he added. "We'll go separately."

I knew where he spoke of. The organizer must have seen me in there a few times. I met the unionist for dinner, and we ate some tamales and drank soft drinks. I scanned the faces of the nearby tables to see if any of the bosses were there. It was no one but us and a few Mexican families.

"Is this about organizing?" I asked. "I'm not sure I want to join the union."

He sensed my hesitation, and like and added a persuasive twist. "What if I can secure your job and get you better wages?"

I straightened in my chair. "I'm all ears. The thing is I'm planning on taking my family down to help them folks from Oklahoma and Texas and head further West. I want to make sure I a job when I return."

"I can definitely help you." He spoke in a matter-of-fact tone.

"I'm not signing up now," I cleared my throat. "I mean, I need to speak with to my wife."

"Of course. I'm checking to see how many people are interested. I know you can lose your job if they catch you on a list. I'm not taking names or anything right now. I don't want to waste my time here. So far, it looks like I'm not."

"I understand."

He stepped out as rapid as he entered. He reminded me of like Early Greene the way he vaporized. I finished my drink and tamales by myself and paid the tab. That was the last conversation I had with the man, even though I noticed him on the streetcar several times. I smiled and tipped my cap toward him, like the other patrons.

I rushed home, peaking over my shoulder, checking if anyone followed me. I acted a little guilty, like I cheated on my wife or swiped some chickens. Someone might have followed me, because a car with a guy who resembled the company clerk passed me twice and pointed my direction. It was hard to tell if it was him or not. I worried a little. When I returned home, I told Lydia, the only person I trusted, about the meeting.

"Oh Papi, you need to be careful who you talk to. They might have hired people to see who wants to join a union, and if you say yes, they will fire you."

"Good point, honey. That's why I didn't commit to nothing. I told the man that I need a little time to discuss things with you and also about our trip to Texas."

Her eyes widened, and her voice rose an octave or two, nearing a yell. "You can't tell these people about the trip, or even that we're thinking about a trip. Sometimes Bo, I think you trust too many people. I hate to say it, but you're like your mother that way!"

I scratched my chin, seeing her point. "Yeah, you're right. I wasn't that way before. When I ran shine, I didn't trust nobody, but now I'm legit I trust a whole lot more folks. Damnit, Lydia, I need to only trust you."

"I'm glad you didn't tell them you want to join." She came over and kissed me on the cheek, while I ate the burgers she made. "Now, tell me again about this trip you want to take."

"I'll tell you after family time." We did the usual singing and jamming, letting the kids sing all the different songs we taught them, until it was sleep time for the kids and private time for us. She ran her fingers through her hair and my curly locks, wanting to know more about the trip we were planning.

"I don't have all the details, but I figured we could drive down to see Pa for a couple of days. After that, we would head over to Texas, hop a freight train and travel with the folks. We'd sing songs and cook them meals. If we time it right, we could even schedule a few shows and try to raise money for them. I'd love to take the train out to California and play for them Okie's that are stuck in government camps. You know them folks we've watched on the newsreels?"

"Sounds good, Papi. Maggie and I are planning something, too. We want to schedule a Cinco de Mayo celebration, a carnival, and another big fiesta. Our people have been threatened, deported and killed. We won't back down. We need pride and I can't think of a better way or date to celebrate it."

"Hey, great idea. Do you need help planning or organizing it?"

"Oh no, Papi. I want this to be my thing. Mine and Maggie's. You did the music festival all on your own."

"All right darling, you guys do everything. I'll concentrate on the vacation, while you plan the festival." I kissed her on the forehead and lips, and we drifted off to sleep.

I worked a half day the next day and picked up Sara from school. On the walk home, I told her about the trip I was planning, about going to Grandpa Cecil's, and catching a freight train across Texas.

"I want to ride a freight train like you did when you moved up here." Her eyes were as big as a harvest moon, all big and shiny. I've never seen her so excited.

Maybe I'll take you on a little trip. Don't say anything to Mami until I make sure it's okay."

"I won't daddy." She tuned a little song on the way home. "I'm gonna ride a freight train, I'm gonna ride a freight train. Going to ride a freight train, across the land."

It was one of those parental moments where you want to smack the child, for disobeying you, but marveled her brain and sense of adventure.

The next night, Lydia and I made love and we rested in each other arms. I couldn't see the whites in her pretty brown eyes, and her breathing steadied, as she drifted off to sleep.

"Sara is excited about taking the train across Texas."

"So am I, Papi." She slurred her words, in her dreamy state.

"Then it's okay to take her for a ride in a boxcar, maybe a quick little run out to North Platte and back?"

"Mmm, I don't care baby."

She was soon fast asleep on my chest, as my mind started wandering. I thought about the folksinger who I watched on the newsreel before the movies. His name was Woody. I began admiring the man. In my dream, Lydia, the kids, Woody, and I would travel across the country on a freight train, singing, and helping the migrant workers. If we had money, we'd donate it, even though those folks probably wouldn't accept it. If there was extra food, we'd cook for them, if we heard about employment, we'd find them jobs. All of the pictures I saw of these folks, none of them smiled. I wanted to make a few people happy. I fell asleep humming a song in my head.

Hopping that train with you, and I'm picking them crops with you.

I'm living in boxes with you, cause we're people just like you.

Stealing some peaches with you, and I'm stealing some chickens with you.

I'm walking the beans with you, cause we're people, just like you.

Cooking over the fire with you, and I'm crossing the river with you.

I'm getting bullwhipped just like you, cause we're people, just like you.

I woke up refreshed after a few hours of sleep and ready to start my day. I scribbled the lyrics on a piece of paper, woke up Lydia, and lit an oil lamp. I showed her the words while I sang it. "Hey darling, what do you think of this song?"

"I love it, Papi," she muttered and rolled back over.

When I got home from work the next day, she translated into Spanish.

Salto que preparan con usted, Recogerlos cultivares usted,

Vivir en cajas con usted, Somos personas igual que tu.

Robo de los melocotones con usted, Robo de pollos con usted.

Paseos a los frijoles con usted, Somos persona, igual que tú.

Cocinar sobre el fuego con usted. Cruzando el rio con usted.

Como bullwhipped con usted. Somos personas, igual que tú.

She played a little riff on the guitar, and I got the banjo and sang along.

"It sounds better in Spanish."

"It must be the way I sing it," she giggled.

"Of course, darling."

A few days later I took Sara down to the railyard. It was the same place I met her mother years ago, and the same place I held my first legitimate job. A few families still made their homes there, just not as many as there was ten years ago. I pointed to Sara where I met her mother. I wasn't sure it was the exact spot, but no one knew any different. I tried being as close as possible.

"No trespassing." a bull shouted. I didn't recognize him.

"Hey sorry, I'm showing my little girl where I met her mother. We'll be taking off soon."

"No worries there, kid. Be safe around here."

"Sir, I got a question for you." I whispered so Sara didn't hear me. "I want to take my little girl here for a ride, maybe a quick one out to North Platte and back. I don't want any trouble. If I slip you some green, would you make sure we don't get arrested or beat?"

"Depends on who's working that night. It can't hurt."

I asked Lydia later that night if it was still okay. to take her for a little train ride.

"What! I never said that, Bo."

"Yes, you did darling. You did half asleep. You probably don't remember."

"You tried tricking me."

"No, I wasn't." I said with tongue in cheek. "I will make sure it's safe, and we'll get off at the first stop, and grab the next one coming back. Don't tell her, but I'm going to bribe the guards a little. You've seen the news reels. Kids her age ride the trains all the time by themselves. I promise everything will be fine. She really wants to go."

"Do you promise?"

"Darling, I promise you I won't put our baby in any danger, and…" I paused for effect and winked. "I'll even make it up to you."

Lydia reluctantly agreed, aware Sara asked all week about it. The trip was set up for the following weekend. It started to get as chilly as early November can get in Nebraska. The north winds howled in full force, like coyotes on the western plains. The temperature remained bearable, but we wore our winter coats, hats, and gloves. I ran into a bull and told him what I was doing and shook his hand while slipping him a Lincoln.

"Yeah Barnum, I know who you are. You're a straight shooter, and I respect that about you. This one over here will head straight to North Platte. Ask for Bill when you get there. He'll get you one straight back." He looked at his hand, and the five-dollar bill in it. "Damn railroads been laying off people. I need to protect the family."

I grabbed a ten and shook his hand again.

He smiled and said, "Stay safe, Mr. Barnum."

"It will be safer this way, sweetie. Sometimes we need to talk to the rail police. There are some places where these policemen are not as nice."

"When you came up here, did you give the rail people money?"

"You saw that, didn't you? Nope, but I got beat up pretty bad, and thrown in jail. I don't ever want that happening to you."

"Let's take that one over there. It looks like it's ready to roll." She started across the yard, running to a train that looked like it was heading south.

"I think we should take this one. I know where it's going. You only take the ones where you don't know the destination if you're running away. We're not running away."

"What if I want to run away with you, Daddy?"

"Then, we'll take one with no clue where it's going to."

"Okay Papi, we'll take this one here." Her lower lip stuck out, as if she wanted to take the other train south with her old man and run away from the rest of her family.

We walked over to the car which turned up empty, so I climbed in and helped her get on. We found a little spot in the back and rolled out a blanket and cuddled up. I unpacked my Marine Band harmonica and blew in rhythm as the engine started puffing, the train wheels rolled, and that old bell of a whistle hollered, waking up the sleeping city.

"Daddy, stop it."

"Here, you try. Put your mouth over the first three holes and breath in twice, then out twice, and keep repeating. See, it sounds like a train." She kept wailing on that harp like an old Southern Negro man, and through her eyes, I noticed she smiled. A look of excitement resonated, however as I felt her cuddle next to me, I knew she became frightened. The train picked up speed when two hobo kids jumped on. Even in the dark, I knew they wore tattered clothes.

"Where you headed?" The older one asked me. He looked to be twelve, while his traveling companion looked younger. They had to be brothers. Their eyes were on Sara.

"Taking my daughter for a joy ride. I used to ride these years ago. Haven't been on one since."

"We're heading out to Wyoming, trying to get work on a ranch. Our Pa whooped us good last night, so we is running away."

"What did you do?"

"We stole some chickens and melons. We were trying to feed the family," the older boy continued.

"You shouldn't get whipped for that. Hell, my pa never cared if we stole food. I stole chickens and melons all the time back in Arkansas. My old man never whipped me at all."

We talked a lot on the trip out. I guess I did, telling them the stories of my youth, and how I used to run shine for my old man. The boys gazed at me like I was Jesus. I saw the whites of their eyes hanging on every word that I said. Sara listened too, even though she heard those stories about a million times.

With me talking up a storm, the trip went pretty quick. I taught the boys to play the harmonica and gave mine to the oldest at the end of the trip. Once the train stopped, the boys thanked me and took off, while Sara and I snuck out of the car. I told her to walk low as we went to find Bill, the bull. I went over and asked the first bull I could find.

"You Bill?"

"Yep."

"I'm taking my daughter for a quick little trip. Looking for the next one back to Omaha. Plus, there were two boys on their way towards Rock Springs. They seemed like good kids, but their pa likes the switch too much. Hoping you can help them out, too." I shook his hand and placed a ten in it.

"Yeah, they sent me a message from Omaha. Here, take this one over here. I'll keep an eye out for them boys and get them in the right car. That damn switch is why I'm out here and not in Denver no more."

It was deathly silent in the North Platte yard, and pitch black. Sara huddled up so close to me that if she got any closer, she would be on my other side. A loud noise broke the eerie silence, someone shouted in Spanish, followed by two gunshots.

A voice resembling the bull who helped us, swore, "damn spics, we keep telling them there's no work in Omaha."

The ride back seemed like it took forever with Sara quiet, and I didn't know if she was sleeping or not. She clung to me tighter as we chugged East. I held on, refusing to let her go. No words were spoken. She knew what happened and must have been too afraid to ask me about it. Her grip all night tightened around my chest.

When the train stopped, I hoped we arrived in Omaha. I never trusted a bull; I still owned a little scar to prove that. He could have put us on a train to Cheyenne or Denver. I didn't recognize the yard at all since the night sky was pitch black. Sara was still asleep, clinging to me, and I patted her shoulder to wake her up, and walk her outside. I struggled with her since she was growing, flipped her on my shoulder and kept walking, on the lookout for a landmark or a street sign, but I couldn't find one. I was pretty sure we were in Omaha, and which way was home, so we headed that direction.

I came across a street sign, and I turned in that direction. My back started aching, so I put my little big girl down. "We're almost home, sweetie. You can walk from here."

When we got home, Lydia slept on the davenport waiting for us. She woke up as we entered.

"Thank God you are home. I was worried about you two." Sara ran into her mother's arms.

"I'm glad we're back, too," I told her. "It was quite the adventure."

Sara turned to me and then to her mom. "It was the best trip ever. I want to do it again." She ran and hugged me and gave me a kiss. "Thank you, Daddy," and she ran off to her and Tommy's room and fell asleep.

"She's something special, isn't she?"

"Yes, Papi, she sure is. Definitely a Daddy's girl. So, Bo, when are you going to make it up to me?" We were in bed laying down. "I said when are you going to make it up to me?" All she heard was snoring.

Chapter 11

"Darling, I thought Mexican Independence Day was in September. I didn't know it was in May."

"Cinco de Mayo is not our Independence Day." Lydia slapped her head in exasperation. It's the day the Mexican Army beat the French at the El Dia de la Batalla de Puebla. We also call it The Day of the Battle of Puebla. It's a celebration and another big festival. They used to celebrate it in Texas, but I haven't seen it here as of yet. I would like to get it started."

I gave a sheepish grin. "What year was that? I think my great grandpa fought in that. At least, that's what Pa told me."

"1862. Your great-grandpa fought for the Mexicans?"

"Not sure, I think Pa said I had a great-grandfather who helped slaves escape. Well, he married one, and they lived in Mexico for a while during the Civil War before he came back and died fighting for Louisiana and the South."

"You never told me." She looked cross that I neglected feeder her this piece of vital information for so long.

I gave her an apologetic look. "I forgot about it, until you told me about the French. Pa said his Grandpa shot a bunch of Frenchman up, and that's why he hopes we never fight for the French, or against them. He's afraid his French kin might remember and shoot us dead. Pa's crazy."

"Your dad is special though. Now, baby, I do have to go plan some things. Can you take the kids out so Maggie and I can get things done?" She wagged a finger at me. "No train trips."

We had a long cold snowy winter that ran till March. The snow began melting and little rivers of water trickled down next to the streets of Omaha. Lydia had about a month and a half to plan. The weather was warm enough that we could grab some sapling and head down to where the Platte and Missouri Rivers met and try our luck at fishing. I always liked to fish in the spring when they were always spawning and hungry, which meant good eating for us.

A little country store stood in Plattsmouth that sold all the bait we needed, plus it carried harmonicas and corncob pipes. Sara approached ten, and I smoked at ten, so I thought about getting her a pipe. She wanted one, but I knew that would probably be the last thing I'd ever get her. Lydia didn't do tobacco at all, it stunk up the house pretty bad, and she said it ain't good for me. She was probably right, but my folks always did tobacco in some sort of way. They either chewed or smoked it. Sometimes both. Of course, most of my kin didn't live long healthy lives either. I didn't think twice about getting Tommy a pipe, and he was seven.

I set up the poles for them. First, I got Tommy's ready and threw the line in the water for him. I was about to get Sara's ready, but she beat me to it. She also beat me to a wad of chewing tobacco I brought. She stuffed in her cheek like I did, and I noticed her pretty little face turn green. She puked it out, and everything else she ate that day. I saw some of the bologna from the sandwiches we had for lunch and some pieces of apple on the ground. She managed to hang on to the sapling while she vomited. I could never underestimate the girl. She didn't cry or nothing.

We fished the rest of the afternoon, until it got dark and we headed home. I told stories about Grandpa Cecil and I fishing on the pond. They heard the stories about a zillion times, but still listened as I went on.

"Grandpa always told us a little prayer before we set out. Grandpa wasn't a religious man or anything, but he said that in the early days a lot of Jesus's followers were fisherman. That is why you have to pray when you go fishing. His prayer went something like this, 'I know I don't talk to you as much as I should, but like your followers, we are fishing today. We need to catch these fish to feed the youngins here. So, Lord, bless us with a good catch today. Amen."

"Daddy, why didn't we pray before we started fishing?"

"I guess Sara, we should have. It might have stopped you from chewing that tobacco."

"I would have snuck some from you sometime."

"At least now you know, you shouldn't chew that stuff."

"Why do you do it?"

"I guess it's a habit. Maybe today I will stop, and let's pray that I do. It can't hurt none."

Sara and Tommy both prayed I quit chewing tobacco. We caught about four catfish that day, all after we said the prayer about an hour into the fishing. I left the chewing tobacco on the riverbank and never touched it since. Now, the pipe tobacco was another thing.

We got home with dinner, but Lydia already cooked up a storm. She usually prepared the big meals when she had a great day, or she used it as a way to relieve stress. I wasn't sure which it was. Maggie, and her daughter, Ana were helping in the kitchen. Enchiladas were baking and the aroma of the beans, chilies, and tomatoes spread all over the house.

"Did you have a good day?" She looked at me, in a sad way. Then it turned into an angry glare.

She chopped meat with the butcher knife, slamming the knife into the pork like she was trying to kill a live pig. My muscles tensed, sweat dripped from my forehead, as she turned toward me to answer, and she grasped the knife in her fist, pointing at me. "You should have been there, Bo. I needed you, and you weren't there."

"You didn't want me there."

"I know," and she put the knife down and came into my arms. "Maybe we can't do this on our own. I might need your help."

"Darling, we're a team. What do you need me to do?"

"I don't know. If I knew, I could do it myself. Maybe these people don't want a Mexican girl organizing a festival. Maybe you can talk to some people."

"I can talk with the new mayor."

"I'll talk to them. I need you by my side. They harassed me, and called me a dirty spic, and accused me of trying to start a riot."

"Who did? I'll kill them."

"At the courthouse. I went in to get a permit for the party."

"I'm coming with you the next time you go back there. I'll be by your side and won't say nothing unless I have to."

A couple of days later, we went down to the courthouse, and talked to the same people Lydia spoke with earlier.

Lydia stood in front of the older clerk at the courthouse. She shook when she spoke. "We want to celebrate Cinco de Mayo in Omaha. There are a lot of Hispanic people here, and we would like to put on a festival. Maybe get a carnival with rides and perform some live music."

"Sorry." The old lady never looked up. "We are not holding a festival for some crazy Mexicans. It's for the city's safety."

"What do you mean?" I butted in. "It was last fall we put together a big music concert for the city, and there was no violence. People had fun, and no one got harassed. It's a way the people can celebrate and enjoy themselves. Nobody's going to hurt anyone."

"The word is no, and I'm not budging. These folks are all wild and rowdy."

I felt like one of them cartoon characters, whose temperature was rising, and ready to explode. "Now, listen here. Does this woman look like she's going to start a riot? Do you think my children are going to start a riot? They're Mexican too. I demand we see the mayor."

The lady turned around and walked away. She never said she was getting the mayor, nor said 'tough luck, spic lover.' She never said anything. We waited in the lobby there for about thirty minutes before a security guard removed us for loitering.

"Well darling, we need to find some people who will make it happen. Maybe we should go to Nuestra Senora de Guadalupe. I think we need to start attending church for the kids' and our sake."

"Good idea, Bo. That was my next suggestion. I'm thinking we could have it on the property." We got on the streetcar and headed home. I thought both of us were getting out at our stop, but when we reached, she kissed me goodbye. "Wish me luck." She rode the trolley to the church. I was home alone, since the kids were in school.

She came home in a much better mood, smiles all around, and the kids remained at school for a few more hours.

"Bo, that's why I love you. You always think of ways to better our lives, our children and the community. I told them at Nuestra Senora de Guadalupe that we'd start attending, and we want to have a Cinco de Mayo festival. Guess what? C'mon Bo, guess."

"They said you can do it?"

"No. They're planning one already. They want me to work on it right away and have a meeting tonight."

"Even though I mentioned it, I'm not so crazy about these church meetings you know, with my ma."

"I know, Bo, but I need to go back tonight. You'll watch the kids, I hope. Ana too."

"Of course, I will. We can get into all kinds of trouble together."

While Lydia and Maggie attended the meeting, I entertained the kids with music. They needed to embrace all their cultures from both parents, so I sang some of those old Mexican work songs, as well as the Negro spirituals and some mountain music. I wanted them to learn that one culture may have its faults, but also has its own beauty.

Sara took over the singing, her voice as pretty as her mom's. That girl was destined to be a singer, or whatever she wanted to be. She excelled at everything she did. Tommy was good at keeping the beat, his rhythm was steady, but he wanted to sing. His off-key and snarly voice drowned out his sister and her friend. I stayed home with the kids for about three nights a week, for six weeks while they planned the festival. The carnival soon got booked, a few bands were added, and it was showtime.

Most of the congregation knew me. I wasn't famous in town or anything but had a reputation. Most of the Mexicans in town respected me, since I stood up for their beliefs. There were a few crazed men who wanted my head because I was making it with one of their own princesas. They didn't give me any problems, only nasty, jealous glares.

Most of the bands were local. The same guys I played with before, but the church got a band out of South Texas that was popular in the Rio Grande Valley to play. I'm not sure how they pulled that off, but I played with the Carters, Lydia could play with Narcisio Martinez and Santiago Almeida. I never heard of them, but Lydia listened to them, and she loved the way they played. The church couldn't pull in the biggest name band in San Antonio, but they pulled in a third-tier band that was getting a good reputation locally.

"Do I get to play?" I tried to cajole my wife.

"No, maybe with the guys you played with before. I'm not even sure I will get a chance to sing with Paulino and Torreon. I'm hoping so."

I was disappointed. When I heard they were getting some band from Texas, I anticipated playing with them, even though I had no clue who they were. I thought they were the big thing out there, but it turned out they were the third biggest in San Antonio. I learnt most of their songs, just like she learned mine. I knew it wasn't the last thing on Earth, and I figured I'd get over it.

"Darling, I was looking forward to playing with them." I broke out the guitar and played like a farmer protesting the government from his one room shanty south of the Rio Grande. I sang in my broken Spanish, as I remembered a young Mexican girl of sixteen singing *"Red River Valley"* in broken English.

"I'm sorry, Bo. I will see if you can play one song with them. Remember this party is for Mexicans. Of course, you will be there. You are one of us."

"Of course, I will be there watching the kids. Tell me, will there be a kissing booth?"

"Of course, silly."

"I know where I will be. I'll drop my change to kiss you."

She rose on tiptoes and kissed me. I didn't let her know that I felt bad about not playing. Soon, it was time for the Cinco de Mayo festival. Lydia and Maggie went to the church early to get things ready, while I walked to church with the kids. Sara and Ana were old enough to hang by themselves, but I made sure they stayed near me.

When we got down there the festival was hopping. Most of the Mexicans in town or across the river attended. I took Tomas on some rides, mainly the carousel. He wasn't too crazy about the big rides or the roller coasters, and neither was I. I didn't mind not taking him on them. Sara and Ana went on the fastest, spinniest rides there. I figured they were fine.

"Tommy, let's go see your mama. She's at the kissing booth."

"Daddy, we just went there."

"Yeah, I know, but you really miss her, don't ya?"

We walked up, and I dropped a few dimes, and shared sweet kisses with my wife. Tommy also gave her some kisses. I stepped aside to study the other people, who dropped coins off, to press their lips against her rose-colored lips. The joke's on them, as I realized I received longer and sweeter kisses for free. These jokers had to pay and all they got was a quick peck.

She closed her kissing booth down a time or two. It was her turn to sing with one of the local bands she booked, and one I booked for my festival. Lots of folks filed onto the dancefloor. I danced with my girl, while her brother danced with Ana. We didn't want any older boys dancing with the girls. Maggie was there, too. She and Tommy took turns with Ana.

All eyes focused on Lydia, as the crowd grew. They hooted and hollered for her. She became an instant star that day.

It showed in her eyes. There's nothing wrong with star-struck eyes, and wanting the fame, glory and receiving admiration from hundreds of onlookers. I do think there's something wrong when you want it more than your family or it becomes your passion. I'm not talking about the music being the passion, but the fame. Somehow, I saw it in her eyes, something different in the way she glowed from the adulation. There was something mysteriously dangerous about the way she smiled. I wish I could put a finger on it, but I couldn't.

I spoke with Maggie about it, and she shrugged it off. "Bo, you're used to the attention."

Maybe she was right. People always cheered for me, or for her and me, but this time it was for her alone. I was a nobody to the crowd, one of a handful of gringos who was celebrating. She joined the second band on stage to do some back-up singing, and she was once again a hit. They had an equally pretty singer, a little more provocative in the way she dressed and danced and gathered most of the attention.

Paulino and Torreon called her up to do a couple of their songs. She sang her parts beautifully, and danced a little dance, too. Rhythmic and sexy, if you ask me. After the songs I needed to hug her and let her know how proud I was of her performance. I went backstage, where she spoke with the Tejanos.

I overheard Paulino or Torreon say, "You are very good. Would you like to join us on tour?"

"No, I can't. I'm married and I don't think my husband would like that."

"Your husband? A pretty thing like you shouldn't be with one man."

"Unless it's me," the other voice said.

There was an awkward silence, as I got warm, and turned red. My clenched my fists, and ready to go pop the guy, but after a few deep breaths, and divine intervention, since we were in a church parking lot, I kept my cool.

Lydia continued, "We're planning a trip through Texas, to support the migrant workers and will also head west to support the Okies. It's kind of what we do. My husband plays guitar and banjo and writes songs and we sing them. I want to play one for you. I translated it to Spanish."

"Here take my guitar and let's hear it." She played *"Te Usted"* for them, and it sounded prettier and more passionate than ever.

"That's very good. We play a lot in San Antonio and in the valley. When are you going to be in Texas?"

" This summer, I'm pretty sure."

"Well, you look us up. I will get you a show. I promise you."

I stomped away, breathing hard as my heart beat out erratic. I slammed my fist into a trash can and kicked it over, and that damn can went rolling down the hill. Wasn't sure if I was a little jealous or I was right about the look in her eyes earlier, a look that would give in to temptation for a little bit of fame. I thought the devil got a hold of her. I walked away and waited, as I paced the parking lot. I already began the clean-up process, but most of the papers I picked up, were from the trash can I tried to demolish.

"Bo, I got good news. They want me to sing in my own show, when we pass through San Antonio this year. We are going through San Antonio?"

"It wasn't on the way. I thought we weren't supposed to tell anyone about the trip, or are those only my rules?"

"Bo, what's wrong?"

"I don't know, maybe a little jealous, but the trip is between us and the kids right now. I figured they told some folks, but you don't know these guys. You shouldn't be telling these strangers our business."

"You were listening? Why didn't you come back? I would've introduced you to them."

"You were busy talking, besides I wanted to start cleaning up."

"Bo, I'm sorry, I should never told them. I was excited from performing. I know how you feel after you play up North and get home real excited. I want to get everything cleaned up and send the kids to Maggie's, so we can stay up all night." She gave me a long kiss, right next to a couple of nuns. "Let's finish picking up."

After our private time, I laid awake that night wondering if I was wrong for feeling the way I did. I knew she deserved the spotlight more than she got. I was the one who always got the attention. Maybe I was right, about the star struck look she had, about the devil getting a hold of her.

Maybe I as wrong, too. Sometimes a man had to know, and other times it's best to wait and see, so you don't look like a total fool if you bring it up. I decided to wait.

The next few weeks I planned our trip through Texas. The traction company granted me a few months off for the summer. It was paid time off, and the trip became a reality. Lydia still acted a little distant. I knew she longed to sing on the big stage, where she had thousands of fans cheering on every note. She had a gift, and the thing about folks having a gift is they need to share it with people. I figured we'd hit San Antonio and give her a shot at stardom. What better way to spread our message than have someone famous speaking out loud? Maybe people would listen to her, cause around here most folks didn't listen to me, no matter how much I tried.

Chapter 12

I wanted to spend a week or so with Pa and revisit the juke joints and little shacks I delivered to before moving North. I thought Lydia and the kids would take a liking to them, especially Sara. After that we'd have Pa drop us off at the train station in Shreveport and head to Dallas and San Antonio. I'd give Lydia the shot of her lifetime. I wanted to take a run to Mexico after that and work with the migrant farm workers who struggled to survive in the Rio Grande Valley. When we got time, after that we would head back North and catch Route 66 and head west, following the Okies who were kicked off their land and struggled to feed themselves. We'd give them what they needed, and that was encouragement and something to look forward to, besides broken dreams and promises.

The roosters started cackling, but we already crossed the river and headed south toward Missouri. The kids yacked it up and played games, while Lydia tried to figure out which songs she'd perform in San Antonio. Me and my hot rod sped down Highway 59 like a bat out of hell, while the rail posts became blurs to me.

We rolled into Fayetteville that evening and stopped at a little roadside motel and diner. The slightly plump, sad-looking waitress came over to us. She wasn't too bad looking, and I found myself interested in her a little too much. My eyes roamed the contour of her face and followed down her body, paying too much attention to her rather large breasts, which she didn't mind giving me an eyeful of when she bent over to deliver our food.

"Bo!" Lydia smacked my arm, not hard, but enough to change my focus.

"What? Oh sorry, there's something about her. I'm thinking about writing a song about her. She got the look that the next trucker might snatch her away from here in the middle of her shift."

"You hadn't written anything about me, not since we've been married. Do you still love me?"

"Of course, I do. I figure it's easier to make up stuff about someone you don't know. Honey, look at the way she walks and looks toward the door when someone comes in. She's looking for something."

"You still like the way I look at you?" She batted them long, brown eyelashes at me, and her smile became a little sinful as she licked her lips and twirled her hair.

"Let's get this to go and get an early start tomorrow. Maybe the kids will fall asleep early," I whispered to her.

The kids didn't fall asleep, so Lydia and I slept comfortably in our arms. I always liked it when she snuggled up against me. I could smell her sweet essence and listening to her breath made me thank God that she was with me. Plus, when we awoke in the morning, the first thing my sleepy eyes saw would be her beautiful face.

"Bo, sometimes I get scared going down to your father's. I'm afraid a big old snake is going to get us."

"That ain't gonna happen. I'll protect you."

I think tu padre is a little dangerous. He doesn't clean up, and he chews and spits right in front of the kids. I wish he'd show a little more respect around them."

"He does want to spend time with them, so let's give him that. I feel, since he's the only grandparent they have, let them enjoy that quirky behavior of his."

"I know, the kids loved him the last time we came down. Maybe he met a new woman, and she's taking care of him. I can't imagine what you would you'd like if you hadn't met me." She turned to me, flicking her long black hair.

I loved it when she did that. The kids in the back got excited when we cruised past Texarkana. I wanted to look up Becky but figured it wasn't the best idea, plus there was no time. We had a busy two months ahead.

We arrived at my dad's an hour later. The place remained hidden, but at least there were signs pointing to Cecil Barnum's General Store, that weren't there before. The old man could afford some advertising, so he must be doing pretty good. We drove through the abundant cypress trees, and I ran over a bull snake that stretched out across the road from end to end. I didn't see it since I hollered at the kids, who were a little too excited to see their grandpa. I shouldn't have screamed at them, since they were singing my song about him earlier, and Lydia and I sang once we crossed the state line. The kids continued it making up their own words and had no pitch at all. They might have scared up some sort of wildlife.

We got there in the early afternoon, and Gator, the old coon hound, waited on the porch for us. He ran out, with his tongue drooping out and tail wagging, barking and yelping at us. Sara and Tommy ran out after him, and the dog, who doesn't forget a smell, gave them big wet sloppy kisses all over their faces. Lydia got out carrying suitcases and almost got run over by the hound as he galloped to the car. After witnessing that attack, I decided to wait on unloading the Model T, and gave that old hound a hug. Pa stumbled out. Age was really getting to him. He walked with a cane and had a few more wrinkles, and more gray in his thinning hair. But there remained that youthful grin on his face. I could tell he was elated to see us.

He wasn't smoking, chewing, or drinking when he came out of the house. He hollered at me first. "Bo, how you've been?" He still sounded a little spry, and wild.

I fought with many a man, and had no problem challenging one, but one look at his face would tell me to get away. I came up to the old man and gave him a hug and he hugged me back.

"Pa, I've been doing good, and yourself?"

"Not so good there. Doc says I got to give up the tobacco and liquor. Don't want to, but I figured I'd give it a try. Surprisingly, the liquor was the easiest to give up. Since I really don't make it no more, it wasn't too hard. It's hard to put this pipe down. Nothing like a good smoke out on the lake after a tough day working here."

I gave up most of that stuff, too. Figured it was best for the kids. I barely take a snort, and gave up the chewing tobacco, too. Just like you, I can't put this pipe down."

We unloaded most of the car, except for a few things, and made our way to Pa's house, which sit's adjacent to the store. Our rooms were on the second story.

"Son, I have a surprise for you."

Out walked an attractive Creole woman about forty years of age, and she carried a pot of gumbo. "This is Angeline. She used to work here years ago, before I owned it. She came back a few months after you came down the last time, looking for work. I lied to her and told her this ain't no who.... I mean brothel anymore."

"I said good. I don't want to service them pigs that came here no more. I want me a real job," she replied.

"So, I said what else can you do?"

"Well I told him: I can cook. I went straight in the back and raided Cecil's kitchen and made him a crawfish pie."

"Best damn crawfish pie I've ever tasted. She hasn't left yet." The old hoot laughed pretty darn loud. "She's another reason I gave up the chewing and drinking. She's making my life worth living."

She bent down and kissed my dad on the cheek. "He makes mine worth living, too. Saved me from a life of whoring. I didn't want to do that no more."

We ate the gumbo, and I saw Lydia eating it down like it was the best thing she ever ate. "Angeline, you have to show me how to make that."

"Oh, you can't make that up in Nebraska. No ma'am. You gotta' get the okra fresh and crawdads fresh from the lake here. Freshest ingredients make it taste so good. I'll share you some secrets. Come on."

Lydia followed her into the kitchen. There was silence and then hysterical giggles and laughter.

Tommy took his seat on Grandpa's lap and tugged his beard like a train whistle. "Ding ding," he went, and Grandpa started doing it to. As soon as Tommy pulled on his beard, Grandpa screamed out, "ding ding."

Sara and I laughed. I never pictured my pa would ever do that. I wondered if he played like that with my brothers and me.

Sara, Tommy, Pa, and I went outside and sat on the porch overlooking Black Bayou. The kids ran around playing, which gave my father and I a chance for some small talk. I told him about the trip we were planning.

"I want to make a little trip cross state to Helena and over to Clarksdale while we're here. Got this old resonator. I want to pick up some spending money for our trip west and sing the Negro songs. Them guys might be the best musicians no one ever heard before."

"Damn right, Bo. Got a few colored boys come over here and play every now and then. I should have you meet these fellas. Good kids."

"Yeah, when are they coming around? I want to teach them a trick or two, or maybe they can show me something."

"They'll be over tomorrow night. I think the furthest they've been is Monroe or Longview. Guys ain't got much money, but hell I hear some crap on the radio, and these kids are better than that stuff. I do run a little juke joint after hours still. People who come here are pretty friendly. Some working girls do come here but they aren't staying. The noise isn't so bad for the kids, since the bedrooms are over the store, and not where the music is. I'll try to run everyone out by midnight. By the way, I still make whiskey for the folks who come. We're down to about a show a month. It was bad timing, but I want you to hear these boys."

We continued to hear laughter coming from the kitchen. I guess my wife and Pa's lady friend hit it off. "It should be okay if it gets too loud, I'll let you know. I'm sure Lydia wouldn't like it if there was whoring going on right next to the kids. Sometimes she's afraid our loving will wake them up."

"Well, Angeline and my room is far away from you guys. Our loving ain't going to bother you." Pa almost laughed his head off, slapping his knee.

Not exactly words I wanted to hear from my old man, but I was glad he found someone to make him happy. "Why don't we grab the ladies and do some fishing?" I asked.

We grabbed the ladies and the sapling and headed out on the dock to catch us some fish. I knew we could land some good pan fish for dinner one of these nights. From the smell of the kitchen I think Angeline already planned dinner. We plopped our behinds on the dock, hooked up some crawdads, and waited for some fish to gather on top of the mudbugs so we could pull them in. We caught about fourteen keepers between the six of us. We ate red beans and rice and fried catfish for dinner. Angeline cooked. No one else, not even Lydia was allowed.

"I am cooking you authentic Mexican before we head north. I'd love to cook for you, Angeline and Senor Barnum. When we come back from our trip, we will get some pork, and I'm making tamales." Lydia told the crowd.

"That sounds good. I will help you. I want to know how to make them."

"Only if you show me how to cook this food." The women shook hands.

It was a nice visit, but I was getting sleepy. I took everyone up to their rooms and Lydia and I laid them down. I told them stories about when I was a kid.

"When I was you guys' ages, I used to run down to the pond and go swimming and fishing, sometimes my brothers and me would play baseball in the fields. They were bigger and stronger than me, but I made up for everything and better than them because I tried harder. When you do the best that you can do, things will work out for you. I always caught more fish than them, and in our baseball games, I got more hits. They hated losing to me and started fights, but I fought back and soon became tougher than them. Pretty soon they were afraid of me, even though I was smaller and younger. Kids, take every opportunity you have to become better, even if someone at school picks on you."

"I know, Daddy," they both said. "I always do." They laughed at each other since they spoke at the same time and started hitting each other on the shoulder.

The next day we hung out and did more fishing and talking. Sara had a snapping turtle on her line and pulled it in herself. She was afraid to take it off the hook, which I don't blame her. They're called snapping turtles for a reason. Fingers can be turtle food with one quick bite. Grandpa and I got it off the hook for her and we threw it in a bucket for dinner later. Her eyes studied our moves diligently. "If I catch another one, can I take it off?"

"You can help us. You can hold the darn thing." My dad said.

Sure enough an hour later, she had a huge tug on her line, and she yanked that sapling up and there dangled another snapper. Cautious and nervous, she grabbed the turtle by the shell, while Gramps cut the line with his knife leaving the hook in its mouth. Sara dropped the thing in the bucket. We were having turtle for dinner soon.

Dinner that night was some fish and jambalaya, a spicy rice dish with some chicken chopped up in it, and some more fish that we grilled outside. Angeline and Lydia were both busy making food for the party. The kitchen smelled good as they also whipped up a pot of gumbo. A couple of Negro boys, a little younger than me, showed up. One with an old beat up resonator guitar and another one with a harp. My pa introduced them to me as Sonny and Willie.

"This is my son, Bo. He can play you guys under the table."

"No white boy can play like us. It's in our blood. This boy don't have what it takes."

"He ran shine since he was sixteen years old, went to Memphis, Clarksdale, and Indianola. He often came home a day late to hear the black man sing. I tell ya, he's the real deal. He drove down from Nebraska. I'm hoping he can sit in with ya."

"Well, go get your guitar, Bo. Your pappy done build you up rather big. Let's see if you can back it up."

"I ain't that good. Got me a guitar like yours there. Let me run up and get it. I'll get my harp, too." I took the walk up and returned in a second. I sat down and played some songs I've been hearing on the radio. They was old blues, and I wailed on the guitar, feeling every note. I howled that old Southern song, like I was sharecropping in the cotton fields or on work detail on a prison farm. The harp player started to toot his harp, while the guitar player jammed with me. We took turn on the guitar doing the scales and soloing and then switched back on the vocals. We made up our own words and did about a ten-minute song. We did another one like the previous one, this time with more blood, guts and emotion. I was feeling it. Hell, I knew I could play the blues.

"Damn, boy, your papa ain't lying. You got some moves there, Mistah Barnum. Thinking you can sit in with us and play a few songs tonight. Watcha' think there, Willie?"

"Ain't never heard no white boy play like that. Most white boys who play the blues tone it down a notch or two. Cecil's boy, man you don't do that. You play some mean guitar there."

I broke out my harp and started the old train whistle and danced around with it. Willie broke his out and we dueled with each other, while Sonny called the gators home on his guitar."

"Damn, Cecil, Let's get this party started. Your boy here is the real thing."

Some cars showed up so the three of us started playing. Angeline fixed some beans and rice, and gumbo and serving some barbeque pork sandwiches for the folks arriving. The three of us blew the roof off the old shack when Lydia came down.

"I want to sing," she said.

Damn, if she wasn't Ma Rainey reincarnated as a Mexican as she wailed her soulful songs. Sonny and I played some good guitar on them and the place rocked all night. I don't think we quit playing until about two. The kids came down and watched, and everyone there ate, drank Pa's whiskey and beer, and had a good time. A couple of the women left with the guys, so there weren't no whoring at the house anyway, and we eventually wound down, knowing we shook up the dry Parrish that night.

Next morning, we didn't get up until close to noon. Everyone slept. Pa had to get up early in case some fisherman stopped by to get some crawfish or other bait or pick up some fishing poles. We didn't hear no one come. We didn't smell the bacon or the coffee cooking, which usually woke me up after a long night.

We decided to hang out at the house another day. I kind of liked it down here. Sara also enjoyed herself. I wondered if there was work in Shreveport and if we'd move down here.

Pa's woman got up late and didn't start making breakfast until after everyone woke. She sleepy, smiling between yawns. Pa wasn't even up yet. He's usually up before the sun. I guess getting older and dancing and partying was too much for the old man. I hoped he wasn't dead or nothing, but soon he came out smoking his corncob pipe and missing one shoe.

"Damn fisherman kept coming at seven, eight, and nine. Don't they know this old man wants to sleep after he does his thing?"

Angeline walked over to him and kissed him. "Go back to bed, honey. The kids will be fine."

"Well I was thinking we drive into Shreveport to see what type of work is there. I could get a job driving one of them oil trucks around Louisiana, or at least work in the refinery."

"Why?" Lydia asked me.

"I was thinking about moving down here. Not planning anything, and I know we haven't talked about it but playing with them boys gave me an idea—that we could get a band together."

"You hadn't talked about it," she snapped.

"Well I didn't know until last night. Plus, I was just thinking about it."

"How about you let me know first when you think about things? I don't want it to be a surprise."

"I'm sorry, like I said I was only thinking."

We took that little drive into the city. It was smaller than Omaha, and there weren't too many Mexicans there. I knew Lydia wanted a Mexican community to live in. In Omaha there wasn't a lot of Mexicans by Texas standards, but the people were close, and they looked out for each other. Even with the oil booming, there weren't a lot of jobs around. I wasn't too crazy about driving the oil rigs around. I didn't want to go out in flames from driving a tank of dynamite.

We got back to Pa's and we ate turtle soup for dinner. Pa caught a couple more. We also chomped frog legs and rice and beans again. Another thing I liked about living in the south, is you could catch some crawfish, bullfrogs, or turtles and scarf down dinner.

Next day we headed across the state to Helena and then up to Memphis. Lots of Blues music was happening, and they even hosted a radio show, which we listened to on occasion. I was able to find the ol' juke joint I used to run to, and the old Negro man who ran that place recognized me.

"Wow, son, you've turned into a man. Haven't seen or heard from you in ages. How's the old man? Where you been? Watcha doing here?"

The questions went on forever. I told him my story, which you know by now. "I want to play some music here if you don't mind. My wife and I can sing the blues pretty good."

"Well, we got us a show tonight. Tiny Walker is going to rock the house down. I suppose you can open for him."

"Can't say I know him."

"e busted out of the farm down in Mississippi about a year ago. Usually plays with about three or four different names so he don't get caught. He's mighty fine player. Gets a little crazy, so don't be too good. He thinks he's the best ever. People said he shot a man cuz he was better on the guitar than him. Don't knows if it's true or not, but he did do time for murder."

"I promise you that we won't be that good. Lydia, let's bring the kids down and play this old man a few songs."

She cautiously came over with the boys and the old man gave them a hug and a Coke to drink. I tuned up, and Lydia stretched her vocal chords and we played a few numbers for him.

"Damn, boy, you're pretty good. You better watch your back, cuz I think you is better than Tiny. He's not God as he says he is. Lots of people don't like him. He's no Son House or Charley Patton, that's for sure. If he were, he probably wouldn't be playing here."

"We'll tone it down a notch then for our safety."

Lydia and I laughed, but the old man didn't. He wore a serious look on his face as a smile wasn't to be found, and his eyes fixed on me. Tiny and his crew soon showed up. He was a short man, barely five-foot-tall so his name fit him. His entourage was two bosomy black ladies and a big tall black man who looked like a bodyguard. The old man introduced us to him.

"This young cracker's name is Bo Barnum. Plays the blues like any kid from the Delta can. Good boy, too. He used to run his pa's whiskey to me all the way from Texarkana."

Tiny's eyes lit up like the old still when he heard whiskey. "You bring some with ya?"

"Nope, he don't run no more," the old man said.

"Then watcha here for? Doubt if you can sing the blues. You don't got no blues in you."

"Oh no. The boy's mighty fine. Him and his wife played us a few songs earlier. These kids got it."

"No honky actually got the blues in him." He looked me over pretty good. "Boy's probably never done more than a day in jail. Probably never been on a chain gang, and never picked no cotton for a quarter a day." Then he stood right next to me and got in my face and stared me down with a menacing look. "Have ya cracker?"

"You don't need that to play the blues." I grabbed the reso, clicked my switch blade open. Flashed it in his face, then played the meanest, dirtiest licks I knew. The licks that raised the dead, while I sang songs of the South. This wasn't no radio songs, but songs you'd only here in the bayous of Louisiana. No two-bit hacker would put me to shame.

"Damn, kid. You are pretty good. Sit down in the old rocking chair over yonder and let me take you to school. I'm gonna be your teacher."

I admit the man was pretty good. Better than me, cause I didn't play fancy. I played mean and dirty. Tiny Walker was a lot fancier player than me. He was a showman and I witnessed why people came to see him play. He was technically as good as me and could be a guitar great if he concentrated on the playing ability and not the style.

"You got to teach me that behind the head move."

"That's my move. I don't share, especially with no cracka." His hardened face broke into a smile, and he winked. "It's a pleasure to do a show with you Barnum."

I reached over to shake his hand.

He yanked his hand away. "I ain't shaking no white boy's hand. You should be lucky I'm gonna share the stage with ya."

We kicked off the show. I did a few songs solo and got good applause from the forty or fifty people there. Seemed like most of them didn't care that I was a white boy living in a black man's world. I thought some respected me more, but there were others who felt I intruded in their little world.

Lydia came on and sang some slower numbers with me. The folks loved her. Most of the couples danced, and the black ladies that came with Tiny shook their goodies. Good times were had by all, and we got a good ovation.

Tiny took the stage about nine and he played loud and spirited. The crowd dancing and hollered. The ladies on stage danced and sang back up, while the other man responded to Tiny's calls, with field hollers. Tiny glided all over the stage with his guitar, doing fancy little walks across the makeshift stage, while the ladies bebopped around, shaking their big behinds to the drunken crowd. I'd say it was quite a show, and the crowd loved it. We were busy packing up the car toward the end of it, and on our way to Memphis to get a fancy motel. We didn't want to test the old man's theory.

We spent the night in the Peabody Hotel along Beale Street. The blues music seeped through the sewer system of the river city. We got the kids in their bed, even though Sara didn't want to sleep with Tommy, and he didn't want to sleep with his big sister. The four of us cuddled up in our bed. I was next to my wife with Sara on the other side of her, while Tommy snuggled up with me. We got us a nice big breakfast the next morning downtown and walked around the downtown streets, gazing at the buildings. The city bustled even around noon, but it was soon time to head down through the Delta and back to Louisiana.

We got back to my dads' place the next afternoon about 3:15 quarter after three. It started to heat up on the bayou. We didn't do too much the next couple of days, just fishing and relaxing. Lydia helped Angeline with the cooking, while Pa, me, and the kids sat on the dock, or went out in one of his rental boats.

I figured I needed the break. We were about to make the long journey westward and hoping to get to California and back in three weeks. Still wasn't sure if we should drive or ride freights. I wanted to take the train, but Pa and his woman packed a lot of food for us to feed the transients, migrants, and the destitute.

A few days later we hugged them goodbye with the car jam packed. We left some stuff at the bayou, as we were ready to head out toward the great desert. First place we planned on stopping was San Antonio. I wanted Lydia to have the same thrill I did, playing the dark man's country music. It was a real treat to play with some of the best and worst musicians in the South. Lydia needed the same opportunity to play with the best in Tejano music in Texas.

It would take all day to cross that gigantic state that laid west of me. I didn't get into Texas too much. It was an old family thing, but I made a few runs to Ft. Worth. Pa always told me not to go west of there, since I'd probably get killed by one of them Rangers or outlaws. He also told me one of my kin got lynched in Corsicana or some other city, for helping slaves runaway. The old coot never liked Texas. Not sure why we always went to Ft. Worth in the first place. I decided to find out since it was on the way. I stopped by the ritzy speak easy that I used to deliver to. I remembered the guys face, but he didn't remember me. I was a seventeen-year-old kid when I delivered there last and now pushed thirty.

"Hey guys, I'm going to get a box of chicken at this little place. I'll be right back."

"I'm Cecil Barnum's boy. Don't know if you remember me or not. I used to stop in here once about three or four months." He looked at me with a blank stare. "You know Cecil Barnum from Texarkana."

"Oh yeah. I know Cecil. Damn crazy son of a bitch. Damn fool owed me for years. Not money just favors. You folks quit feeding me the whiskey, but I heard what happened. Heard the Klan got ya."

"They didn't get us but forced us on the run. Say what do you know about all of this."

He reached for a stick and picked his teeth with it. "I probably know more about your history than you do. I bailed your family out on more than one occasion. I think it went way back to his grandpa. Not sure if you knew this but your great-grandpa Robert married a black woman, a slave that he ran away with. Basically, stole her right from his uncle's plantation. That made Cecil's dad, and your grandpa. a Negro in many parts. Makes you a nigra in these parts too."

We took longer than expected. Lydia came in with the kids, after they used the toilet. The man continued talking as he saw my family enter. "They your family?" he asked. He stretched his neck, glancing around the club. He nodded to no one in particular.

"Sure are, damn proud of them."

He handed me a book of matches, pointing to the cover, Words were no longer spoken. I glanced at the cover and tossed it in my overall pocket. "You know it ain't safe here. Bourgeois all over this area, especially down by Huntsville." He nodded to a lanky man with a white Stetson pulled over his eyes hiding his face. I didn't recall him in the lounge when I entered.

I followed his glance, and noticed the lanky stranger turned away from me. I signaled to Lydia to get the kids. I wanted to skedaddle out of there.

He boxed the chicken up. Eight pieces, plenty of grub for the road, and we purchased soft drinks also. "Like I said he's way down there in Austin, if you're down that way give your cousin a look up." His eyes shifted toward the white capped stranger.

"We gotta run darling." I hollered across the diner. "Get the kids in the car. She left, I waited for any further instructions, before making my departure.

"We don't allow her kind in here. That man is my enforcer. See your cousin, he's a welcoming man. Now get." He waved his hand, almost blowing me out the door. I fired the hot rod up and headed south.

The drive south was silent. Even the children who sat in back yacking all the way remained quiet, as they peered out the window absorbing the sights of The Lone Star State. I glanced at my wife. She bit her fingernails, a habit I never noticed before. "What's wrong darling?"

She peaked at me, then returned her focus out the window. "Why didn't you speak up, say something. You rushed us out the door."

"I didn't feel safe in there."

"Did you notice there were no Mexicans in there. I even noticed a sign in front. I wish you would have said something. You didn't defend me, or our children." She continued looking out the window.

Darling, I need to pick our battles. Something didn't feel right. That's why we needed to skedaddle. I got me a cousin in Austin that feels the same way, we do and it's on the way. I pulled the matchbook out of pocket and handed to her. She yanked it from my hand, glanced at it, and said nothing. Three hours from leaving Ft. Worth, we pulled into Austin and hit downtown. We fell behind schedule a bit, but I was hungry, and I had a like-minded cousin, I discovered. I found the café and pulled over.

We walked in and ordered tamales. Even though the place looked a little boisterous on the outside, the people were friendly. The customers were integrated, and people were drinking beer and whiskey and dancing. Negroes, Mexicans, and whites were part of the customer base. The waitress, a half-Mexican-looking girl came up with our food. She looked at Lydia, then the kids, and finally me, and smiled. Her smile seemed a mile wide.

"Nice friendly place you got here," I told her before scarfing the tamales."

"Well, it has to be. Anyone causing problems are going to be shot. Not sure if you saw the sign behind the counter." She smiled and walked away. I smiled as I watched her strut away. We finished our dinner and the waitress came back. I swear she could have been Sara's big sister. She stared at Sara and me as she returned to collect our plates.

I called her over. "Say, you don't know an Isaiah Barnum, do you?"

"Hey, Stranger, how do you know him?"

"Well I don't know him, but I think he's kin to me."

"Shhh." She put her index finger to her lips. "People are always looking for him, kin or not kin. I got to be careful. Daddy's pretty much wanted around here. So how are you kin to him?"

I handed her the book of matches. She looked inside as if there was a secret message inside. She disappeared into a back room, and returned in a minute, waving us to follow.

If I were an older, dark-skinned man, I now knew what I'd look like. There was my cousin, Isaiah standing in the dark, with only a flickering lantern revealing his face. He led us to a back room, behind his already darkened, private quarters. This time there was light. He looked us over pretty good, especially Lydia.

"What is your surname?" He asked. "I bet you have status."

Lydia stared at me, I guess wondering if she should answer. I shrugged, letting her know she was on her own. She stared at my distant cousin, like they played some Texas hold 'em, waiting for him to give away his bluff. My kin did not budge.

"Fuentes," Lydia proceeded, sounding out every letter, staring at Isaiah waiting for him to flinch.

My umpteenth cousin lit up a fat cigar and took a puff. "You're not the lost daughter of a Jorge Fuentes, who was murdered in cold blood up in Omaha?"

It was my turn to jump in. "Wait a minute, how do you know that?"

"Senor Fuentes was murdered in Omaha and had a daughter. You told my daughter you were from Omaha, and a Barnum. It was pretty easy to figure it out. You see, Bo, lots of folks don't like change. Lots of folks don't like seeing these blacks and Mexicans with rights and good jobs. They still think we should own them. Since our heritage is mixed up, like a mongrel puppy with whatever race Great-grandpa Cletus decided to create I can't hate no one, and I got a feeling you're the same way."

"So, you think I'm responsible for her parents being shot? Hell, I didn't know they were important until after they were dead. I had nothing to do with it." I studied my cousin's poker face. His daughter hurried the kids out of the room. "Do you know a man named Early Greene?"

He stared me like he held three aces in his hand or a nine high. That cool son of a bitch wasn't giving in. I tried being as cool as my cousin, but I began to think that son of a bitch knew something about Early and Lydia's parents. The longer he took to answer, the more my impatience grew. I peeked at Lydia who was turning red, her jaw clenched, and eyes squinted, while glaring at my relative. I glanced from him to my wife. Lydia stared at me and then him. No one said a word. The silence made me boil inside, and I almost saw steam coming from Lydia's ears and nostrils. She waited for me to say something.

"Cuz, I never heard of the man," he spoke with a rapid inflection. His eyes shifted to a painting that hung crooked on the wall behind us.

"Liar. You know something about mi padre's death. I know you do." The Latin temper, which I rarely seen from my wife began to show. "What do you know about it? You know something." She stood up and walked straight toward him and got in his face. "I want to know everything, Senor Barnum."

"Okay, I know all about Early Greene. He's a hired hand. He works for the side that pays the most money, fighting for the

Villaistas and against them. He fights against the Klan and for them. He doesn't care, as long as the money is right. I do know for a fact that he did not kill your parents, but I can tell you he was involved. How, I do not know."

"Who killed my parents? Was it the Mexican government or the US government or the Klan?"

"Lydia, what I will tell you will us both killed. People try to kill me every day, so I keep a low profile, running this little joint. I barely go outside of this damn diner. When I do, it is dark outside, and I run to my small house. I quit practicing law when my office was burned down. I'm tired of living in fear and I've kept this a secret in fear of my life." He got up to check if anyone was listening. His daughter and my kids were still out in the restaurant. He returned to his seat and took a sip of water. He swallowed and wiped his brow with his bandana. "It was all three. The Mexican and US Government were in on it. They paid a couple of Klansmen to do the deed. The reason Early Greene went to Omaha was to assassinate your folks. That I can't prove, but it was a Klansman from Arkansas who killed your parents. I heard he was hung, but I don't know for sure. I really think Wilson was behind it."

"The President?"

"Of course. The US government wanted to get rid of all agitators. What I've read about your father is the Mexican government sent him to the US so he would be assassinated."

"Was I supposed to be in Omaha too? I mean was there a reason Early took me up?"

"I think so. The Klan has been after the Barnums since the war. They've either recruited them or tried to have them exterminated. That's all I have to say. You guys need to leave now. It's not safe here. Make sure you are not followed."

Lydia left with the kids, while Isaiah kept me in for a few seconds. "Bo, be safe. Watch your back," and I departed with my family as we snuck out to the car, hoping we weren't followed.

We would get a room in San Antonio tonight, and tomorrow, Lydia would try her luck singing. I thought about changing our plans, since I no longer trusted anyone. Soon the kids were asleep, or at least I thought they were, and I looked at Lydia. She looked back at me, but we said nothing. Finally, I asked her, "Do you believe Isaiah?"

"Bo, I don't know what to believe. I'm afraid. I think we need to go somewhere where no one knows us. Texas isn't safe. I'm not sure if I trust Isaiah. We just met him, and he knows a lot about us."

"Should we turn around or do want to hit San Antone and sing? I do want to hear you sing in front of everyone at the show tomorrow."

"Oh, Bo, I want to so bad. It's one of my dreams. At least I can blend in. I don't think anyone knows me down there, so I want to give it a try." She leaned over and kissed me on the cheek. "Thank you so much Papi." She smiled at me, in a way I never seen before.

Chapter 13

"Daddy," Sara said from the back seat. "Is that the same car that's followed us from Austin?" I glanced behind and she was kneeling, looking out the back window.

"What?"

"I was looking out the window, and this car has been following us since we left that diner. I fell asleep though. I'm not sure if it's the same car."

I've been running from people since I sixteen, traveling the roads outside Texarkana, but I ain't never been this far into Texas. I didn't know these roads, and I had no idea where I could find protection. This could be nothing, since I'm sure lots of people drive from Austin to San Antonio on a Thursday night, but I needed to be sure. I wanted to floor it, test how fast this coupe would go, but hell with that, I didn't know if those lights were from a Texas Ranger, a state trooper, or a hit man. We weren't committing a crime. I hoped to get to San Antonio and find a motel so we could crash for the night.

My right foot got a little heavier on the gas pedal, but not too much. I wanted to get that car out of sight, so I could pull over at the next stop. I sped the car up about ten more miles per hour and asked my girl if she could still see the lights. Finally, she said they were gone, and we came across a small town that had a motel with vacancy. I pulled in backwards by one of the vacant rooms and waited for the car to speed by. We were safe that night.

We checked into the room and put the kids to sleep. Lydia and I lay in each other's arms. I held her close and we talked.

"I want to get out of here quick. I think its best we get to Louisiana. I know we're safe there. I don't trust no one here."

"Bo, you're getting scared. I don't think your cousin knows what he's talking about. No one knows us here."

"They know of us; we're a mixed family and the last name is Barnum. People hate us here."

"Bo, you're talking crazy. We came this far; I think you owe it to our kids and I to let me sing. You owe it to yourself, to the people leaving their homeland. This was your dream. You can't let some far-fetched story scare you from your dream."

Maybe she was right. I kissed her forehead, and we made love to each other while the children slept on the bed next to us. The lovemaking wasn't passionate or explosive as normal, just enough to let each other know how we really felt.

We ate breakfast at a diner across the street. The waitress stared at us, scoffed with her lips curled up, but she served us anyway. I was tempted to ask if she spat in our coffee but didn't. We headed down to San Antonio. We were about fifteen minutes away as we pulled in. The show was held near the Alamo, and we were ready. I hadn't seen this many Mexican folks in my life, and Tejano music played everywhere. Before I met my wife, I had never heard the term Tejano, but now I listen to the music more than my down home, old timey, bluesy sound. Can't help it since she sings it all the time around the house. We wandered around and found Paulino and Torreon.

The two Tejano singers reached out their hand to me first, which I appreciated. It showed they respected me as a man and as her husband. They ushered us to the backstage waiting room. In their broken English Spanish, they said, "Lydia you go on at 4pm. We'll need you to rehearse a bit with the band before you go on. Meet us back here about 3pm. But for now, walk around and enjoy the sights of the city. Don't forget to visit the Alamo, where we took care of them gringos. Pardon me, Senor Barnum." Paulino or Torreon laughed hysterically across the backstage area.

Three o'clock rolled around, and I walked Lydia backstage where she planned to meet-up with her band. First Tommy, then Sara, and finally I gave her a good luck kiss. Mine was much longer than the kids, and all three of us gave her a family hug. She disappeared behind the door. I wanted to wait outside the room until it was time for her to perform, instead we wandered out into the festival. We got right up front, center of the stage, and the kids impatiently waited for their mother to take the stage as I anticipated my wife's debut.

From the time she took the stage, I knew there something wrong. Her radiant smile was replaced by a scared version of nervousness. I knew she would be nervous, but usually she would have a grin a mile wide to compensate for her apprehension. She stared down at the kids and forced a smile, and then to me, and I saw tears shimmer in her eyes. They weren't of joy. I kept my children close, but I longed to grab her off the stage, and make a run for the Louisiana border right then and there.

She sang seven songs brilliantly, but my worry increased about her safety. I moved the kids toward the area where we dropped her off, and I heard a scream, "Bo don't. They will get you, too. Keep my babies safe and take care of them. Te Amo, Bo, Sara y Tomas." Then she screamed again and collapsed. Sara and Tommy's eyes covered up as I pressed their faces to my chest. They didn't see what happened to their mother, nor did I. The crowd screamed; I just held my children tight. If they weren't there, I could rescue my wife or at least die trying, but I couldn't put my children at risk. The only two people I knew were Paulino and Torreon. I had no clue which one was which, and I suspected both of them did this to Lydia.

I glanced up on stage, and I saw an old familiar face shoving something in a fiddle case. Someone I trusted with the kids before, however I'd never trust him again. Early smiled that crooked smile right at me, and then fled the stage as rapid as I thought I saw him.

When the bedlam died down, I went to one of the cops hanging around to ask if they knew what happened. The one I spoke with looked at me like I was crazy. He had no idea what I was talking about. "My wife got killed or kidnapped right on stage. Didn't you see it?"

"Could care less what happens to all those 'spic singers. Not sure why they have these festivals anyway."

I shoved him to the ground and walked past in search of anyone who looked like they'd help. I flagged down a policeman outside the festival, and he actually listened.

"It's the Mafia. The Mexican Mafia. They are more notorious than Al Capone and John Dillinger. Clyde Barrow would cry like a baby dealing with them. Would have given them Bonnie and turned himself in."

"How do I see them? I want my wife back."

The police officer stared at me and then Sara and Tommy. "Senor Barnum, I am sorry. You might want to come with me."

"I'm not letting them out of my sight."

"I understand, senòr. She is dead. She was drugged, and then they chopped off her head. I suggest you leave San Antonio as soon as possible and hold on to your children. Barnums and Fuentes are bad combinations in San Antonio. Leave. Get out while you have a chance, I will escort you to your car."

"What about the body? I want to see the body."

"All that's left is the head. They took the body with them. I'm sure you do not want to see her head. Mow leave. When we recover the body, we will ship it back to Nebraska so you can bury her. Get out before they get you."

We got in the car and were ready to head east. Getting out of this state was my priority. No one spoke a word. I think my children were still in shock, as I was. I blamed my children for being there, I blamed myself for not listening or acting on things. I blamed Lydia for wanting to sing so bad. I blamed Isaiah for putting these conspiracy theories in my head. I blamed Paulino and Torreon for setting us up, but most of all I blamed Early Greene. He's the man who bailed me out many times.

Was this all a set up? I wanted revenge, and I was going to get him.

Part II

Chapter 14

I sat in the car for about ten minutes, stunned in disbelief. Tommy wailed his eyes out, even though he wasn't sure what happened. Sara kept screaming for her mami.

"Don't leave without her. I want Mami back, Papi. I want my mami. Daddy you can't leave without her. Why isn't Mami coming with us? Dad go get her. Get her now!" She stared at me with big brown eyes as she sat beside me in the front seat. It was her usual place when her mom wasn't riding with us. I looked at her, and all I saw was a younger Lydia. I wanted to be strong, but had a hard time controlling myself. I hugged Sara, hoping to comfort her, but it was me who needed the hug from my little girl.

"She's not coming back with us. Your mom was murdered, the police say."

"No, she wasn't, Dad. I saw her as we were rushed out. I know I saw her. She blew me a goodbye kiss."

My eyes widened and I pulled back to look at her face. "When was this, honey?"

"When the police guys took us away. She isn't dead. We have to go get her."

"Well, baby girl, maybe your mami wants to stay down here for a while and sing, but we need to get back to Grandpa's. I don't feel safe at all in Texas. It's my job to take care and protect you. Mami will come home to Grandpa Cecil's and head back to Nebraska in time. Pa always said nothing good comes from Texas, and I guess the old coot was right. We ain't coming back here anytime soon, but I promise we will get Mami back."

I drove all night, and all I remembered crossing a long bridge over the Sabine River, where the river is at its widest right before it empties its waters into the Gulf of Mexico. I also recalled driving aimlessly down some dirt road, but that was about it. The pounding on my windows woke me up. It scared the bejeebers out of me, but I knew I felt safe in Louisiana. Something about this state made me feel protected, like God put a big blanket around me, and I was armed with a double barrel shotgun. Even on my deliveries, when I was a kid, I never feared getting run down by the law or the mob. I'm sure Pa had some folks bought out, still, folks were different here. At least they were up northern part of the state. I was about to find about these Southern Louisianans.

I raised my head slowly, and realized I was in the middle of a small railyard. I might have dozed for a bit, but luckily, I wasn't parked on a train track. "Looking for work, boy?" The big-ass white man asked me. "We might be hiring in a bit down here."

"Huh?" I struggled to get an answer out, then noticed Sara and Tommy grabbing coke bottles out of the machine. "Where am I?"

"Vinton, Louisiana," the man spoke in a heavy Southern Cajun drawl. "Ya got to move the car there so we can get some work done."

I looked around and noticed again where I was. "Oh sorry, sir." I felt my twang coming back in my voice. "I had to get out of Texas in a hurry. Didn't do nothing wrong, but my pa never liked to do business in Texas, and I can't say I blame him. We ran into a lot of trouble in San Antonio and drove all night to get here. Guess I dozed off when I got to town."

"Well park your car at the diner there. I'll open it up and cook you up some biscuits and gravy and some grits. I know you gonna like it. I spice the gravy up real good."

Ma, for a Southern woman, wasn't the best cook around, at least I didn't think so. She wasn't the worst cook the world has known, but her dishes lacked the spice. Lydia always cooked me up tortillas and beans, but I missed that real Southern cooking.

"Want to tell me what happened over in San Antone son?" The man asked me.

I realized I might be a widower and that thought sobered me in a hurry. I wasn't sure if I should tell this stranger anything and didn't even want him to know my name. The world had seen way to many Barnums pass through lately. I looked at the man straight in the eye, and he was staring right at me, too. He had an innocent look of sincerity to his eyes. I could tell he was a trusting man, but I wasn't ready to tell what happened, at least not in front of my kids.

"Sir, I can't tell ya right now. It was pretty bad. It has to do with my wife, so I ain't gonna talk about it none."

He got a little pushy, at least I thought so. "Either way, it will do you a lot of good to talk about it. Not good to keep things inside there, young man."

I guess the stress got to me cuz, I snapped at the nice man. "I said I ain't talking about it! Not in front of my kids, anyway."

He held up his hands. "Okay, boy, I'm sorry. I'm here if ya need me. Say where you headed to?"

"Shreveport to visit my pa for a bit. Then head back North to where I live, pack my stuff and move back down to Louisiana somewhere. I need to start over."

"If you want to take a walk with me, so we can do some conversation in private. I'd be game for that."

"No, thank you, sir, I ain't letting my little ones out of my sight."

"I appreciate that son, I want you to know we are friendly folks here in Vinton. Say, what kind of work do you do?

"I drove a streetcar in the city, but always wanted to drive one of those big rigs." I stared at the large diesels parked across the highway.

"I'm sure I can get you a job driving one of those log trucks over there." He pointed to a few of the big trucks by the tracks.

"Like I said, we're headed north, up to Shreveport to see my pa for a bit, and then back home to Nebraska. I plan to sell everything and make my way back here. I'd like to take a shot at driving a truck. All I know is I ain't crossing the Sabine ever again. Bad stuff happens over there."

"They take a lot of timber down to Texas. You might have to."

"In that case I have to think about it. Besides my kin is from Northern Louisiana. Not sure if I can get used to this Southern part here."

"Lot nicer down here."

Tommy got in the back seat and stretched out, not missing sitting next to his sister one bit. Sara climbed in the passenger seat, looking as radiant as her mother. The man watched them climb in the car and he walked me closer to the soda machine and whispered, "What happened to your wife anyway, son?"

"Pretty sure she got murdered in San Antone, but the cops whisked me away and then threatened me. They said it was for my protection. Not sure if I believe them or not."

"Yeah, can't trust them folks there across the river. It's best to stay here."

I looked around and saw a man in a longer coat and hat, holding some sort of case, sneak into the woods.

We took a slow route up to Caddo, stopped off in Coushatta, so I could see the plantation I heard about it in tall stories, about my kin who freed a couple of slaves. Pa mentioned this a time or two when I was a kid, but at that time I didn't care none, but he mentioned it again when I was older. I wanted to see it all. It's where I got my stupid morals that were going to get me killed one day. I cursed and thanked my heritage.

We arrived at the bayou early evening, taking the makeshift back roads to my pa's place a little later. Pa and his hound were there to greet us with his shotgun in hand.

"Back so soon, and where's Lydia?" he asked.

"Not sure. Take the kids in, and I'll tell you what I know."

He took them into his place and came right back out. I cried for the first time, and he hugged, a rare sign for him since I can't remember when he touched me lovingly. I definitely remembered times I got a switch on my ass but can't remember when he actually showed me affection.

"You have to go get her back. I think she's a good woman there."

"Damn state is a jinx. I ain't never crossing that river again."

"I understand. Wouldn't be too hard to round some people up. Got some cousins all over that damn state. We could get her back."

"I think she wanted to go. I think she ran away. Sara said she saw her, after the cops said she was dead."

"Then let her come back. Ain't no good to chase a woman that don't want chased. All you do is waste time. Protect these kids and get on with your life."

"I don't know if I'm still married or a widower. Thinking I like being a widower better, at least that way I can move on."

Angeline spoke to the kids, telling them some old swamp stories about life on the bayou and life down in New Orleans. She probably was telling stuff twelve and nine-year-old kids don't need to hear, but they stared at her intently, as if she were the school ma'am, telling them great stories about the great war between the states.

"Angeline, are you telling them about the times down at the old whorehouse again?"

"Na Cecil, I was telling them about voodoo. I know how to make someone appear who disappeared. At least we can know what really happened."

"I don't want to hear that, and they don't either. Stop this witchy crap."

"Cecil, watch your mouth. This is proven to work."

"No, it ain't. You know I don't believe it."

"No, Gramps. We want to hear it," Sara spoke.

"Sara, Tommy, you really want to hear this junk?"

"Of course, we do."

Angeline went into her backroom and invited me. I wasn't sure what to think of all that nonsense, but figured if it gave me closure, I'd listen to the witch for a while. I wondered if Lydia was waiting for the right time to make a run for it, or was she brutally assassinated because she was kin to the revolutionary leader, Jorge Fuentes? I didn't want to hear about either one, but I had to.

She prepared the candles and incense and all that other weird stuff as she said to me, "Bo, the moon is perfect to get the results. Did you notice the waning moon? It should give you the results you need." She took out a little doll, looked like the one Sara had a tantrum with when she got one for her birthday. Then my Dad's friend started poking it with her needles. I grimaced every time the poor doll got stuck. Angeline was like a doctor as she was giving this poor doll her shots.

"Hey, don't cause her no pain."

"The needles are not to give her pain or to cause harm. They're trying to reach Lydia's spirit, so she will talk to you."

I thought this was crazy, but I went ahead and listened to her talk and maybe hear Lydia, too.

"The spirits are saying she is alive, Bo. They said that she was tired of the life she was a leading and wanted to live in Mexico and be a star. She wanted the fame that eluded her, living the life with you. Also, don't go looking for her, or your life will be in danger."

"Really? Do you believe that?"

"I don't always believe in the magic, Bo, but I think this time it is right. You robbed this girl of her innocence, as well as the people who took her parents life. You gave her the life you wanted, but this girl was destined for more. I believe she is alive. Let her go, and she will make her way back to her family as time fits. I don't know if you will see her again, but she will see her children. The spirits also say, if you see her again, she will be the last thing you ever see, since your love for her is so strong."

After a sleepless night of tossing and turning and dreams about Lydia, some of them horrid, I talked to my pa about what Angeline had seen and told me.

"I don't believe that crap. She makes some money with that shit just to give some people hope, but I think it's all a bunch of crap."

"I agree, but I guess I have to file for divorce or something. I don't want to marry two women."

"One is bad enough son."

"I thought we had a good marriage, but I reckon not. I think I'll stick around here for a few days and try to find some work. A guy I ran into down South said there was some work driving a logging truck. I was thinking about checking that out."

"You don't want to move down there. I know I could hook you up. You and the kids can stay here and make your living off the land. Lots of folks come down to do some fishing on this old bayou. I know this place like the back of my hand. I'll teach you everything you want to know. You could a guide or something since you were always the best fisherman. Hell, you can always run a little shop too. Maybe a legal one, or maybe you can take this place over."

"I wouldn't mind that. Hell, I was thinking about doing a little juke joint. I'd cook up some gator and catfish down near Coushatta, near the old Barnum plantation or over near the Sabine."

"There's great fishing down there. I think you could run a little place like this. I'll tell you what we're going to do. We are going to take a little trip there and I'll show you the historic Barnum places that ain't in no tour guides and find you some land and we'll get that little juke joint, café, bait shop, and whorehouse going. You're going to do a great job."

The next day Grandpa Cecil, Angeline, the kids, and I took off a little later and headed down toward Coushatta. We packed a picnic lunch and brought all kinds of fishing stuff in the car and headed south. We drove around and down the Sabine River. Grandpa Cecil commented, "there's some good land here that's for sale. Right down there is where my great-uncle Cletus Barnum hung out. There's all kind of tunnels and stuff. Not sure who owns the land, but I bet we can buy some for ya."

Sure, enough as we drove back near town, Sara squealed, "Did you see that? It said land for sale."

"Do you want to live here, honey?" I asked over my shoulder.

"Sure do. It's awful pretty down here. I want to go fishing all day." Tommy seconded his sister's comment.

"I do, too. I will check out the schools around here. You need to be book smarter than your old man. Doubt if you'll be street smarter than Gramps here, but we can work on that too. Best education in the world is learning to do things as you grow up, and to learn them from reading. Now tell me kids, what do you want to do when you grow up?"

Tommy answered first. "I want to play guitar and sing, just like you, Daddy. I also want to make whiskey."

Grandpa and Angeline laughed. Sara and I didn't.

"It's legal now. I ain't taking the recipe to the grave. I'm sure we can teach him how someday. We need to teach him business in darn schoolbooks, so he runs the place properly when he's older," Grandpa said.

When all the darned commotion died down, Sara looked at us all and prepared her soliloquy, "I want to be a lawyer. I want to fight everything you and Mami dealt with in the courts. I want to make all of this stuff illegal that people do. I want to see some of those people who won't serve us in restaurants arrested. I want to see the people who killed my friend's dad arrested. I don't want to live in fear, because Mami was Mexican. I don't want people to die, because of their race and where their ancestors came from. My grandparents and my mother might have died because they were Mexican. Papi, I remember you told Mami about the black boy who was lynched by a mob after the police started a riot. I want this to end. I want to go to college and become a lawyer."

My eyes teared up, and I looked at her. "Honey, you'd be the best. Do you want to live in the country or city?"

"I want to live in the country, then go to a big University. I want to do this for you, Daddy. You shouldn't have to fight so hard for everything."

I looked at my dad and saw some tears in his eyes. He must have figured he did a good job with me, and I did a good job with Sara.

"Bo, I've never been prouder of you in my dad-gummed life as I am right now. Not sure why your brother ran off and joined the Klan, not sure why your mother did too. I never raised a word against them colored folks, probably because I knew I was one of them. My pops didn't preach to me nothing bad about Negroes neither. So, Bo, I'm so goddamned proud you were fighting for something you believe in. It could cost you your life, and probably sacrificed a marriage, but damn it, you did right, and that makes me feel good. That's all this old man could ask for his children to make them proud."

Really never heard Pa talk that way about me, but I never gave him the chance. When I was growing up, all I thought he cared about was delivering the whiskey and getting back in one piece and getting back alive was secondary. I started to tear up and brushed that salty water away from my eyes. It was settled, we were going to stake out our new home.

We drove up along the edge of the Sabine, looking for land for sale. We didn't see nothing else, so we purchased that land Sara had seen. It was just out of town and a plantation, good for cotton and such, but I didn't want to own no cotton. I wanted to have a garden, and grow some food to eat and sell, and maybe raise some chickens so we could slaughter them up, and sell a few, too, but I didn't want to do that for a full-time job. I figured I could turn this little place into a juke joint and get some of my people playing all night. I wanted to play too, I still had the call to be a musician, and I could make Pa's whiskey. Sabine Parish was a dry parish after all.

The kids were enrolled in the white school in Zwolle. Both would attend middle school. All that was retrieving our stuff back from Nebraska, so we'd be ready to head back and start our new life. We hung out at our new place and tried to figure out where everything would go. Which part would be the living house, which part the juke? I also thought I could build a place, too, if I wanted to run a little whorehouse. I didn't want to, but I was starting to get lonely. The emptiness would change with a bunch of cute lil' Creole women running around my place. Hell, maybe I'd remarry, if anyone caught my fancy.

After a couple of days figuring things out and a few good fishing stints with Pa, we took the long road up to Nebraska to get my stuff. We took our time on the drive, helping out hobos when we saw them cooking some stew, and I'd play some songs on my five or six string. Sara was learning to play guitar, too, and her voice continued to sound like her mother's, but for some reason it sounded more beautiful. It took us about three days to get back to Nebraska.

Most people would have been in tears, others would be livid, stomping and cussing and ready to kill someone. Me, I looked at my children and laughed when we got to 23rd and F Street in Omaha and saw the ashes of our home. We contacted the police and fire departments, and they knew nothing about it. Again, that wasn't much of a surprise. I knew folks wanted me dead, cause I owned a reputation as an agitator, but I'd also earned the respect of the boss man and mayor, because I wasn't afraid to stand up to them. So, staring at the gray ashes that used to be our house had little effect on me.

We looked for Maggie and Ana to say goodbye but could not find them. One of our neighbors said both had been deported. There was only one thing to do, and that was to return to Louisiana. The kids napped in the car while my eyes grew heavy, so we drove down to the river and set up camp.

I rested on the sandbar that nestled along the Missouri River when Sara, all cool and unaffected by all of this nonsense, came up to me.

"See, Daddy. This is why I want to be a lawyer. You don't have to go through this. It's going to kill you. You are too smart to let someone shoot you, but all of this fighting is going to make you an old man pretty soon. I bet when I become a lawyer, I can make it illegal for people to do this to you." She kissed my cheek, and we fell asleep listening to the river run.

The bull frogs quit chirping, roosters cackled, and the catfish leapt in the Missouri River as my Model T sped down the Iowa highway. My past life behind me, I watched Omaha in the rearview mirror since all I kept were my two kids, and what was in the car. Everything else was ashes, stolen, or back in Louisiana. I thought about Lydia, her folks, Early, the race riots, lynchings, and all the Mexican and black folks that lay dead because of hatred do to skin color, or where people come from. Sometimes I thought all of my efforts were in vain, but when I looked at my precious half-breed children, one asleep with his head rested on his pillow, the other with dreams of changing the world, I knew I may pay the price for their freedom. Nothing I did was in vain, nothing I did was wasted, and if I met an early death for the sake of my children, it would be worth it.

We took our time going down as there was more sight-seeing to do. The kids and I were more interested in watching the hobos on top of the boxcars and seeing the people work the land. We spent the first night outside Springfield, Missouri, where we set up camp in the Ozarks. Sara bought a live chicken, and I showed her how to clean it. We cooked it up for dinner, along with some beans we had. After the meal, Sara grabbed my guitar, I played the banjo, and Tomas wailed some blue's harp. He did a great job. Sara sang along, too, making up some unmemorable lyrics. I can't remember them, but they were dedicated to me.

The next day we got on the main road and decided to get to my daddy's place as soon as possible. We hurried on down highway 71 and passed cars like they stood still, and I didn't slow down until I was north of Texarkana. I debated calling on Becky and wondered what she was up to, whether she'd be willing to give herself to me again. It's been awhile since I saw her, but I thought different about it. These kids were my life, and I figured I shouldn't teach them more bad examples but instead a more appropriate way of life. Besides, if my past was behind me, I should bury all of it. Becky McCormick was part of my past. Although, my innocence, the playfulness in which we had sex, the uncaring and unloving way we went about it, should also be obscured. I cruised around town showing the kids some of the landmarks I remembered as a youngling, and headed to Louisiana, the state I longed to be my new home.

I pulled into Grandpa Cecil's place about four that afternoon. As a custom, Gator came out barking at us, with Pa limping right behind him.

Grandpa shook his head when he saw us and gave a wry little smile. "You got here pretty early. Thought you be packing for a few days."

"Nothing to pack." I said in a matter-of-fact tone. "We can't carry ashes. Some folks burned the place to the ground."

The old man laughed for about ten minutes straight it seemed. He sounded like Santa. "Come here, son," he said giving me a hug. "Chip off the old block, ain't ya?"

Chapter 15

The old man bought me that swamp land west of Zwolle, stretched all the way from the railroad station down to the Sabine. Legend had it that this is where Cletus Barnum lived. The only building still standing on the land was an old juke joint and whorehouse, away from the neighbors and the river, but close to the train tracks that traveled north a mile or so before they crossed the Sabine into hell. The rest of the land was a mixture of savannah grass, caves, and cypress trees, with the occasional gator sprawled out in the backyard.

No idea how the crusty old moonshiner paid for the land. I'm sure he didn't invest in anything, but the old man probably had boxes full of stash buried in old snake holes that sprawled all over his property.

Sure enough, he hobbled to an old cypress tree along the shores of the bayou and pulled out a box. "This is also for you. Got a couple more for the kids when they are older. Open it up," his eyes twinkled.

Too stunned to speak, I counted all the paper money, and there must have been about twenty thousand dollars there.

"Now go move into your new home," he said while slapping my back. "I don't want my boy and his kids in my space cramping my style. I'm still a player down here and always will be." He winked at me and the kids and then he hugged us. "We'll be down tomorrow to help you guys get set up."

We headed down in the direction of the swamp with the deed to our new land and a steel box filled with a lot of green. We passed the lonesome rail station and headed out to the forest where our new home awaited. It wasn't ready to live in yet, but we brought our sleeping bags and stuff, and slept in the same room as if we were camping. We were about to make this place a home.

The building would become the juke joint after we built a nice little house closer to the river for us. The main room would face west, toward the river, and most important, toward Texas. I wanted to look at it when I left the house, so I could taunt the Lone Star State, and laugh at it since it was across the river. It will make a good fort from which I'd wait for my enemy on the front porch, ready to shoot them down like my kin knocked off the yanks near here 70 some years earlier. I wanted to pick them off one at a time as they paddled skiffs across the Sabine and shoot the people straight out of the water if they tried to swim across. The land was all mine, from the roadside to the banks of the Sabine, and nothing, nothing and no one, especially from Texas would intrude. It was the perfect place.

When Pa arrived, he walked around the land pretty good. "Son, I didn't know your land here went all the way to the river. We might find some of Great-uncle Cletus's tunnels lying around. Bo, kids look!" He pointed at a large cypress, with unusual markings on the side. The markings looked like a signal, as if a torch was carved into the bark with a knife. "I think that's the tree he hung out in. Legend says there is all kinds of stuff in this old tree here. Bo, can you climb in the river and see if you can get in it?"

I jumped in the muddy waters, climbed into the tree, and saw gators peacefully sleeping. I climbed up into the tree, though it looked like it was about to collapse into the bog. I caught sight of a little hollowed up section of the tree, big enough for scrawny fifteen-year- old kids to hide in. I wasn't sure if a scrawny thirty-three-year-old man could fit in.

"Can't climb into this hole. Not sure if I can fit." I hollered down at them.

"I'll go," screamed Tommy.

"No, you're the little brother," Sara shut her brother down. "Besides there's alligators down there. You might scare and awaken them. I'm going." Sara bravely climbed that old cypress tree, like a bayou river rat and found a small crevice where she climbed inside. "Daddy, there's a ladder in here." She must have climbed up it since the next time I saw her she was about ten feet higher in the tree and waving her skinny arms at us.

"Damn, this must be Cletus's old tree he lived in. Hey sweetums, can you see anything in there? Any markings?"

"It's too dark Grandpa. I'm afraid to see what's in here."

"Climb out of there honey," I said. "I don't want you hurt. You're not a swamp girl yet, but I bet soon you will be. In fact, you will be whatever you choose to be."

"I want to be a lawyer and not a swamp girl," she screamed as she neared the exit. I could only tell by the sound of her voice. Her little head popped out of the tree and her eye darted all around, like a bird in those new cartoon shows. "How do I get down?"

"Not sure, sweetie. Jumping in the river is not a good idea. It's not that deep, but I don't want to make them gators angry. Guess the best thing to do is slide down until it's safe to jump." I looked down and she already jumped off the tree and was rolling in the savannah.

"That was scary, I couldn't see a thing. I felt the ladder with my feet and hands, and then there was like a table up by that hole there. If someone lived in that tree, that's probably where he watched out for people. I thought I saw some other stuff in there, some markings and other things I couldn't make out. If I wasn't so scared, I'd go in with a lantern and search around."

"That's okay, you don't have to," I assured her as we walked toward the old house.

"Daddy, I know I don't have to, but I might need to go in there. It could hold clues, too."

"Clues to what, sweetums?" Grandpa asked.

"Clues to everything. Clues to Mama disappearing, clues to Grandpa and Grandma Fuentes, and clues why people want to kill Daddy. I'm going to look in that tree one day and see what is in there."

"I'm not sure an old cypress tree holds the answers, but you never know, honey." I told her.

"Oh well, I'm going to make my way into that tree again sometime. I'm going to get me a lantern and. bring Tomas too, so we can look together. He's got a good imagination, and I bet together we can figure out all of this."

"I bet you will."

We returned to the spot where I planned to build the house. I ain't never built one before, but I helped Pa put up a barn once, so I recalled we needed to dig a place to start a foundation. Pa said the foundation is the key for a strong house, so we got our shovels and spades and dug. I went into town and got a load of bricks and started to put down the foundation.

After a few months of building and pounding and bricklaying and nailing, we had a complete house, with plumbing and electricity. It looked like one of the fancier ones in town and had a concrete driveway and we even a garage for the car.

I was kind of proud of myself, and the next step was to get my little multi-purpose bait, tackle, and juke joint/whorehouse going. It didn't need much, a good coat of paint on the inside and out, and to add a few bedrooms, in case some of our customers wanted to get a little action. The still was already cooking the whiskey. I can thank Pa for that, and by Christmas of 1937, we were ready for business.

Business wasn't the best for a while, as I the main entertainment. I played my best old-timey and country blues but didn't have anyone else playing and not too many people showed up. Unfortunately, while running an illegal business, it's hard to advertise, but I tried my best to get people to show. During the summer of 38, things started to pick up. I had a string of musicians stop by to jam with me, most of them black musicians from all places East Texas, and a few guys from Mississippi. I played with them when I could keep up, but mainly entertained the gathering crowds, while doing my best to be a good host.

I had some women around to entertain the guests and musicians. The musicians usually got twenty bucks and the lady of their choice, and the other ladies received twenty bucks from the customers. I only hired about eight ladies and they were nice, pretty and friendly. All were colored girls, and I found them quite charming, though I never indulged.

Leaving the kids with Pa, I took a run to Clarksdale to drop off some whiskey for an old family friend. The man a scruffy old man liked his Perique tobacco and adored Pa's shine. On my return I spotted a Stella guitar, already beaten up, laying on the roadside. I tossed it in the back of my coupe and returned to the Black Bayou.

After a short visit with my father, I grabbed my kids, and we drove home. Approaching the Cane River Bridge, we spotted her, a young gal of about sixteen, and she tossed objects into the river. The girl stood short and scrawny, but still pretty. I wondered why she stood all alone on the bridge and hoped she wouldn't jump into the river. We all knew gators cruised the waters near Natchez.

"Where you headed?"

"Anywhere."

I pushed the car door open. "Hop in. We's going somewhere."

She grabbed her bag, as she piled in the back seat next to Tommy.

I looked back at her and she stared at me swatting her tears away with her right hand. "Sorry for crying, sir. I had to run away from that old pig. I worked for a man who hired a bunch of us to do some sharecropping. And dat old cow made me the maid, and one of my duties was to take care of him and his boys. Dey raped me every night."

My lip curled up. I raised an eyebrow, taking in her big brown eyes and her jet-black complexion. "You're too sweet looking for anyone to do that to you. You come down and work for me? I think I need me a maid."

"How do I know you won't do the same?"

"Not sure, but I guess you gotta to trust me." I smiled, the first time I smiled at a young lady since Lydia vanished, and she smiled back. "I need some help with these kids and some cooking and cleaning, too. You won't have to do much. I'll give you five dollars a week, plus room and board." I had no intentions of pimping her out, I employed older gals for that, plus she was off limits to any of the musicians who frequent the establishment.

"My name's Bo Barnum, and this girl is Sara, and that's Tommy you're sitting next to."

"Hi, Bo. My name's Miriam, and I guess I'll go with you for a while."

"Now, Sara, she looks fifteen, so you guys will get along."

"Miriam glanced at my daughter, who glared back. I wondered if this would be a good idea. They tended to avoid each other, while my son became infatuated with her.

A year later the juke joint hopped, but I let most of the girls go. I didn't feel right running a little whorehouse in front of the kids. I tried to quit but didn't quite. Too many of the musicians and customers wanted to hook up, so I ran it on party nights. The money I made would pay for the kid's college. The juke joint stayed active and folks came and went at all hours three nights a week. The kids stayed in the house with Miriam as we played music until three a.m. every Thursday, Friday, and Saturday. On rare occasions where no one showed up to play, I performed solo. I wished I knew a singer or someone to accompany me, and sometimes the guests might step in and try to rock the house down. What I didn't know, some young lady listened to me play.

I thought Miriam was a pretty little gal when we picked her up while returning home. I thought she was Sara's age, so I didn't want nothing to do with her that way. I didn't want to be a creep like her previous employer, and I missed Lydia, my one true lover. I missed a woman's touch.

There were times in passing, when we both cooked dinner, or I helped her with her chores. She'd grind her hips against mine. It wasn't sexual, maybe a bump here, and our arms brushed against each other. I devised a plan to get her attention even more. I gave her the morning off, and I'd make breakfast for the four of us.

Miriam cooked the way we liked our food, added enough red and black pepper to give our meals a swift kick, not too hard, nothing that would knock us on our bottoms, but enough to let us know there was good Louisiana seasoning.

I shook like the pecan trees scattered along the Sabine during hurricane season. I wanted her to want me, but I forgot how to ask. I cranked the pepper in like I cranked my wrist playing my five-string. I did it in rhythm with Cripple Creek and I sang along while twisting my wrist on the grinder. There was way too much pepper in the gravy when I finished.

I smiled, my trap set, and waited for the prey. They came down the stairs one after the other with Sara in the lead, followed by Tomas. Miriam stumbled down the stair minutes after my boy. They all sat at the table as I threw a package of bacon in the cast iron skillet and stirred the gravy, and then grabbed eggs from the icebox.

Still nervous as a red fox, I could not stop my arm from shaking. I felt like a kid, when I courted Becky, and when we skinny dipped in the shared pond for the first time. The gravy needed more water and I grabbed the measuring cup, but it fell into the cast iron pan. I reached my hand inside the simmering gravy, got burned, and dumped flour on myself.

Laughter came from the table, as Miriam rushed to me, stroked my arm and pressed her hips to my groin. She tasted my gravy and spat it out. "Mastah Barnum, you put way to much pepper in da gravy. Here let me show ya how to make it."

"Miri, I think I'm overcompensating for Ma's cooking. She didn't like the spicy stuff. Pa wanted to bleach us up a bit, to give us kids a fighting chance. Figured we could pass for white boys if he married a white woman."

"No offense, your papa is a fool, Mastah Barnum."

"None taken but I can pass, and so did my brothers, but one is in the Klan, guess he got too much bleach in him, and da other one still missing."

Even though I knew how to make the gravy like she did, she showed me how to cook as we gleamed at one another. The kids and I loved her cooking, and we finished breakfast. Later, I gave her the afternoon off, and she ran around the land, while I gave Sara her guitar lesson.

I noticed the Stella was missing and rushed outside, abandoning my daughter's lesson. She played better than me anyway, better rhythm and did her scales faster. I headed off the porch with my banjo and heard sweet sounds of the south, but in the local rhythms. I didn't see no one, so I headed to where the guitar and sweet and gritty voice came from.

No one was there; however, I heard the singing from another corner, and I attempted to chase her down. Once again, the singing stopped but returned from an adjacent corner.

She sat playing Come on in My Kitchen, a Robert Johnson classic on the Stella I found. I loved that song, and he was a great singer. Too bad he ain't with us anymore. No one knew how he was killed.

"Bo where you get this guitar? I think there's magic in it." She smiled as she ripped another blues song and switched over to the sound of the Creole. A sweeter, and upbeat sound with similar progressions. I tapped my feet, figured the rhythm and started cranked my banjo as I *approached her.*

"What's dat you playing, Miri? I like the sound."

"Dey call it Lala De Creole, some folks call it Zydeco." She played and sung a few tunes, while I figured out the rhythm.

She gleamed at me, as we played and sang.

"Don't you go messing with my mojo,

Don't touch you above my knee,

Don't be messing with my mojo,

And keep your hands of my gris-gris."

She paused, waiting for me to join her in a duet. At the drop of a hat I came up with the second verse of our first duet.

"I don't want your mojo,

It's not your mojo that I want

"I'm not after your mojo,

Mwen vle fe seks avek ou."

She skipped a beat on the guitar, and stopped for a second, gleamed at me smiling. I got that smile I once received from Lydia and she continued. I'm not sure where the Haitian Creole came from. It might have been magic.

"Baby don't mess with my mojo

You touched me above the knee

Dat's messing up my mojo

And don't mess with my gris gris.

Baby don't you mess with my mojo

You know I had plenty of dat.

Oh baby, don't be messing with my mojo,

Eske ou vle danse.

I stopped playing to watcher her roll through the thick grass. "What's dat mean?" I asked, my accent thicker."

She laid in the meadow, on her back, legs ajar with the guitar on her chest. She giggled. "I asked you to dance with me."

"Of course, I'll dance with you, I dropped the banjo to the ground, reached down, holding her hand, and lifted her to her feet, and twirled her around. I held her in my arms, and smiled, as she returned the grin, I wanted to take her to an upstairs bedroom in the juke, but we needed to finish the song. I changed the rhythm up a bit and sang.

"What if I'm that man
That you're supposed to see
What if that little red mojo bag
That you call gris gris
Now red is the color of love
Maybe we is supposed to be
This comes from the Lord above,
And that bag you call gris-gris."

We both yearned to finish the song. There were other ways to communicate what we felt. Singing, playing and dancing together was mere foreplay for our intentions. Miriam finished, repeating the chorus thrice, going slower each time.

"Baby you mess with my mojo
Touch me above my knee
Baby you can have my mojo
Thanks to my gris gris.

We retreated to the juke. I chose the master suite, which was more glamourous than any bedrooms inside the house. The brass bed lay empty except the clean linen that hadn't been used for weeks, since business was slow on the Chitlin' Circuit.

We held each other, both wanting to make a move, but scared. I inched towards her lips. Her face moved towards mine, and then drifted away, before returning towards me again. She tasted sweeter than my homemade wine I experimented with. We continued for hours before drifting off to sleep, satisfied as any person who walked the planet.

We laid naked as jaybirds, cuddled up after we finished. "Don't really seem right doing it in here, does it?" You know I used this as a whorehouse, not a place where a man and woman make righteous love."

Her head was on my chest, and her firm breasts pressed into my stomach. She sucked on her finger, cuddled up next to me. "So, you love me? Does that mean I can sleep in your bed?"

"Of course, pumpkin. I ain't one of them guys who come here to pick someone up. I'm a one-woman man, and I don't like sleeping around. Not sure if I want to get hitched, but I can think of you as my girl, if you don't mind?"

"I don't mind, Mastah Barnum, I mean Bo. I got one question." She raised her head slightly to look at me. "Why did it take so long to notice me?"

"Pumpkin, I noticed you, but didn't want to be like your last employer. I didn't want to take advantage of you. Notice how I kept you out of whorin'? Guess I didn't want to see anyone else with ya, either. So, let's gather up our stuff, go to the house and finish up our sleep."

"I'm too tired to get up." She stretched out, her head on my chest and fell asleep. I held her all night and felt ecstatic. At last, I felt alive.

Chapter 16

"Daddy, I don't like her. She's not mi madre." Sara's first reaction to the news that Miriam no longer worked for me but was my lover. "She's not good for you, and this place isn't good for you. Maybe if you worked on music and sang songs about what you believe in, I'd support it. Getting these folks drunked up and partying all night has to go. I know people are having sex, too. You shouldn't be doing this, Daddy. You're too good for it."

"Sara, this little club here keeps us alive and puts food on the table. It also keeps me alive. If I went out there fighting for what I believed in, I'd be dead by now. I don't want you two to be orphans."

"Ma ain't dead. I know it!" She yelled back as sassy teenagers do.

"Well, where is she?" I crossed my arms to show her who is the boss. "She left us. She's either dead or ran off. So, she's dead to us."

"Maybe this is why she left. I'm sure Mama would proud of you, making the whiskey and selling girls and everything. I'm sure mi madre knew exactly what you really were."

"She left you guys also. If she thought I was nothing but a lowlife pimp and whiskey runner, she would have taken you along. Now, I don't want to talk about your mother no more. I don't like you talking back to me, but sometime honey, you have to start cooking from scratch. Losing your mom made me start my dream all over again. This here ain't a full-time gig. I got rid of all the girls but Miriam, who was never supposed to be a whore. I hired her as a maid, and someone who can watch over you when I'm not around. Now, the whiskey is for the people listening to the music. I want to entertain.

People have a good time when they come here. I'm laying low right now. Too much bad stuff happened, and I feared for our lives. Honey, I'll be back. I ain't done fighting. I might try to record some of my songs, you know like that Woody Guthrie fellow. What do you think of that? I want you to apologize for talking back to me, but I love that you care."

Sara stood silent for a moment. She stared at me rolled her eyes and exhaled. "I'm sorry, Daddy. I know Miriam ain't mi madre. I don't like all these people coming by the house. I love you, and I like that you are going to make a record someday. I want to hear you on the radio."

All I knew was that the next few years were going to be hard. The cuter and smarter my daughter got, the more yelling and screaming there would be. She was usually right, but I was her papi. I would always be correct even when I wasn't close to being right.

Tommy liked Miriam. She spent more time playing with him in the yard. They played ball, and she taught him how to play music on the washboard. I think the main problem with Sara and Miriam was they weren't too far apart in ages, and my darling baby girl was a little jealous that her daddy had a new flame. There was going to be a new number one girl in his life. It didn't matter how many times I tried to reassure her, that there was only one number-one. I was happy there a number two.

I closed down the shop for a few days so we could head down to the peninsula to see Miriam's father. Sara didn't like taking trips with Miriam in the car because she was delegated, once again, to the back seat with her baby brother. She sat in back with her pretty pouty face, and her lower lip jutting out, arms folded across her chest.

It was a good drive to the peninsula with its trees and wildlife. We drove down southwest from New Orleans and made our way through the swamp. Folks hung out on the front porch, dancing away and playing music. I wondered if this could be our next home.

Once we got into town, Miriam took over in helping us find the way. We took several turns and crossed a big bridge and finally stumbled upon a little shack with a couple of black men who looked about fifty years of age sitting there. One had a washboard, the other played the accordion. They didn't seem to notice us, but Miriam yelled at me to stop the car.

"Miri, is that you sugar?" The man playing the accordion stood up and slowly walked over to his daughter. He hugged her when he was close enough. "How de hell you been doing Miri? Haven't seen you since you ran off." He turned to his musical partner and said, "this here my baby girl, the one I'd been telling you about."

"You ain't done tell me you had a daughter." His partner put down his whiskey bottle, after swallowing a dose of poison.

"Told you lots of times. Now, Miri, you coming home to stay?"

"Nah, Pappy. I came down to visit. This here is my new beau; his name is Bo. I call him my Bobo."

I stretched my hand out to meet his. He wasn't shaking hands.

"I don't like you messing with them older, white men. I got your letter from Shreveport, Miri. I don't trust this man as far as I can throw him. My age Miri, I can't throw that far neither." He took another shot and laughed like one of them hyenas.

"My Bobo ain't like that, Pappy. He's real sweet to me. He picked me up hitching from that place at Shreveport and hired me as his maid. Don't pay me that good, but he never made a play on me for over a year. Plus, he's a musician. We play and sing together real good, too. Bobo, grab your banjo and let's do some lala for my pappy. Pappy, you guys need to join in."

We did our duet and a few more standards that Miriam taught me. Her dad and his partner played along, and Tommy came out too and danced while Sara sat in the car, obviously afraid to have any fun. After a while, she got out and sat on an empty bench, across the street from their house.

"Sara, come on sing a song!" I hollered at her. "Which one do you want to do?" Her eyes focused on the man's accordion. She stared, probably trying to figure out a way to break into conversation. She remained silent.

"Mr. Landry? Is this Creole music all you play? My daughter is Mexican, and her mom always sang that Tejano stuff you hear over in that godawful place west of the river."

"My last name ain't Landry, and, please, don't call me mister. Damn her mother, kept her name and she didn't keep my name. Damn that woman. Maybe I should have been around more. I don't play nothing but Creole music there, boy. Only music around these parts."

"Pappy, can you follow along? What if we play something, can you figure it out?"

"I can figure anything out on this thing. I just don't know no Mexican songs."

I took Miriam's que and started playing those old folk songs I first heard Lydia sing when I arrived in Omaha and living in a box car. Miri followed along on her guitar too, and we made eye contact with Sara, who walked across the street and started singing. Miriam's dad followed up on the accordion, and here we were in the swamps of the New Iberian Peninsula, where 99.99 percent of the population is Cajun or Creole, and I don't think there are any Mexicans around, and we sounded like a mariachi band. Folks opened their doors, looked out at us and applauded, as we did about four songs.

The old man smiled and whooped it up and we hugged and shook hands. "Damn Bobo, glad to meet you there, sir."

"Pappy, Bo runs a little club up north, by Zwolle, and I thought you can come with some fellas and play some night, and we could get caught up. They don't play much lala up there. I want to hear some and play some, too. Come up, please."

Miriam had a way of getting what she wanted. She would stick her neck out, almost kissing, and a big pretty grin, and then her big brown eyes would get even bigger as she begged. I couldn't resist, now I checked on her pappy. I'm sure she wasn't the temptress to her old man as she was to me.

"Damn, Miri, okay. You have a way about you, don't you? When I was raising you, I could never say no, even when I was passed out on Toulouse Street in the city. Now, you folks will spend the night. We going to cook up some crawfish and make some jambalaya. Give that Yank a taste of real food."

The neighbors and them, they cooked up a feast and we ate, drank and partied. Miriam and I snuggled up and were kissed a lot, when I noticed some Creole boy and Sara dancing a little too close for my liking. Sara was about the same age Lydia was when I met her, and I was kissing and loving her mom back then; however, I didn't want Sara to be fooling around with guys until she was at least twenty-one.

I didn't want to break them apart, but I didn't want it to go further than the dance and hugs. I'd have one eye shut while kissing Miriam, and the other on my daughter and her new friend. Miri's kisses made that hard to do because soon, her kisses carried this old boy to places that were only dreamed about. That girl had a way about her. Not sure what was happening with Sara and her new friend, but I finally decided to make some rounds and check on her. Arms around our waists, Miriam and I wandered through the neighborhood and found her in a secluded part, sitting on blankets under a huge tree in the bayou. She wasn't alone as the boy she danced with, was kissing my little baby girl.

My brain deluged with thoughts. Was this her first kiss, or were there many boys before? Did they start kissing, or were they finishing up something? If they were, what were they finishing up? Who is this boy, and how many girls has he kissed? Why is this boy kissing on my girl? I know she's the most beautiful girl in the world, but damn, what gives him the right? Who made the move to sneak out, was it him or my angel?

I wasn't sure how to act as I stood in awe. My eyes caught Miriam's and she grinned. That wasn't the look I hoped for from her as I yelled at Sara to stop. The boy ran, he slipped into the darkness, like a thief who stole a heart. Guess it was time for an awkward adult conversation with my baby gal.

"Papi, I'm sorry I was having fun. I ain't never kissed a boy before. I saw you and Miriam kissing and figured I like that boy and he likes me, so I tried."

"Well, Miriam and I are in love." Sara rolled her eyes around and sighed. "What?" I screamed back at her. Miriam left to join the party.

"Daddy, you ain't in love with her. You like her. She's pretty and talented, but you don't love her. At least you don't love her like Mami."

I glanced around looking for my lady. I didn't see her anywhere, so I figured it was safe to say this. "I'll never love anyone like tu madre, you know that, maybe you're right on the other part, too. I might not love her, but I do like her a lot, and have gotten to know her over the last year. We were friends first. Now, you just met this boy and already you're letting him kiss you. That's what I have a problem with." My arm went around her shoulder and pulled her close. "Baby girl, I know it will happen, some boy will steal your heart, and you won't be able to say no to him on anything. I don't want it happening for a long time. Hopefully you'll marry that guy, and believe me, I want nothing more than for you to marry some great man. I ain't ready yet."

"Daddy, can I say something, and promise you won't get mad?" She waited for my approval and said. "You haven't done the best job teaching me morals."

Silence settled over the bayou. The bullfrogs and pelicans announced their presence, and one could hear a gator cruising up the river. "You're right, but I'm doing the best I can. What kind of morals do you think Grandpa Cecil taught me? What makes you think that old man I call my pa taught me right from wrong?"

"Of course, he did, just like you have, but I'm sure mi abuelo taught you wrong. Just like you've taught me wrong, and when I have kids, I will teach them the wrong way to live too, like I'm going teach them the right way." She hugged me. "I'm sorry, Daddy, for letting that boy kiss me. It was the first time, I promise, and he just kissed me, he didn't touch me nowhere else. I love you, Daddy."

We walked back to find Tommy dancing it up with some little black girl as he played a washboard. Sara and I smiled at each other.

We spent the night down at Miriam's dad's little place, all crammed into his one-bedroom house. Sara and Tommy slept on the floor, while Miriam and I slept on a davenport, but with one head on each end. I tried playing footsie with her, but she resisted. We got up the next morning and ate a good breakfast with some mighty fine biscuits and gravy that must have had a ton of pepper in it, and some piping hot coffee.

Miriam kept bugged her father into following us up to Zwolle, and he and his musical partner, got in a broken-down wreck of a car and followed us home. They could stay in the former brothel. That same boy who kissed Sara must have snuck in their car unnoticed, but he was the first one out of their car once we drove past the rail station and down the gravel road through the bayou until we got to the clearing known as Barnum Manor.

The boy walked up to me, and his thick accent said, "I'm sorry, suh. I shouldn't be kissing on your daughter like that."

"Well, son, I guess I can't blame ya. She's a pretty thing."

"That she is, but I guess I was disrespectful to ya. We was just kissing. I didn't even try to touch her. I hear we're going to play some music here in a couple of nights."

"We?"

"I brought my guitar with me, I bet I can play better than you."

"If you put it that way, we should jam a little. Besides, I think we should practice a lot before the show."

He went back to the jalopy and whipped out his old broke down guitar and started playing lights out on it. Kid probably sold his soul to the devil or something because he played like no one I knew. I seen and heard a lot of guitar players in my life, and damn if that kid was the best of them. "Okay, you win, I can't hold a candle to you, but let me teach you a thing or two." I whipped out my dobro, and really got the ghosts of the bayou singing along as I put that old switch blade on the neck and slid it up and down the strings. Snakes and the gators sang along as they slithered along the swamp while that guitar wailed through the night.

"Wow, Daddio, you can tear it up, too. I still think I'm better but we're going to make dem boys and girls dance and cry all night. With Pa playing the accordion and Uncle Leon on da washboard, Miriam, and you, we going to tear this roof down. Hey Pa, Mr. Barnum can play! You ain't all white either, are ya? You got some Negro in ya there don't ya?"

"I actually do, and that old man's your Pa? So, you and Miriam are brother and sister?"

"Hell yeah, Pappy's got kids he don't even know about. I'm thinking I'm the youngest, but hell I don't know. All I know is I'm ready to play."

There was something about the kid I liked, but it's hard to trust a kid who was over-confident. Then again most young kids are fools, and one could blame it on age. While I admired his talent, eagerness, and presence, many would want to see the young fool fail. They are turned off by the boastful arrogance that this boy distributed. I reckon an innocent fifteen-year-old girl could be impressed. Caution was needed this next week, but then again, I'd be tearing it down on a guitar and banjo. When this old man gets in the mood and throws a five or six string in my hands, look out. Caution ain't in the goddamn dictionary.

All of us rehearsed on our little stage. Miriam's dad and the blind washboard player took the center. Tommy grabbed a chair in front, while Sara and Miriam stood on the right of everyone, since they'd do most of the singing. Me and the boy hung out on the left. It worked better that way. Plus, I didn't think I'd appreciate the boy near my precious girl again. The way he wielded his guitar might draw Sara over the edge.

We rehearsed for about two hours trying to get the perfect rhythms, sounds, and vocals down. "Damn, we're sounding good. That's as good as it gets."

"You don't know crap about lala, boy." Miri's dad said. "This ain't close to perfect. We got a lot of shit to work on. Da music is all about the rhythm, and you are off a bit. Keep practicing, son."

"In all respect, sir, we don't want it to be perfect. We want the music sloppy but good. That's how we played. People come here to drink my whiskey and dance and maybe some guys want to meet someone for the evening. This music does that. It makes people want to party. Hell, I want to party."

"Mr. Barnum, I respect your opinion. However, I'm a professional musician. Man, I got me several records out and played from New Orleans to New York City. People dig on all types of colored folk's music. You never know who the hell is gonna show up to watch a performance. There might be some record producer arrive tomorrow night. You never know. If you are too sloppy, he might walk away unnoticed and that was your lone chance. You're mighty good on that old banjer and dobro, I like the way you play, but you are off on the rhythm a little bit."

"Sir, I never played music to record, or even to get a recording contract. I play so you and me can play together, so me and Miri can sing together. I play it for everyone so they can dance with each other, to teach them that blacks, whites, Mexicans, and others can stand together and sing and dance. I started playing to woo my neighbor girl up in Texarkana. It Goddamned worked. Hell, that's why we play. If I never make a dime off my songs, I don't care."

"I do care. I'm a black man, living in a depression. I ain't got no other way to make no money. You're right it's about fun, but for some of us it's survival. It's a mother fucking, goddamn shame, but for me it is. Let's go through the set again and do it better. We haven't played together, so the more we play, the better we'll get."

I took offence by Miriam's pappy because it's my gig. It's been a long time since I relinquished the control to some guy. It went back to the days of the Carters and Early Greene.

The Zwolle folks were reluctant, but the Morgan City folks were all fired up. Even though I was averse to the second round of rehearsal, admiration for the men and boy, for their passion for the music and the way they went about their business was earned, as well as respected. About a third of the way through our second set, my playing came alive, like spirits that that rose up each night on the bayou.

"Goddamn, Bo, What the hell got into you?" Miriam's sperm donor asked me.

"I felt something deep inside. Think I finally figured out what this was about." Passion, rhythm, and technical ability, I always had. Magic came from the guitar, too, but this time it sounded different. It wasn't coming from the banjo or dobro anymore. The music came from the swamps. It resonated from the ghosts of my ancestors, from the spirits of the runaway slaves that fled across the muddy swamps and hid in dug out cypress trees.

We hooted and hollered after that second set. I never noticed when Sara and Miriam sang, *"Take Your Hands off My Mojo,"* Sara gleamed at the boy. I didn't notice because Miriam stared deep into my eyes like I hypnotized her because she put a spell on me. Sara was right. I wasn't setting a good example for my daughter.

After relaxing with some good grub some shots of homebrewed whiskey, and beer and sweet tea for the children, we let the Morgan City crew hang out in the club. A few unused beds sat upstairs. While us, Barnums and Miriam, retired to the house. Tommy went to his room, while Sara went to hers, and Miriam and I went to ours. I hoped that's where everyone spent the night, since Miriam and I refused separation.

The show the next time was incredible. Miriam brewed some good old gumbo, and we hauled in a string of catfish that we caught from the Sabine that day and cooked up a mighty fine feast. A batch of shine waited, along with some home-brewed beer. We were prepared to take on the night. People from all over West Louisiana and I heard a few folks from the peninsula showed up and they needed to party. As a band, and hosts and hostesses, we didn't disappoint. We played a lot of the Creole music that was so common down south and a lot of East Texas Blues, prevalent to our area. The whole club was packed, and we rocked the night away. I wasn't even afraid folks from Texas crossed the river to hear us.

The party went on until 3a.m., when this old boy headed to bed. The old man, his partner and the boy kept at it for another hour or so. We heard the jamming from my house while Miriam and her Bobo lay comfortably in bed with each other, doing our thing. We curled up together, not wanting to be more than a few inches apart at the most, as she ran her fingers through my curly locks and I laid my hand across her breast, resting it there, and not tantalizing it. We confessed our love for each other and vowed never to part. The music stopped playing, and the only noise we heard was our hearts beating and the bullfrogs croaking.

The creak of the steps got louder and kept me awake. They soon went past our door and grew faint as they approached Sara's door. I thought I heard the faint sound of a girl crying as they passed by our bedroom. Poor girl didn't know that the more careful you are trying to be quiet, the less you succeed. She didn't learn her sneaking in and out from me, that's for sure.

I debated going to check on her, but I was spent, in a relaxed state, exhausted after a wonderful session with Miriam. I liked the way we made love. Can't say she was better than Lydia; but can't say that Lydia was better than Miriam. Tossing and turning for an hour after hearing the crying and creaking, I decided it was best to check on my daughter.

I knocked before bursting into her room. She still cried on her bed. "I heard you come in, honey. Don't try to be so quiet." I told her as I brushed the tears away.

She wrapped her arms around me and tucked her head into my chest. "Daddy, please don't punish me for sneaking out. I wanted to see him real bad."

"I know you did. I saw you looking at him. I know that look."

She pulled her head away from me and stared into my eyes. I taught my children always to look into one's eyes, so you knew they told the truth. She took a deep breath and sighed. "I went up to his room and knocked on the door." She paused for a minute. "I heard moaning and screaming and such." There was another short gap, and she continued. "I figured he was with someone, and I heard another lady giggling. I sat there crying for thirty minutes when one came out." She stopped again, this time even longer. She crushed her head into my chest and collected her thoughts. "One of the women came out the door and saw me." She sniffed, and really broke down. "The lady said to me, 'Girl you too little to handle that boy. He needs a real woman. That man boy will shred you apart. Go back home and play with your dolls princess.' She started laughing." My poor girl cried her eyes out. I spent the rest of the night with her as she cried herself to sleep on my chest.

Chapter 17

Locals were pretty laid back and warm to our shows. We lived far enough from anyone to not bother the neighbors, but most of them showed up anyway. On a great night, fifty people arrived at the bait shop, juke joint, and former whorehouse to enjoy a night of homemade beer and whiskey, catfish, red beans and rice, and, of course, some good music. When the whores still worked, I think we had over a hundred people in that place at one time. Luckily, about ten were upstairs in the rooms that were set up. Cutting the brothel out made me feel a little more legitimate about the business. It was a good gig, almost legal and people had fun. We still had some regulars from the days of the old whorehouse who tried to use the rooms upstairs if they met a woman willing. It usually happened.

We were scheduled to play another gig that night. The musician and host in me wanted to play another show. The father in me, wanted the Morgan City clan out of Dodge as soon as they got their asses out of bed. I figured on a compromise. My kids would stay in the house, and we'd cut the show off early. I hoped to get everyone out by midnight. What people hope for and what actually happens is always two different things. That night was no exception.

Miriam and I called it a night about midnight, hoping the rest would follow suit. The old men and the boy kept the party going by themselves and partied all night. I often questioned myself for running the business, but we made some decent cash and folks had a good time. There wasn't a thing wrong with that. I soaked it in, knowing I was safe with the law. I'm sure Pa made that happen, since he had connections everywhere. I kept a low profile, no wild civil rights or Klan fighting. That could got me killed down here in the South. Us Louisianans tried to keep that stuff west of the river.

I didn't miss the fight. I brought whites and colored folks together through the music we'd play. Our audience was mainly black folks, but we had a few mixed folks and white people digging the sounds we made. There wasn't any trouble ever, so I felt I met my goal of racial harmony.

We had another good show the following night. Sara decided to stay in the house. She didn't want to mess with that boy no more. Poor girl got her first broken heart, I'm sure it wouldn't be the last, but my baby girl would break a lot more in her time. She probably broke a few already up in Omaha and slaughtered some up in half down here in Zwolle. During this last year with my time with Miriam, I knew I wasn't the dad I needed to be. That afternoon while the band performed, I figured it was time to become the father I was capable of. No more hopping freights, no more touring the country, helping the depressed, and no more juke joint touring. I would start that after tonight's show.

The show was a repeat of the previous night, the lala gang had it going on, and Miriam and I had a kindred thing happening. We knew when to stare at each other, when she would sing, when I was going to sing, when she would rip into a solo, and when I was going to rip into one, too. We became magic, like some voodoo queen. Not like Angeline, but some real princess down in New Orleans, casting up magic potions that naïve and desperate people spend some good money on. We retired early and spent another magical night. Heading downstairs in the morning we discovered the old men discussing the fiddle player who showed up late in the evening.

"I ain't seen no one play the fiddle like that man."

"Not since the 20s when that drifter came passing through. Dat boy could sure play."

"Played with him before Miri left, and never heard from him again."

"Suppose that was the same guy?"

"Could be?"

I interrupted. "What did this guy look like?"

"He was shifty, about forty-five I'd say. I thought he had a scar across his cheek. Maybe two."

"Did he mention a name?"

"Nope, didn't ask."

You didn't see which way he went did you?"

"Hell, we didn't see him show up. Seemed like he popped on stage, took a swig of whiskey, and said this is the best shit ever. He played a few songs with us and vanished into air. You know this guy?"

I motioned Miriam to take the kids into the other room. Only Tommy went. "Yeah, it was Early Greene. Used to know him well. Haven't heard from him in a few years."

The other old man, the blind washboard player, looked my way in disbelief. Sara came close to me and held my hand, as the blind man said to Miri's dad and the man child, "We must get our asses out of here. I heard stories about that man that can awaken a dead gator. We best be running. Thanks Barnum, for the gigs."

The three of them disappeared, and I didn't hear from any of them again. I wasn't sure if they made it back home, got ambushed somewhere in the swamps of the Sabine, or they got lost in the vast state across the river. Miriam never heard from her father or brother either.

Well, he still exists. I still had no proof of him doing anything wrong. That son of a bitch found me, and never said a word. I knew we wouldn't be partnering up again, and I wasn't sure what to do. Running wasn't an option, even though I figured I could torch the place and make a clean getaway, but that man would find me since he had the nose for whiskey like a coon dog can sniff out a varmint.

When I needed advice, I knew I had to run up to Cecil Barnum's place on Black Bayou in Caddo Parrish. It was the best little place I knew next to mine. Then again, I was afraid that mad man would follow me up there, and I didn't want his place to be torched to the ground again. My old man didn't need that happening, but that damned Early Greene probably knew where Pa was at anyway.

I slowly got out of the juke joint business, since it was time to retire from clubbing, but the music played brought a smile to my face. I could throw a show every other week with some top-notch entertainment. Sometimes, our little house parties were made up of some pretty dreadful musicians and other times there were some pretty good players, like me, looking for a place to engage in some good music with other like-minded musicians. Top performers stopped by with their six strings and harmonicas and taught this old boy a lessons on the Blues.

Miriam wasn't too fond of me stopping the shows. I guess she was like Lydia and wanted to perform and be discovered. She bitched me out, cursed me out, and when she was nice, she just yelled, but I wouldn't let her have her way. This was my place and she was my gal, and even though she loved me up right every night, I never thought of her as my partner. I figured she was there for the ride. I really didn't love her, I knew it, I liked being with her, and there is a big difference and she knew it. told many times I was doing this to bring my kids up right. They didn't need to see this drunken debauchery happening three to four nights a week. Every other week was good.

There weren't any signs of Early Greene for the next two months. I was no longer Miriam's Bobeaux, or Bobo, however she spelled it, but instead the guy she crawled in bed for some passionless loving. Things picked up when I booked that famous blues man from across the Sabine. He was from the state I didn't want to book any one from, but over in East Texas they had some of the best singers coming out. I could do some promotion and get that man over here to wail a bunch of songs and give him some good money. Since I wasn't in Texas maybe nothing would happen. The show was a success. Lots of people flooded the café like the Sabine was damned up to run electrical power in the valley. The ladies threw themselves all over the stage for him. Undergarments littered everywhere but he didn't take a liking to any of them. He took a liking to one little gal who played onstage with him. I watched the famous blues man tear away in his Cadillac convertible, and she tossed memories of me out the back of the coupe as they bounced down the gravel road. She left everything I got for her, except her clothes.

Miriam's elopement didn't bother me that much. That young lady had her life to live and so did I. We moved in two different paths. She wanted fame, and I wanted justice for all. I wanted to raise my kids, and she didn't want kids. She chose the limelight, while I wanted nothing to do with it. I thought of it as another chapter in life's betrayal, death, and abandonment. I rolled on with no regrets. I wondered what might happen next.

We spent the next several months alone, Tommy, Sara and me. The house shows all but ended. I raised my kids alone, even though courters dropped by the house with batches of biscuits, cornbread, and gumbo. Black, white and Creole women arrived with their goodies, offering food or themselves, but I didn't give them the green light. Never even made a move on any, even though some of the ladies threw their pots in disgust. I even managed to dodge a thrown fry pan aimed at my face. I had no idea what I wanted and didn't want to confuse myself or any of these ladies who brought me breakfast, lunch or supper.

Soul searching was what I needed. One spring day, the kids and I drove into town and headed to Zwolle Baptist church. It was mainly a white church but there were a few colored people there, much to the dismay of some members and much my delight. I liked to see the people blend, and I saw a few mulattos there, too. The church was pretty friendly until the pastor started talking about the devil being present, and all eyes turned on me. I pretty much wanted to grab the kids and scoot on out of there, but I noticed Sara and Tommy's eyes stared right at the pastor like he had them hypnotized.

Maybe it was guilt that made me want to leave. Never thought of myself as the devil, but never thought of myself as a hero either. I aimed to do good all of my life, but deep inside I knew running a brothel and a saloon in a dry parish was something Jesus wasn't too kind about. Even the townsfolk, some of them were regulars, didn't approve of me being there, as they made comments when I went over to greet them and shake their hands. Seen a few of them pull away from me as if they I carried sort of strange contagious ailment or the scaly red man himself. A few women there who brought me food, one who was with her husband tried to get with me one lazy sunny afternoon.

Her comment when she saw me at church, "Shame on you, coming in this fine church and trying to corrupt the children and these good folks here."

Really thought this place was full of hypocrites, but something brought me back week after week. It might have been Tommy's and Sara's insistence that they learn more about God and Jesus. So far, they hadn't learned a damn thing about religion from me. Maybe it was a higher power telling me I needed to get my spiritual life in order.

The three of us soon became regular attendees of the Zwolle Baptist Church, and I cared less what the other church members thought. The more we went, the lesser the confrontations with the greetings. I still got up and walked around, giving my half smile to the Barnum haters and greeting them with a half-hearted handshakes. The mulattos and blacks who attended became my friends. We shared something in common as we sat in the back pews of the church. The more we went, the less talks about the devil infiltrating the church the preacher did. Most sermons were about how everyone needs to be forgiven, the adulterers, the bootleggers, the prostitutes, the brothel runners, and murderers. He looked me dead in the eye, when he said the bootleggers and brothel owners. He looked straight at the lovely lady to my right when he mentioned the prostitutes. We both locked gaze when he finished. I invited her over for dinner when the service concluded, and she accepted.

She sucked down some gumbo I made, and then said. "I don't turn no tricks since I left a house down in Narleans a few months ago. Settled here to stay with my sister, who ran away from the same house last year. Sissy moved up north with her man but left me alone. I figured I'd start heading to church. This is the closest one to my house. I don't care if it's a white church or not, I like going to."

"I used to run a little juke, and had girls taking care of the singers and customers. I figured folks like music, whiskey and women, and I had the best of all three. I got tired of the life and retired, from it. I'll still throw a show or perform myself, but no more whoring of the girls. It's not a good atmosphere for my kids."

"Mastah Barnum, you're probably right, but peoples still needs to work to make some dollars. I'd be willing to make some arrangements, if you up for some business. I ain't got no man of my own right now, and I still can shake what I got. I don't want to be no maid no more either. I get tired of cleaning that Thibodaux place."

"You work at the old fat lawyers place on the edge of town? Dirty son of a bitch tried to run me out of here. Funny thing is I've seen him take one of my girls up and always drinking the hooch. Guess that fat old man wants his hooch and hoochie too. He ain't no Klan man, is he?"

"I don't know, Mastah Barnum. I don't think so. He's just a fat old lawyer as far as I know."

I tried staring into her sad, dark eyes, but she turned her face to the lantern that cast the only glimmer of light in my parlor room. Damn lady must be lying.

"Mastah Bo, I really think you should go into business again. Good way to make some more money, plus I really need extra coins and such. I'se be willing to helps ya. Really Mastah Bo, I want to work at a joint again."

Now this lady was no Miriam, and if she was, I wouldn't allow her to whore herself out anyway. I didn't want that lifestyle, plus I didn't like her pushiness. Thought it was kind of strange for a church woman to beg to be a whore. Like I said, she weren't no Miriam, but she shouldn't be begging to be a whore either. Maybe I was getting smarter as I got older, but I felt something wasn't right. I think it's the same feeling Lydia had with Early Greene, the mistrust feeling, like if you give out too much information. My kids and me could be gator bait in the musky bayou that crosses our land and flows out to the Sabine and down to the Gulf of Mexico. Figured some shrimper would scoop us up in one of his nets and sell me to a market back East.

"No, ma'am. I'm sorry. I ain't gonna do what's illegal anymore. Brewing the juice cost me my wife, and I ain't going to screw nothing up again. I'm trying to get a fresh start in life, play some music, do some farming, and throw a show on occasion. That chicken shack is officially closed." I gently escorted her to the door, but she gave me long deep kiss, the type that would make any house mastah give special privileges. My knees jerked, enjoying her touch. I kissed her back.

"Daddy, what are you doing?" Sara entered the parlor, to return my guitar in which she practiced with.

I pulled away. "I ain't doing nothing. Just escorting Miss Toussaint out the door. Didn't you say you wanted to learn a new song?" I winked at my girl. "Thanks for reminding me, sweetie."

Sara took her cue and sat in a wooden chair and started playing some scales.

"Like this, Daddy?" Her chopping was better than mine, as she worked her way down the neck of the Montgomery Ward's special.

She started some shuffling as I went for my slide, couldn't find it so I broke out the blade and flashed it at my neighbor before I slid it down the strings, making an eerie, swampy sound that could only come from the back 40 of my place. I was oblivious to Miss Toussaint, my former prostitute neighbor, who I believed was trying to frame my skinny, mixed ass for whoring and making whiskey. Once again, my brilliant and psychic daughter shredded the strings and singing made up songs. She belted out a blues song, like Bessie or Memphis Minnie could only do. I wished my baby wasn't so talented. I wanted to get rid of that old bag who claimed my neighbor, but she sat in my chair, eyes focused.

When Sara finished her song, she looked at me. I smiled, knowing years of practice and being around music all her life paid off. The applause we heard came from Miss Toussaint. "Play some more, Sara, play some more stuff. You're a magnificent player."

Sara looked at me for approval, but I wasn't sure why since my little girl was smarter than me. I'm thinking if she was looking for my answer, then do the opposite, knowing 100 per-cent her decision was the correct one.

Sara started another song, a little Creole piece that she's been practicing. She played it loud, so she could wake the gators floating like logs in the bayou. She screamed the lyrics, so those damn Texans heard us. Damn bitch kept on clapping her hands and got up to dance, Sara took the lead and started walking out the house, dancing off rhythm to some old jig that you only heard in Louisiana. I followed her out in a different rhythm, still off beat but my baby girl and I headed out the door toward that old whore's house. She followed us closely, dancing to the rhythm we played, and we shuffled past her fence, still playing that same song we improvised. Ms. Toussaint invited me in, and I turned and headed the mile home down the swampy road that connects the two residences.

I hoped she got the hint that I didn't want to deal with her. I wasn't in the mood for her foolishness or her demanding whorish self. She wasn't following us as Sara, and I danced our way home. We played and sang "La Cucaracha."

Once we stepped in the parlor room, we practiced, unsure who taught who. My girl could play better than me, so our practice sessions kept turning into jam sessions. Tommy came down with his maracas and shook them in time. The boy had good rhythm, but couldn't sing or play a lick, but my boy kept the beat. We played for about an hour and finished up my gumbo on the picnic table behind the house, that looks over to that miserable place that always caused misfortune to old Grandpa Robert Barnum's clan.

Soon the kids went up to their room, and I stayed outside and went out to another table toward the Sabine. I grabbed my guitar out and felt like writing some good old lonesome blues tracks since I missed Miriam, Becky, and especially Lydia. I prayed one of these beautiful ladies would come to me. I wished one would come back to me, one would come back to make this poor man free. I wailed the blues shuffle, added variations, kept making up words and sang to no one in particular, when across the river I heard noises. They were screeches of treacherous fear, followed by a single gunshot. Hell, it came from Texas, so it could have been anything, but the deathly silence that followed made me think someone was killed.

I wasn't sure whether to head inside or investigate what the hell happened. So, like the fool I am, I grabbed that old banjo and strolled through the forest toward the river. I heard the faint splash like paddles from a skiff, slashing through the muddy river waters. As I got closer, the splashing became closer, like a train chugging down the tracks. It was a perfect rhythm, like Tommy playing his maracas or Sara and I playing our guitars. I reached into the pocket of my overalls and out came my harmonica, as the banjo sat strapped across my back. I played the old train rhythms I taught Sara way back in Omaha years earlier when we took our ride in the box car.

The skiff and I did some good call and response, as I chugged, and the skiff splashed. The sounds were a perfect mix, and I figured there was some old blues man running from prison, in search of freedom. I wanted to meet this person. as I walked toward the river's edge, eager to meet this person. Soon, my feet were wet as I waded through the swamps. The splashing ceased. Through the haunted silence of the bayou, I heard, "Bobo, are you there? I heard you playing. I need help, Bobo."

Damn, it was Miriam. I still couldn't see her, but I knew where her voice came from. Sounded like she was about 100 yards to my south, which would take us down to that old tree where ol' Cletus Barnum stole the slaves, loved them up, and sent them on their way. I made my way down there, playing the shuffle on the guitar and harp. Her calling soon became the music, as I responded to her. We soon met by the tree where many women found their freedom. Miriam found hers.

Chapter 18

Miriam tackled me, knocking me to the ground with her incredible hug.

"Bobo, I need help. I'm so sorry I left you for that old dirty singer. Take me back to the house, and I will tell you what happened." She continued her story as we walked through the forest and over the grass land that leads to my place. "I sang with dat dirty ol' bastard, and he and me did get it on a time or two. After playing a show up in Tyler, this guy tried to rob us. Though he didn't get nothing since we didn't have no money anyway. We spent the money from the show on booze. Well dat ol' mother fucker shot him in cold blood, right in the back, after he was walking away. We was arrested I was sent to the farm in Goree, him to the men's place."

"Did you escape?"

"Hell yeah, and der is more. I'll tell you later. Anyways dat son of a bitch came and got me when I was picking cotton on da farm, He shot a guard, and we ran across fields and fields. We hopped a freight, stole a car and headed towards here. I realized where I belong and wanted to come home. I was scared and shaking all da way. Cops kept on our tail, but he outran them. He hit a cow in some town, I jumped and ran, knowing we was close to da river. He chases me down. He turned to me and asks, 'are you wid me babe? We're in dis together, you know.'"

"I goes 'No. I didn't kill no one. You now killed two folks. I ain't got nothing to do with it.' He smacked me across the face, and then throws me down on the ground and tries to rape me. I got lucky, grabbed his gun and shot him right where his thing is. I knew there was a skiff nearby, and I paddled madly across the river. I knew this was your place, Bobo. I knew it."

She got a hug from me. The hug that says I ain't ever going to let you go, as she clung to me like a leach in the muddy waters. We walked to the house.

"Bobo, I needs me a bath, and held all night. You was always so good to me. I loved you but didn't know it."

Then she pounded my chest as she sobbed. I held her close as we walked through the back door and into the house. I led her to the bathroom. I ran the bath water for her, while she slithered out of her torn and wet sun dress and stood naked before me. "Hold me, Bobo. Please, just hold me."

There weren't no kissing or fooling around. Just two people showing extreme intimacy for each other. We were motionless, except she tried to get closer to me, and I caressed her shoulder. Her small firm breasts pressed into my chest. She wrapped her leg around mine and grinded tighter toward me, as the water filled up the tub.

She climbed in and looked me with those irresistible eyes. I needed me a bath, too, so I undressed. figuring I had my lover back as I climbed in the tub with her, and the intimacy continued in my room, long into the night. We pledged our love for each other, and I forgave her for running off with the other man.

Next morning, Sara and I made breakfast.

"Need to make an extra biscuit and some more gravy, honey. Miri came back last night."

She smiled. "I know, Daddy, I heard." She grabbed the flour and put an extra cup full in the bowl and in the pan for the gravy. Then she grabbed the pepper and shook it like it was stuck. She smiled at me again, "Miri always liked it spicier than you."

Miriam crept down the stairs, wrapped in a blanket. She walked ashamed and looked like she did a few of the mornings when she partied too much. When she stayed up late, she always smiled and laughed while looking like death worn over, but this morning she just looked sick.

I didn't notice the bruise on her face the size of the fist right below her eye until now. I didn't notice the redness around the neck from a bastard that must have tried choking the girl. I didn't even notice the black eye she had on the other side of her face. I don't think she did either, until she got a good look in the mirror.

She grabbed a cup of coffee while Sara gave her some grub. "Thanks, Sara, I'm starved. Now, Bobo, last night I told you there was more."

Sara and I stared at her. "Yeah, I think so."

Tears ran across the bruise below her left eye. She sniffed. "Sara and Tommy, it's about your mother. She's still alive. She's at Goree."

"The prison?" I asked.

"Yes, I met her there. She looked familiar, from your pictures of her. Did you know they had a prison band called the Goree Girls? She was one of the singers. I auditioned after one of the girls was paroled and was a guitar player and singer. I asked her name since she looked familiar, and she answered me 'Lydia Fuentes.' I then asked her if she ever married to a guy named Bo. Her eyes lit up, and a huge smile came on her face."

" 'You know Bo?'" she asked me.

"I told her, yeah, I stayed at his house as his maid. He thoughts you was killed.

"No, I wasn't killed. These guys kidnapped and kept raping me while we went on tour throughout the valley and Northern Mexico. They threatened to kill my family if I ever escaped. I tried to escape many times and almost made it once while we were in Austin. Bo has family there, and I made it to his restaurant and tried to get him to help. Either they followed me or knew exactly where I was going to go, because as his cousin walked out the secret back door, two men waited for us. They shot him dead and shot me in the leg so I couldn't walk. They also handed me the gun as I lay bleeding on the ground and that was the last, I ever seen from them. I was taken to a hospital and charged with the murder of my husband's cousin and sent here."

"How long ago was this, did she say?" I asked Miriam.

"Well she's been in for a few years, I was in for about a month when she told me this."

"If she's alive, we need to get her out."

"I tried to get her to leave with us. She said she liked it there. She was the star and wanted to stay."

I stared at Miriam and my kids. Tommy's eyes were wide as Miriam told her story, while Sara had a curious but determined look on her face. Her eyes darted back and forth, and her lips twitched. "We need to get her," Sara slammed her fist on the table. "We need to do it now!"

Tommy clapped. "I want to go; I want to go."

I figured he was too young to help his mama escape jail. Sara was probably too young, but I needed her, since she was my common sense. "Miriam, what's the best way to help her escape?"

"Well, that bastard came and got me, and we started running. It was early evening when he got me. He escaped from Rockwell the night before. He knew when I worked the fields, so he damn snuck up and grabbed me."

Miriam continued, "Lydia, she only works the fields in the morning, so we can get there at night and grab her as they go to the fields. She don't even wear shackles around her ankles. She's the princess of the farm. I knows you guys don't want to hear this, but some girls thinks she fucking the warden. I don't think that, I thinks she gets special treatment cos she's one of the singers. I knows where to goes on the farm, so I can takes you guys there, but I needs to stay hidden."

"Of course, I said. "I bet Pa has ideas, so we're going up to Caddo, to speak to Pa, also to drop Tommy off. I think Tommy is too young to go with."

Sara stared right at Miriam as I said that. Guess she was looking for a clue on what was going on. I bet she wondered if this was a trap or not. Miriam's eyes didn't give anything away, so Sara gave me a slight nod of approval.

"Daddy, what about me?"

"Of course, I need you there."

Sara's brown eyes turned blue as she smiled. "I'll get Mami back Papi."

Tommy smiled; aware he would see his mother again. I had my doubts. I would have to enter Texas again, and that's something I didn't want to do, but this old boy had to do it. "Okay folks let's head up to Pa's. We're spending the night with Grandpa Cecil."

Tommy was excited. Grandpa Cecil was the man who taught him the most in life. Now, one of my regrets was not treating my kids the same. I admit, Sara was a precious girl. I heard somewhere that if fathers give their baby girls their full attention, they wouldn't be working in some whorehouse somewhere in the swamps of Louisiana. I knew my gal won't be doing that even though she was raised in one.

Before we left, I got in the skiff and paddled across the river into that hell of a state, Texas, and hiked up the shores of the Sabine. There was a railroad trestle a few miles to the north, and I would hike across that and meet my family there. Sara knew the route and so did Miriam, since me and her sometimes drove out there for some fun. Hell, I knew the train's schedules, pretty much, so I didn't have to worry from being in the middle of trestle when that engine hollered and splashing into the river. I got to the trestle after a couple of hours after leaving the house, my timing perfect, like dawn and dusk and the roosters crowing back home. I saw the train chugging across the bridge and got out of the brush as it got its ass out of Texas. I got on the tracks and went across the iron path to meet the jalopy waiting at the other side.

Sara climbed out the driver's seat, and I got in and took paths I didn't know. Finally, I hit a main road somewhere near Mansfield and soon got to Shreveport, then went to Pa's by the road I knew by heart. I was always careful when going to Pa's since I saw Early at the club. Lately, Early Green sightings were as common as gator sightings in the bayou. We needed to be careful.

Pa opened the door, this time walking with a cane, and his beard longer and hair thinner. I hoped I didn't look like him when I got old. I still had all of my frizzy, curly hair and kept my beard trimmed. Well Tommy took off like a white tail to his grandpappy, and Pa gave him one of his hugs. That man loved his grandson, too. He's probably teaching my boy the family business. Something he didn't teach me. I learned it by osmosis.

The old coon dog was nowhere around, and Sara, Miriam, and I walked up to the car. Grandpa Cecil gave Sara a big hug and commented on her height, which surpassed Lydia's and definitely

Miriam's. "Watcha need, Bo? You never come running anymore unless it's important."

"Two things. I need you to watch Tommy for a few days and also it's about Lydia."

"What about Lydia?"

"She's alive. She's over in Texas at the farm in Huntsville. Got framed for murder. Me and the ladies are going to get her out. Miriam says she met her there in the prison band they have. That's why I want you to watch Tommy, and I need your help."

"Both your kids are too young, son."

We walked outside by ourselves, "Sara needs to come with. She's my common sense. Without her I'd do something stupid. I ain't as smart as you are, Pa."

"I see where Sara might work in your plan, whatever that is. We will go ahead and discuss it tonight."

Miriam joined us on the dock. "Bobo, before we get her, you might want to make sure she wants to escape. She seemed happy there. I think you guys need to make a run to Huntsville and check her out. I can't go in, but I can show you where the best place to grab her is."

"Good idea," my Pa said. "We can go visit and get comfortable with the area. Know where to hide, where to tunnel if we need to. We'll check out the back roads and freight schedules. You can't just go get her."

"Yeah and Bobo, she was happy there. She was the Queen, getting everything, she wanted. She told me she missed her family but hated being on the run all the time."

"Well, she got two kids and me. We need our family back, but you are right. We need to plan this and go inside first to see how we can get her out."

"That's right, son. We can take one car and hop a freight back to your place. I think the train goes right by your place. It will be best to strike quick after getting a lay of the land down there. Miriam, do you feel safe down there?"

"Yeah, plus I'm little and can hide about anywhere. Don't ever want to go inside that place again."

"I don't blame ya. Prison ain't no place for a pretty lil' gal like yourself."

"I'll do what it takes to help her get out for her protection, too. Some of the other ladies wanted to kill her, cos she was da Queen, and they wants to be Queen Bee in there."

"We could drive down tomorrow morning and take one car. Pa, you and Tommy can drive back after we meet her, and once we nab her, we can hop the freight back."

Miriam smiled at me, I trusted her, and so did the rest of the clan. This should be simple. Grab her off the east end of the farm and make a run for home.

Angeline made us a good dinner that night, crawfish creole and cornbread. The kids took in some night fishing off of Pa's dock, like they did when they were little. Sara caught her some catfish and a snapping turtle. I was proud of the way she removed them from the hook and threw them in buckets. Tommy caught a few keeper panfish and took them off the hook himself and tossed them in his bucket.

That night, Black Bayou was in motion as the devil called a lot of folks home. Strange noises yelped all night long. Noises I ain't never heard before, and I couldn't explain. Miriam sat wide awake, afraid to be held. She was damn near shaking in my bed as I laid motionless, staring at her.

Next morning after grits and coffee, we piled in my car and headed southwest to Huntsville. It took us about five hours to get down there. Tomas was real excited about seeing his mother. Sara was excited too, but she sat in the car quiet, while Tommy chatted it up left and right, singing, "We're gonna see Mami, We're going to see Mami." He got annoying. I looked at all the others and they had the same reaction. I guess I can't blame anyone of them.

It was around lunch time when we got there so we found a little diner. Miriam now hid in the trunk of the car. She didn't want to be discovered, and for that, I can't blame her. I didn't want to see her body hanging from a tree.

I looked at everything. Escaping didn't look like a possibility, but I saw the bus coming up, hauling the women back from the cotton fields. I also noticed a forest to the west. Before Miriam hid in the trunk, this is where she said they took off. She also told me that a freight train went straight from Huntsville to Louisiana and crossed at the same trestle I did the day before.

After that, she crawled into the trunk through the back seat, and we hit the diner for some burgers. I always hated Texas, but damn those burgers were always the best. I grabbed an extra one for Miriam, and we returned to the car and checked in at the prison. I asked to speak with Lydia Barnum, but they said no one was there by that name. "Lydia Fuentes?"

"Who wants to see her?"

I sighed. "Bo, Sara, Tomas, and Cecil."

The guard looked us over and left for a few minutes. Back and forth we paced. Surprised we didn't crash into each other like they do in race cars. Yeah, we were nervous but soon the guard returned and took me to a back room. There she was in a plain old baggy white, unflattering dress that left everything to the imagination. I looked at her and tears cascaded down the side of my face, and I could see the redness in her eyes and the water droplets on the side of her face.

"Bo, I want to hold you and kiss you so bad," she said as I got closer.

"Lydia, darling, I thought they killed you. All the police said that. They even showed me body parts. I tried to rescue you, but met with swords, guns, and knives.

"I'm glad you didn't. They would have killed you and probably kidnapped the babies, too. Bo, you did the right thing."

"Mami, I've always felt guilty about it." I looked around. I didn't have a long visit with her. I didn't see anyone around. I lowered my voice as I asked her, "Is there anyone around?"

"No."

"We're going to set you free, tonight or in the morning, when you are on the farm."

Her lips parted and raised a bit, as a brief smile formed. Her large brown eyes brightened, and I knew she was excited. Then she looked around nervously. Her eyes shut for a moment. They opened back up, but not as bright before. The little smile she had on her face dissipated once she exhaled. She looked at her small feet, then stared straight at me.

"I can't. I'm somebody here...."

I interrupted her. "You're somebody on the outside. You're a mother to Sara and Tommy."

She cut me off, like she had a machete. "Bo, you don't understand. I'm no longer on the run here. I'm not afraid for my life. I'm the star. I'm on the radio and have freedom. There is no freedom for me on the outside. I don't want to look over my shoulder anymore. I have it good here. Baby, I don't even feel like a prisoner. I get to sing and perform, which is what I always wanted to do. I can't go away."

"You have to come. We have dreams. We have children."

She sobbed now. "Bo, in here is the most freedom I've ever had, even when we were married, and that has nothing to do with you. It's always been that way."

"I'll be right back." I motioned for the guard to bring Sara in. Soon, Sara strolled in to meeting area, and I watched Lydia look at her. I looked back at Sara as she stared at her mother. Both were in tears.

Lydia gathered her composure. "Oh my God, you're taller than me, baby. I want to hug you so bad. How's Papi treating you?"

"Papi is the greatest. Mami, I want to be a lawyer and a singer. I want to play and sing for you someday."

"I'll be here for thirty years."

"Papi and I wrote a song for you, and we want to play it for you soon."

"I want to hear it, really, but I'm stuck in prison, baby."

"Mami, we want to help you." She whispered. "Papi has a plan."

"Sara, baby, Mami can't go. It's good here."

I looked at Sara and nodded. She went and got our secret weapon and returned in a minute. Lydia took one look at Tomas and cried like a hurricane. I smiled and knew we had her.

"Bo," she whispered. "I'll be at the end of the cotton fields, about 200 yards from the railroad track tomorrow or the next day. There's a tunnel under the wire fence. You should camp in the woods the next two nights."

"There's an eastbound train that goes by at 1 pm."

"I know, Bo. Every time I see that train go by; I think of you."

"We live in Louisiana, the other side of the river."

Her eyes lit up. "I could have ran several times? They don't even shackle me, I come back and pick cotton, and I don't have to pick much."

I leaned further to her, so no one heard us talking, not even the kids. "Have someone create a diversion, a little fight or something, and crawl under the fence and run like hell. Sara and I will be waiting for you. Tommy came with Grandpa, and they're going back to his place tonight. We can pull this off, Mami."

"Bo, I've wanted to leave every chance I had, but I'm too afraid. I don't care about being a Gorree Gal. I want to be Mami again."

"We'll get you back safe."

"Bo, it will either be tomorrow or the next day. I'm not sure when I will be there."

"We will be waiting."

"I know." I leaned over and kissed the glass that separated our lips. Sara and Tommy did the same since our visitation ended. We walked out confidently, knowing the job was well done. Now round two of the job had to be perfect. Most of that was up to Lydia.

We bought some supplies, and Sara, Miriam, and I camped out in the woods adjacent to the railroad tracks. We built a little fire, not big enough to be seen by the prison guards, but large enough to keep critters away. Miriam fell asleep on my lap. I wondered if she knew that if this escape succeeded, she would be relegated to houseguest and maid, and no longer a lover.

Sara and I chatted most of the night. "Papi, why haven't you recorded any of your songs. You're a lot better than a lot of those folks you hear on the radio."

"Well, baby girl. My music comes from my heart. I like to share it with folks when I perform them. If I record it and people listens to it out on the radio, it ain't coming from my heart. It's coming from an electronic box or from recording I made in a studio. They ain't hearing the real me."

"I did record some stuff you and Miriam did before she left us. I really like listening to you guys play. You sound so good together. I think your music is better than yours and Mami's."

"You think so? Actually, I do, too. Mami and I mainly played the old folk songs. I think she does a better job than Miriam on them, but when we get a little rowdy, Miriam can really get at it."

"Yeah, I like that style best."

"Sara, baby. I'm not the kind of person who likes to write stuff down, but I've kept a journal of my life. I have about ten of them in a storage box. Not even your mother or Miriam knows about them."

"I found them."

"What!" I smiled.

"Yeah, they are in the bottom drawer in your room. I was folding clothes and putting them away. I didn't read any."

"Well, I want you to keep them. You and Tommy are my legacy, you know what I leave behind."

"You're not leaving nothing behind. You're not going anywhere."

"Baby, you never know. People are trying to kill your mother, and they're trying to kill me too. You know that."

"I know."

"One day, they might get me. I ain't that bright you know."

"You're the smartest guy I know. Smarter than all my teachers, plus you care about people. You are the best." She kissed my cheek, rolled over, and curled up and went to sleep.

I stayed up and kept guard most of the night. I snuck out, and headed to the railroad tracks, to see if anyone could see us. I dashed through the woods, like a kit fox, out to the clearing by the tracks. One time I almost burrowed back under and behind a tree as searchlights brightened the area. I snuck up all the way to the fence of the state prison. I found the tunnel that ran under the fence. I knew this was the place Lydia would come out. I snuck back to camp and found our camp as graceful as I left it.

Both Miriam and Sara were asleep, and I shut my eyes for a while. We awoke to sunlight flashing through the forest, and still undiscovered. Miriam made a small breakfast over the campfire, and when we finished, we put out the fire and snuck up near the railroad tracks and waited. A long freight train passed us by while we sat on the forest edge. I timed the speed, knowing we could easily jump on. There was another one coming in two hours. If she was escaping today, it would be soon. We looked down the line for the caboose but still could not see it.

The train kept chugging and chugging along, and I smiled at Sara and Miriam, and they both smiled back, wishing I had a harmonica.

Finally, the train passed, and we saw a woman struggle to get through the fence. Sara and I ran across the track and up to the gate to pull her through. Her clothes stuck on the wire, so I ripped her dress, and she pulled her through with the assistance of Sara's strong hand. She ran like the devil chased her, and maybe he was, as we took shelter in the forest. The next train was in two hours, and we worked diligently at finishing a little pit to hide the women in. Miriam, bless her soul, started digging already and started the cavern. Soon both of them were covered and Sara and I watched carefully. I watched the farm and Sara looked for some steel wheels we could hitch a ride on.

It was quiet on my end, so I retreated to get the ladies. We approached the edge of the forest and steam appeared in the sky. It looked like fog at first as gray smoke penetrated the sky, so I went out to the rail and laid my head on it as if on a feathered pillow. I felt the vibration and I looked down the track to see the sky get blacker. Soon the sounds of the engine were legible, and I could see it. All three of them joined me along the tracks as the train was clearly visible.

Lydia changed clothes into a sleeveless sundress that was way too small for her. Miriam must have given it to her, and she burned the prison garb in the campfire. That freight steamed as it passed us. We ran east, timing up the box we wanted, and I got Miriam on, then Sara, and finally Lydia. I was last and all of my ladies helped me in. Miriam held my right hand tight while Lydia had my left in her grips. My wife struggled to get me up and lost her handle on me. I slipped a bit and dangled down by the side of the train as Miriam and Sara struggled to pull me up. The train pick up speed as I hung on with one arm while, waiting to get a grip on something. I felt a fifth hand on my right arm, and soon I yanked into the boxcar. Slowly they pulled me up, and I nestled into the car and reunited with my wife. The star of the Goree Girls String Band escaped jail and was on her way to freedom.

It was great to be with her. It was about six years since we had been together, and I wasn't sure if we were strangers or partners. We had to get reacquainted. Also, it was an unusual feeling looking across at my wife, whom I thought was dead, sitting next to my lover, in her undersized dress. Sara was with them also, and it was a beautiful sight. The only sounds we heard were that lonesome whistle and the rattling of the box cars. There was an awful silence in the car.

Before we crossed the Sabine, I jumped out first, and attempted to catch the ladies, or at least break their fall as they took the plunge at fifteen miles per hour and tumbled down the hill leading into the bayou. No one got hurt, and we wandered down to the river to get into the skiff that will take us to my place. The ladies helped me cover up the boat, and we walked up the hill and through the swamps, dodging beavers, muskrats, and gators as we brought Lydia to freedom.

Again, silence, words were not spoken as Sara and I led her mother and Miriam home. We snuck her in the back door of the house, in case folks searched for us. Not sure if anyone knew the escaped prisoner was my ex-wife or not, most folks around here didn't care. She looked at me, with her beautiful piercing eyes, "This is our house? I like it, Papi."

"Yeah, and there's more. I don't want you outside that much right now, but I'd love to show you around the place. We got a lot of everything here. It's kind of like Pa's, but we ain't directly on the water. I got another building up yonder where we put on some shows and such. I'll show it to you tomorrow. Right now, I think we'll get some rest, and I'll let Pa know we made it home."

Miriam went into the kitchen and started cooking. I guess she realized her place already. She was our maid again and soon whipped us up some fried chicken with beans and rice and cornbread. "Bo, who is this girl, and how well do you know her?

"She stays here. I found her south of Shreveport after you disappeared. She worked as a maid, but the owner was using her. Saw her on the highway and hired her as a maid and to watch the kids."

"Is that all?"

I didn't want to lie to her, "Mami, we all thought you were dead, so yes after a while, we became closer, then she ran off."

"I don't want her here. Not sure if I trust her."

"She got you back to your family, didn't she? I trust her, and Sara trusts her. Hell, I trust Sara. She's intelligent and has common sense. Things I don't have."

"Bo, you have intelligence, but I think you are too trusting at times. That's usually a good thing, but not when you get mixed up with a lot of crooked people."

"Honey, I ain't mixed up with no one. This is our place and our land. We do some farming, host some shows, and record some folks. I run my own business. That other place is for shows, partying, and recording. We've been making some records. I know you just got out, but I think the four of us can put something on record to see what it sounds like."

"I don't want to sing with her anymore. We sang in prison. Bo," her tone quieted way down, to a whisper as she moved close to me and whispered in my ear, "she tried to replace me in everything. She tried to be the queen of the prison. I feel she's trying to replace me here."

"She ain't gonna replace you. You're my wife. Ain't nobody takes your place as long as you're alive Mami."

"She's shaking her bottom at you all the time. I've noticed."

"She can shake it, but she ain't getting me, cause I got you."

"Bo". She was silent for a few minutes. I didn't like that. "We've been apart for a few years. Do you think I'm going to give you your loving? We need to get to know each other again."

"Exactly, we need to do the things we loved to do. One of them was to sing. We have three singers and three people who play guitar or banjo. We should put something down on a record."

"Bo, you don't know what it means to be the Prison Queen, do you? It means that I haven't been faithful to you either. I have to go back, but I need to spend time with Tommy and Sara."

"Well, Pa should be down with Tomas tonight. I told him to meet us here. Baby, I need you to stay with us. Tu eres mi esposa." She always loved it when I spoke Spanish to her.

She cried. Damn waterfall flowed from her eyes. I tried to put my arm around her, but she pushed me way. She retreated to the corner next to the pot belly stove. Then she screamed at me through her tears. "Bo, we are not married anymore! I signed divorce papers and remarried."

"What?"

"I had to," she continued, as she sobbed. "I married the warden to spare my life. When my sentence is over, I will stay with him. Judge Bourgeois signed my divorce papers. You are not my husband anymore."

"Mami, you were forced to do it."

"Bo, you got me into this, you and Early Greene. Judge Bourgeois said that Barnum's ain't no good anyway, and I shouldn't be married to him."

Once she said Bourgeois, I knew something was up, but this was my wife and mother of my children. Something said to let her go back to her so-called freedom in Huntsville, but I still took my vows serious. I wanted to make the best of everything and fulfill our dreams when we slept in that cold boxcar in Omaha. However, my thoughts stayed with me.

Suddenly, we heard a car pull up. Sure, hoped it was Pa. My dogs howled and yapped as Sara ran to the door. Lydia hid, in case it weren't Grandpa and his grandson, Tomas Robert Barnum. There was rapping on the front door. Then silence for a few seconds, and the door kicked open. A gasp came from the closet where Lydia took shelter.

"Woo hoo, is she here? We got the grub, now let's party down. Angeline made tamales, so let's eat. Woot woot woot. Grandpa was fired up, dancing a jig even. "Where's my daughter-in-law?"

Lydia came out somber and almost lifeless. Tommy walked up to her, and I thought he would change her look and attitude. It did a little bit, but the woman still emotionless. She gave him a big hug and kissed, and held him for an eternity, and they sat at the table still quiet.

"What's wrong Mommy? You don't seem happy to see me." Tommy said.

"It's grown up stuff, Tommy. I'm confused right now. I wish I knew how to act."

"Mami, you should be happy to with me, Daddy, and Sara. It's been a long time. I really missed you."

"Baby, I miss you too, but I'm so confused right now."

"You're home. I'm always happy when I'm here."

"I've never been here before. This doesn't feel like home yet. Now, that I see you, it does feel more like home."

The rest of the clan came into the dining area, Angeline brought the tamales and Miriam brought us the jambalaya. Most of us threw the food down like no tomorrow; however, Lydia, in her dazed state, nibbled on a tamale but refused Miriam's jambalaya. She did have some of her cornbread.

Most of us feasted it up pretty good, and Pa suggested we go to the other building and play some songs. I hoped some good old folk songs would bring a smile and life to her body and soul, and Sara did, too. Tommy already ran upstairs to grab his bongos and soon came down with them, playing them in rhythm.

"I'll watch," and she strolled toward the door, her eyes searching around like they were spotlights at Huntsville searching for escaped prisoners. I figured she sought for her own escape route from here.

We walked into the tavern and grabbed our playing guitars, and one by one, Sara, Miriam, and I tuned up while Tommy sat in back with his drums. Sara sang a tune I taint never heard before. It was a little bluesy, a little folky, something only she or I could write. Miriam and I picked it up pretty good as I played slide and Miriam did solos on her guitar.

Mama, you've been gone so long,

Mama, you've been gone so long,

But you ain't done nothing wrong.

Mama, I'm glad you're home,

Mama, I'm glad you're home,

I hate seeing Papi all alone.

Sara screamed the blues, like her old man and the creatures that live in this bayou.

Mama, never leave us again,

Mama, never leave us again,

Papa wants you through the end.

Miriam and I exchanged solos and tore it up. I loved playing with my two girls but not as much as I loved performing with the lovely spectator back when we lived in Nebraska. We played a couple rowdy songs, and Lydia still acting the same. Pa and Angeline hooted it up, trying to liven up the party, but Lydia looked as if she was one of the fake models you see in the department stores. Sara looked at me, and we played Lydia's favorites, *"El Sol Que Tu Eres"* and *"Por un Amor."* Miriam stood on stage, but since she didn't know these songs, she stood and smiled. We looked at Lydia, and she cried.

Without notice, she took off running for the door screaming, "I can't, I can't stay here. I need to go back."

Sara, Tommy and I chased her. She got in my car and headed north toward the railroad tracks. She didn't know the land, so I'm not sure where she was going. The kids and I cut through the cypress trees and swamp land and went straight toward the tracks. About a mile up, we saw the car, crashed into a cypress tree. No one was in it. I saw Lydia in the distance running, and I sprinted faster leaving the kids behind me. I witnessed steam coming in the eastern evening sky. That train came quickly. Lydia stood next to the track as the locomotive slowed down to hit the bridge. I was close behind, calling her to no avail. She hopped the freight, like I taught her, and chased after her. I struggled to get on and eventually climbed into the car.

Part III

Chapter 19

Sara Barnum

The train chugged along, oblivious to the body that fell from the boxcar. My brother and I watched it tumble down and splash in the Sabine. We stared at each other our mouths were stuck wide open like we were saying the letter O. "That body was either Mom or Dad," I thought, as I'm sure Tommy did too. I was in charge, so I led my little brother down the small hill toward the river. We couldn't see too much, but I still wanted to get out and swim.

"No, Sara, we need to get the sheriff."

It was too late as I went swimming in the evil river that Daddy dreaded so much. I got about 100 yards out when I realized I didn't have a chance of finding the body. The water, as always, was a gloomy green, plus the sun was setting. I turned around, determined to make it back to shore. Tommy stood on the shore crying, as I struggled across the murk. The splash of my arms is all I could hear. The train vanished into Texas and was on its way toward Huntsville. I made it to shore and my clothes and body smelled like a combination of catfish, copperheads, snapping turtles, and alligators. I fumed that I couldn't find anything.

"Sara, we don't know if that was Mami or Papi that came out."

"Tomas, I know. I know who came out."

My brother wiped his eyes. "I know, too."

We sprinted to where Mami crashed the car. It wasn't wrecked that bad, and I got it started. Daddy gave me driving lessons, so I knew what to do even though it was on desolate roads and I never drove in the swamp before. We got down to Zwolle and went to the sheriff's office. I woke up the sleeping deputy who sat kicked back in his chair, legs sprawled and feet on his desk, snoring away.

"Wake up, Mr. Bourgeois. I think Daddy got thrown in the river. We have to search it, now! We got a boat. C'mon, Mr. Bourgeois. It was up by LeDoux's trestle. C'mon!"

Tommy kicked the deputy and threw some water on the man who woke up disoriented and grabbed his revolver. Now we were known by most people as good kids. It was our luck it was Mr. Bourgeois, who was always on Papi's side when it came to his business. Papi probably gave him some good stuff and maybe a woman, since the deputy was unmarried. The deputy never busted Daddy when we knew he could have.

"Your Pa got thrown off the train? Now what de hell was your ol' man doing on a train?"

"Can't tell you that." Tommy said. "We ain't even sure it was him. We both saw somebody fall from the freight."

"It was the same car he got in," I cut in. "Papi had to sneak into Texas, and he don't like to be followed there you know."

"Yeah, I know about that. That's one reason why I liked your pa. He was always good for keeping the riff raff out west. Always liked it when he sat by the river with his shotgun. Now, follow me, we heading up there."

We got in the deputy's car and we pointed to where it was. It was totally dark now, but both Deputy Bourgeois and I were what locals call swamp rats, and we headed down the riverbank with my little brother close behind.

Tommy wasn't the swamp rat I was. He only liked to get a little muddy and wet, so he followed carefully as the deputy shone his flashlight along the shoreline. We followed the shore till we got to the edge of our property, and as Deputy Bourgeois flashed his light toward Cletus Tree, we noticed something floating in the water. It looked to be about a football field away from us as I took off sprinting. I knew this shoreline better than Pa, since I often ran out at night and paddled the skiff up to the trestle and back looking for enemies of Pa's. The deputy ran with me, and Tommy got there right behind us. I climbed into the skiff as the deputy handed me a long pole and he climbed in. We paddled down the Sabine quickly chasing the floating body. I still couldn't make it out, but I already knew. I wondered if I could save him. Finally, we reached it, and I gave the long pole back to officer, and he pulled the body next to the boat and lifted him inside the skiff.

In torn overalls his body lay inside the skiff, soaking wet. An arm was missing, not sure it was bitten off by a swamp creature or cut off by an enemy. Worse was the slash across the neck, as his head rocked back and forth, as if he was sleeping. Tears filled my eyes, and if I leaned over the boat, the Sabine fill with salt-water. I couldn't control myself as Deputy Bourgeois paddled his way back to Cletus Tree. He took the body out and set in on the dry land. "Anyone home?"

"Yeah, Grandpa, Gramma, and Miri were there when we left."

The deputy lowered his head. "Damn shame. You guys and your gramps, havin' to see your daddy this way. Come here baby girl, and c'mon, Tommy."

We needed to head up to the house. I wanted to hold my little brother, but I needed held. Tommy stood speechless and not in tears while I tried to being brave, but I created a deluge with my head bowed down low, like I was praying. I felt sorry for the deputy. He carried Daddy's dead body and comfort the two of us at the same time. We took the slow walk to the house where it was quiet.

The lawman knocked on the backdoor, and Miriam answered. "Is Cecil there?"

Miriam looked at me and my brother first, and then at the human carcass that was our father and her lover, and back at Deputy Bourgeois. "Come in, suh," is all she said, and soon sobbed buckets onto the back porch.

Grandpa Cecil made his way to the back and noticed all of us, heads down, and in tears. He saw the drenched torso, and his eyes met mine. He stared head at the dirt floor in the kitchen and muttered something unintelligible. I wasn't sure if he prayed or cursed, since I felt the same way. I focused on him for some reason. Parents ain't supposed to bury their kids, like teenagers aren't supposed to bury their parents. We locked gaze our faces tilted toward the ground.

Grandpa walked out kicking the floor, and he knelt by the body. He put Papi's head in his hand and mumbled. He looked at no one in particular and screamed to the sky. "He was the only one who came out right. He's the only boy who came out right. Why, Lord?"

The wind picked up and the noises from the bayou became deafening. In came the murky, swamp sounds that Daddy loved so much, and the evil spirits that infatuated me. They must have called Daddy home.

Except for Grandpa's scream, no one spoke. We stood in silence, staring at my father. Grandpa held Tommy and me while Miriam sagged in Angeline's arms. Deputy Bourgeois watched us look at Papi.

"We'll take him to the morgue," the deputy said, "and an autopsy to see what happened."

"Do you know what happened?" Grandpa asked us.

"I do, Grandpa. He climbed on the freight to get Mami, and he got thrown off the train over the river."

"Your Mami?" Deputy Bourgeois asked.

"We can't talk about it now," Grandpa snapped.

"No, she'll know what happened," the deputy replied.

"Mr. Bourgeois." Grandpa looked at me, knowing I had something to say, but it was probably best not said.

The deputy has seen that look from this family many times. So, he put his arm on my shoulder and led me out of the kitchen.

"Whatever you say will be confidential."

"Mami escaped from Huntsville, and she was escaping back. Daddy tried to stop her. We can't question her about it, otherwise she might get more time for escaping prison." I looked at Miriam and she hid behind the wall. I saw her dark skin and her dark eyes disappear around the corner.

"More than likely she witnessed it. We'll need to talk to her. Your daddy got murdered. From what I heard, he a lot more enemies than friends. Lots of people wanted him dead."

"I know, sir, I want those murderers found."

"We'll find the killer or killers. Right now, I'm taking your father to the morgue, and you can start making arrangements."

The deputy took Daddy to Zwolle in a bag, while we watched, afraid to look at each other, afraid to speak, or stop crying. We sat all night in the parlor. No one slept a wink. Cecil sat in the rocking chair while Angeline sprawled out in a big comfy chair next to him. Miriam and I took over the davenport. Tommy sat close beside me, and his head nestled on my shoulder.

"What are we going to do?" he asked quietly.

"I don't know. I justice. Whoever killed Daddy will pay, and I'll make sure they do."

"Me too. I want to be a police officer and arrest them."

"And I still want to be a lawyer, making sure they never see daylight again. Tomas, the best thing we can do is finish our education and go to college."

"I'll take care of the house. You guys just go to school," Miriam added.

"You guys going to stay here or come up to my place? I can get you in the Shreveport schools," Grandpa asked.

Tommy answered first. "We want to stay here."

"Wait, Tommy, I think we should go to Grandpa's. People know we live here, and it might not be safe. I think its best we move out after we bury Pa."

"Sara, I agree," Grandpa said. "I got plenty of room for all of your junk."

The next morning Miriam made breakfast and she looked at Grandpa. Guess she reckoned she's going to be sent packing after the funeral. She looked at him all sad.

"Miriam, you are part of the family, too. You ain't going nowhere but with us. Let's have a small funeral in the next day or two. Get your instruments and clothes and let's torch the place. It would be fitting."

"Where are we going to bury him?"

"Got to be near Cletus tree." I told my brother.

The next couple of days we planned the funeral. We didn't want a lot of folks around, but Daddy always said he wanted a party with lots of music. I found all of his songs he put down as well as his journal. Miriam was able to round up some musicians, and Angeline and Miri did a bunch of cooking.

About 40 or 50 people showed up, mainly town folks and a few strangers. There was the man with the fiddle and a scar across his face, and another man who looked like an older, whiter, uglier, and fatter version of Dad. There was also an older white woman with them, and she looked at us like she wanted to talk, and then vanished with the two men after shaking Tommy's and my hands. They never introduced themselves. None of them acknowledged Grandpa.

We spent most of the day cooking and playing music, Miriam and I led most of the performances, along with Miri's dad who came up to pay his respects. We threw a party near the river and near Daddy's final resting spot. When we got done playing, Grandpa and the preacher both said some words.

"My son, Bo, was a great man. Here is a man that fought the injustices of the world, not only with words on a page or notes on his guitar, but by his actions. He did not see color, but people." He called Tommy and I up and put his arms around us. "These two children are all the proof you need. I believe these children are destined for greatness. These children will change the world, and if they do, there lays a successful man in that casket. Bo loved his music, I know he thought he could change the world with his guitar, I know he thought he could change the world with his banjer, and he did. If he got some Mexicans talking to whites, or whites talking to Mexicans, or if he got blacks and whites talking, then he changed the world. I'm a living witness to my son, Bo, changing the world for the better."

The preacher was next, and Daddy wasn't a religious man, even though we were trying to go to church there near the end. "From everything I heard about Bo Barnum, he wasn't always a righteous man. All of us in Zwolle knew what he was about, but we still honored the man because we knew what was in his heart. What was in his heart was pure joy, and he worked for the common folk. He worked for the black man, the Hispanic, the poor, and for his children. All this man wanted was to have everyone get a fair chance in life, and for that alone, he is punching his ticket to heaven right now. I don't know if Bo had a favorite Bible verse or not, but let us bow our heads, while I read *Psalms 116:15 "Precious in the sight of the Lord is the death of his saints."*

More prayers, and tears, and soon the townsfolks laid the casket in the site by Cletus Tree. They threw the dirt over the box, and soon daddy was gone. I still remembered the first time we took a train trip together. We sat nestled in each other's arms, and my daddy taught me harmonica, but deep inside he was teaching me the rhythms of life.

After the funeral, the guests took off for their peaceful homes, while I looked around the lonesome, desolate house. I wanted my daddy back already, and knew he wasn't coming home, but I needed to know what happened. I packed a bag, took off for the train tracks and waited for the westbound freight. I hopped on, intending to ask Mami what happened. I knew she was a witness or possibly she threw Daddy off the train. I had to know.

I waited until I saw the smoke rising through the bayou and heard the rhythm of the train chugging. It was going about ten miles per hour, so it was an easy hop. Once inside, I sat by myself amidst the drifters who occupied the same car as me. I took out the harmonica that Daddy gave me and played the chugging train as it picked up speed.

I knew how long the trip would last from the previous time we made the trip, so I sat alone and timed it out with my little reeded toy. The train made its stop in Huntsville, and I ran off quickly since I didn't want to join my mother in hell. I found the prison and went in past the guards.

"I need to speak to my mama."

"What's her name?"

"Lydia Fuentes, or Lydia Barnum."

"We have no one here by that name."

"She was just here Friday. She's part of the band."

"Sorry we have no one by that name, never have."

"I want to see mi mami!" I screamed at the fat guard. "She was here."

"I'm sorry little girl, she's not here. Now run along." The asshole guard patted my butt as he shooed me out the door.

I turned and glared at him. "Never, ever do that again," I shouted and hitchhiked my way back to the track that goes by the back end of the prison farm. I sat in the forest, wondering if Mami would come out. I waited for two days, and a woman prisoner came out by herself unshackled and looking into the forest. I climbed out from my hiding place and walked toward the fence. The women looked like me and walked like me as she made her way to the enclosure. I quickened my pace and ran across the railroad track, toward the fence.

"I knew you would search for me, Sara, however this is where I belong."

"Mami, I'm not trying to get you back. I want to know what happened with Daddy. "

"I don't know. Two men tied me up." Then she stared right at me. "I saw it all, baby. I think it was your Uncle Zeke, another man, and Early Greene. He tried to get me off the train, and he was attacked by a guy in a white sheet. Your dad grabbed his knife and stabbed him, and then your Uncle grabbed your father, and Early whipped his machete out and cut his throat. Your uncle pushed him out of the car. I was screaming the entire time. Early looks at me, 'And you are next, Senora Barnum. I'm not sure when.' They hopped off the freight a short time later, after pushing the third man out of the car. Sara, you have to go. Protect yourself and Tommy. I'm sure they're after you."

"Well, they will be. I will bring Daddy's killers to justice if it takes all of my life."

"Be careful, honey, I have to go now. Come visit me."

"I will, Mami."

She took off, and I hid in the forest waiting for the Kansas City Southern freight train to carry me home.

Chapter 20

I got back late that night. Miriam, Grandpa Cecil and Angeline waited for me.

"Where did you skedaddle off to, young lady?" Grandpa asked.

"I went to see, Mami. She knows who did it."

"What?"

Mami said there were three guys in the train. One was Early Greene you guys were talking about. There was my Uncle Zeke, who I don't know, and she didn't know the other guy. She said Daddy stabbed the other guy.

"What? Zeke? I knew he was with the Klan, but that's all I know about him. Haven't heard from him in years. Your mom said it was him?"

"Yeah, she said my Uncle Zeke was there. Mami also said Zeke shouted out you killed my older brother."

"That's why he was at the funeral. He knew your pa died, and he brought their mother."

"I didn't know I had an uncle. Daddy never talked about the rest of his family."

"With good reason, kiddo. Now finding Early Greene is going to be tough. Son of a bitch is shifty and will disappear without a trace only to show up when needed."

"Wasn't he Daddy's friend?"

"Yeah. He was with him the night our Texarkana place got burned down. I think he works for the government, a paid assassin. Not sure why Zeke is running with this clown, unless the Klan is up to something."

"We need to get out of here. Does Zeke know where you are living now, Grandpa?"

"I don't think so. I ain't sure he's ever been there except when he was running the shine. We need to gather our stuff and get back there tonight."

"Okay, Grandpa. I want to go through Daddy's stuff, too."

I sat in Daddy's room going through his belongings. In his wardrobe, behind his overalls, I found about seven recordings he did, and in his dresser, I found his journals. I continued to look for more, but didn't find nothing, so I gathered up the goods and stuffed them in my bag. Then I went up and cleaned out my stuff, which consisted of four pairs of overalls, two ripped sundresses, and one nice dress Pa made me wear on Sundays, even though I always threw a hissy fit.

I got Tommy to get his stuff, and we packed Grandpa's car, and made a run to his place. Then we came back and grabbed the rest of our possessions. Whatever didn't fit in the automobile was soon going to be ashes. Grandpa lit his corncob pipe and tossed the match in the brewing alcohol, and the night sky lit up like the Fourth of July. Sabine Parish was a memory as we headed up toward the Black Bayou.

Grandpa drove as I looked out the back window, and I didn't see no one following us. It took us a couple of hours to get back to Grandpa's place. Even though I didn't want to leave our place in Zwolle, this swamp gal knew it was for the best. I knew if folks wanted Mami and Papi killed, they also wanted me and Tommy dead. Wasn't sure where to run to, but Grandpa Barnum's place was hidden back in the woods, right on the bayou. You had to know where it was to locate it. Heck, once I started driving, I stumbled across it the first few times coming back from Shreveport Central High.

Chapter 21

Ten years have passed, and my little train trips to Huntsville became less frequent with time. I was now a civil rights lawyer living in Baton Rouge, and Tommy was an FBI agent in New Orleans. We had both been busy in our careers and haven't spent as much time together as we would have liked. I hadn't visited Grandpa for a while either. I was too wrapped up in changing the world and fighting injustices. But I decided to visit my mami. I hopped the freight as I used to and met her the following morning after camping out.

"What I can tell you, will help find your father's killer and my parent's murderers, too. Tommy knows."

"Mami, I want to know about your parents, mi abuelo y mi abuela. What role did they play in the revolution? I'm an attorney working for the Civil Rights movement. Is this because of them or Papi? I want to know."

"Both, my darling. I can't talk now. Tommy knows all."

"Tommy knows? Where is he? I hadn't heard from in years. Last I knew he was in Narleans, but I hadn't seen hide nor hare from him."

"Yes, Tomas knows all. I didn't want to tell you because I don't want to get you involved. I want you to live the full life that God planned for you."

I looked at her, my chin on my right hand. I stared at her lost eyes. "I would rather die young and help change the world." She still gazed into space, as my left hand also became a chin rest. I didn't think she heard me. "Mami, I would rather die young than live the life you are living. Just look at yourself. You have no idea what you are even looking at. That ain't living for me."

She got up and walked away, and I never saw her again. She turned her head, gave me a smirk, and bowed her head like she was crying or praying.

I left with a combination of disappointment and excitement. I didn't find out what I came for, and that was to know more about my grandparents, but now I had to find Tommy. I knew he worked undercover for the FBI, but I guess I had to go out and look for him. I hoped he was investigating the Klan; or trying to jerk a knot in ol' Early Greene's head.

I had my Woodie wagon all packed up, and ready to skedaddle down the road, in search of my little Federal Agent brother. I wondered what Grandpa Cecil or Pa thought about little Tomas being a Fed. I had just backed out of my driveway, when a black Caddy pulled out with two well-dressed black men.

"Ms. Barnum, where you headed?"

"I'm not sure. I'm heading out looking for my brother."

"I know you are heading to Topeka. We are on our way to integrate the schools there. Some folks challenged the separate but equal law and thinks that schools should not be segregated. You need to be in Topeka by tomorrow evening for a dinner meeting. Good thing you're all packed."

I got out of Baton Rouge quicker than a frog snaps a fly and headed up north to Topeka, but something told me I wouldn't end up there by tomorrow night. Not sure what it was, maybe it was the beastly Louisiana summer, or Daddy's spirit that rose from the bayou. I headed up the highway and soon by the old place, down by Zwolle. I stopped and got some gas, used the white people's toilet and decided to get my grub on.

Cigarette smoke filled the diner like it was on fire, and the establishment smelled like stale cigars, cigarettes, and fried fish and chicken. I got me a fish Po Boy and a coke, and the old white waitress looked me over from head to toe. Then a smile appeared on her face, and she asked. "Ain't you little Sara Barnum? What you doing with yourself?"

"I'm a public defender down in Baton Rouge."

"Funny, I just saw your brother yesterday. He looked finer than frog hair but was also dirtier than a nigger. Not sure what was up with that boy. He had to run off, I reckon. Say Ms. Barnum, you says you're a lawyer. Well, they be talking about damning up the Sabine. Your Pa's old land going to be underwater one day."

"That needs stopped. Say, did Tommy say where he was going?"

"No, but he headed out west, toward your old land I think."

"I need to find him. Haven't heard nothing from him in years. Say, can you wrap up this po boy? I'm going West."

I headed west past the cypress and magnolia trees and found the remains that used to be the old house. I hadn't been there since Grandpa Cecil torched the place, and no one else moved in or squatted on it either. I drove as far as I could until my Buick wagon started getting stuck in the mud. I set off hiking toward the river and more important to Cletus Tree. I knew my brother was there. I don't know how or why, but as a kid that was the place, I always went to find any resolution.

Sure enough, just like a snapper eats a small fish, my little brother, the Fed, was sitting up in Cletus Tree. He hopped down, and we sat on the riverbank and watched the driftwood float by.

"Remember when we used to do this all day?" he asked me.

"Yeah, sweet times, I miss those days, and now this will all be under water. Cletus Tree will no longer be a Barnum family monument. It's going to be a place for bass to get eaten by a fat gator."

"Yep, I miss it here too, and we could fight the dam. They just talking about it. I really miss Caddo and fishing with Grandpa."

"I might stop there on the way to Topeka."

"You ain't going to Kansas right away. We need to go up to Caddo. It's about Grandpa."

My heart stopped a bit. Tears gathered in my eyes and I covered my face with my scrawny fingers. I rubbed my eyes and flicked the salty water toward the river and repeated the act. I hadn't been the best granddaughter the last few years and hadn't written or visited him as much as I wanted. There were times I wished I was more like my little brother, who kept in good contact with Grandpa Cecil and even our mother. I was glad Miriam and I stopped to visit a couple of weeks ago.

"What about Grandpa?"

"Grandpa died."

"How? Was he sick? Can't imagine that ol' coot getting sick."

"Well, he was sick, had cancer throughout his body, but that ain't what killed him." My eyes grew wider, as Tomas piqued my curiosity. My brother took a long deep breath before he gave me a long hug. He squeezed me tight, with his strong arms, and I felt his tears on my bare shoulders. "I witnessed it but didn't catch the men. They was gone like a flash. Sons of bitches disappeared into the fog. I followed them down here, but they stole the skiff and went down the river toward Lake Charles."

"Was it two of them?"

"Yeah, they were looking for the still and the recipe." Tommy reached into his overall pocket and pulled out a piece of paper. Then he smirked, gave a great big smile that the women loved. "Grandpa Cecil gave me the recipe." He laughed, and I smiled back. "Sara, the men wanted to steal it. Grandpa knew he was going to die, and I think he set up a trap for Uncle Zeke and Early Greene. I heard them talking outside by the still while I was in the house watching from the bait shop. Gramps refused to give them the recipe, and I saw Early take out his machete and swing. I jumped out the window and chased them down, but they were quicker than snot. I stopped to check on Gramps, but his head was half off, just like dad's. That little break must be all they needed cause I followed them down here. I saw the skiff floating downstream and no sign of the car either. After we bury him, we need to get those two. I need your help Sara. You are smarter and more devious than me."

"Where's the other boat? The one I always took up the river."

"Damn, I just remembered the skiff. I wonder if someone stole it. It's been what fifteen years? I doubt if the engine even works."

"Well what if they took it up the river and let the skiff go. Those guys could be anywhere. Might be back at Caddo. I ain't got any idea how we gonna find them."

"Me neither, sis, guess we need to start looking for clues or something." Then we glanced at Cletus Tree, and back at each other. "I bet there is an answer in here. Not sure if I can fit, but you're still scrawny."

Tomas knelt while I climbed onto his shoulders, and then I reached up and grabbed the branch and pulled myself up. There were a few branches missing and the ones there were not as sturdy as I remembered from so many years ago. I got to the part where it hollowed out and made my descent, the same way I did as a child and the way Cletus Barnum did a century before us. God knows how many others made this old tree a hideout.

Once inside, I found the wooden steps and I carefully stepped down to where the tree widened. The old wooden seat was replaced with a new one. There were about twelve carvings on the tree that looked like notches on a belt. I moved my flashlight around looking for anything else that might be different. I saw it. It was a blood drop cross, the logo of the Klan. I pointed my light down below toward the tree trunk and there were two machetes on the ground. It looked like a couple of white robes were also tossed there.

I crawled up the steps, knowing damn well I discovered something big. The wooden steps creaked and one broke when I went up. I slithered like a snake through the thin opening, and looked for my brother, but could not find him. I slid down the shaft of the tree, methodically getting to an area where I could jump. There was still no sign of my brother as I reached the last branch. I called for him, but there was no answer. I took the plunge onto the wet grass and looked around. Now the wind picked up, and it sounded like a cross between a freight train and an airplane taking off. I clung onto Cletus Tree like it was my savior as the wind gusted and blew my sundress up over my head. The breeze suddenly simmered down, like someone put on the jake brake to it. I still hadn't seen Tommy, so I ventured north along the banks of the Sabine. I saw his tracks in the mud and followed them like Pawpaw's old coon dog.

I stuck to the path and found him searching another Barnum family landmark, Barnum Cave. It was a small dug out cave not fifty yards from the river. He looked up. When he saw me, he smiled that big smile of his. He could have been a movie actor. He was such a charmer, when he wanted to be. "Sis, come here. Look what I found in the cave."

I ran up to him, and he held a cut off horse tail and a branch with a lot of saw dust on the ground. "This was all freshly cut."

"What's this for?"

"A fiddle bow maybe? They're made from horsehair and wood. These magnolia trees work pretty good, I reckon."

"How can you tell it's fresh? Is it still warm?"

"Shh. He might be trying to trap us."

"You got a gun?"

Tommy shook his head like he creaked his neck. He whispered, "Never carry one, except when I'm hunting."

"I ain't got one either," I whispered back. "We have to trap him, I guess. Wonder if those ol' traps are here."

"Pa had gator traps?"

"Yeah, Pa took me trapping a lot."

He looked at me in disgust. "He ain't never took me trapping."

"Reach in your pocket." Tommy pulled out the whiskey recipe, smiled that charismatic smile of his, then stuffed in back in his top overall pocket.

"Guess we're even now, sis. You ain't getting it."

"I don't want it. I ain't a drinker."

"It's big business, sis. We could make it legit. Grandpa has showed me the ropes, and I took some business classes in college. Come here." I walked towards him, and he whispered to me. "Go get them gator traps, we will trap us some gators. They know I got the recipe, and they want it bad. They killed Pa, for it."

"There's one more landmark, Daddy told me never to share with anyone, not even with you. You can't even see where it is. I promised Papi."

"I'll go to the car."

I slithered my way through the tall savannah grass and found the last remaining hideout, the one that hopefully only Cletus Barnum, Pa, and myself knew of its existence. We called it Cat Burrow, after my great-great-grandma, Catherine Barnum, the former slave. Pa hid a lot of stuff in there. I needed to remember where it was. I walked about 50 feet northwest, angling toward the river. A smile came to me, the type I flashed when I won my first big case. I knew I was going to get our men. I returned to good old Cletus Tree, my faithful friend from childhood, and crawled inside through the bottom. I picked up one of the machetes and headed back to Cat Burrow, cut the thick savannah, and climbed into the tunnel. There were the traps, all five of them. I slid the machete back into the natural passageway and carried the snares up to Tommy.

"I got them, and maybe if we get these guys and sentence them, I'll share with you the other secret spot."

"Well, if you share the secret spot, I might hire you as my partner in the whiskey business." We shook hands.

"They like to strike at night, at least that's when Pa and Grandpa got it. Run into town and get us some food to cook or a few sandwiches, and we'll have ourselves a little family reunion here. Maybe a lost uncle and an old family friend will stop by. Get enough chicken for four. You know gators taste like chicken."

While Tomas went to town. I set up the gator traps and set them near the old rusted picnic table that we used to eat dinner on back in the day. They were hidden good in the long, tall, uncut savannah grass that you could lose an eight-year-old in. Tommy soon came back with our dinner. He got a bunch of fried chicken and beans and rice with some good old cornbread.

"That woman at the diner asked about you. Told her you were going to catch us some gator for later. She laughed cause I was a poet and didn't know it."

"I really miss this place, Tommy. Even though we were born in Nebraska, this is where we grew up. It's a shame it will all be under water one day."

"I'm sure you'll protest it. Hell, Sara, I might protest it. We could stand in front of the bulldozers."

"We're Barnums. Them bulldozers will dadgum run us over."

"We're the next generation of Barnums. Tain't nothing going to stop us. We need to pick our battles. Fighting off hydroelectricity probably ain't the best choice. Gotta get these folks into the 20th century."

"These yokels wouldn't know what to do with it. I think most of these folks are waiting for the Civil War to begin." I replied, staring at the water. "Tomas, I need to ask you something, and I ain't going to get your permission. Mami said you know all about the family, her parents and everything that went down with Daddy and the killers. What's going on?" I was ready to grab his shirt and shake an answer out of him.

My brother smiled, "I can't tell you everything right now. Mami knows you would have gotten yourself killed trying to get those guys. I've been chasing them down from Nuevo Laredo. Do you remember Judge Bourgeois, the man that married Mami and the warden? He has a place in Mexico. I've been on their trail all this time. That's why I haven't been around."

I looked at my brother and then glanced down the river and back north and watched a big hunk of driftwood pass. I grabbed some of the grass and tossed it into the river. "Do you think Mami had anything to do with it?"

Tomas put both hands behind his head and exhaled and turned his head slightly, staring at good ol' Cletus Tree. "I'm not sure, sis." He bit his lower lip and gazed down the banks of the river.

"Liar. You know something. Mami was distant when I talked to her last. She said you know all."

"I do, and that's why I quit the Feds. We are going to do this ourselves. If the Feds were involved, we'll have to take her down too." He grabbed a small log and tossed it into the river.

We downed the food and didn't save none for Early and Zeke. I grabbed the containers and took them up to the rusty old trash can and tossed them in and lit a match. I noticed there was another empty package of food tossed. It sat on top of my po boy wrapper. "Tommy, come here!" I hollered at him. "This yours from earlier?" I held the match next to my mouth and like I was kissing it and blew it out.

"Ain't never seen it before. Besides, I don't eat no burgers anymore." He mouthed, "we ain't alone."

He nodded for me to go to the table. I had other plans though and took off for Cat Burrow and then the Sabine. I had traps set up and the machete waited. "Let's go to the river. I know where the skiff is Tommy." I took off and he followed me. I sprinted, pushing the long grass away from my chest with my arms as my long legs splashed through the muddy swamp. If I was a horse, they would call me a mudder. In high school, they didn't call me swamp girl for nothing. Tommy was close behind, following in my path, running carefully since he didn't want to be gator bait.

Two men, one a fatter looking brute of a white man, came down into the river valley. The other one, who was mean and had a scar across his cheek, sliced the tall grass with a machete came down also. It was them. I snuck into Cat Burrow and grabbed the blade, ready for action and went on the attack. I went for Early first, because I figured he had the brains since Daddy told me about Uncle Zeke. I came up to him with both hands on the machete, slicing up the savannah as I went. My eyes fixed on my target, who was the killer of my family. He came closer, and I ran to the riverbank. He followed me, and I heard the snap of a trap shutting and down he went. Tommy grabbed his machete out of his hands, and I stood above him with my foot on his chest and blade at his throat.

"You killed my pa, now you going to die the same way he did, but slower."

"You can't kill me!" he protested.

I trailed the machete to his chest, and carefully carved a Klan cross in his chest. Blood splattered, but it was just a trace of red. "Before I kill you, you gonna talk." With one swing, I cut off the button of his trousers. "I' will cut something else off next if you don't start talking. I could cut them in half or get them both with one swing. What do you prefer?"

The proud assassin's voice sounded a little timid as tears fell from his eyes. His voice cracked. He sounded like a fifteen-year-old boy, and I cracked a smile. "Why torture me if you are going to kill me?"

"I might not kill you, just cut you up and toss you in the river. Sound familiar?" The machete slashed another button off his shirt and accidentally cut his bicep. "I know you killed my daddy, and my grandpa Cecil. I got witnesses on that." I placed the machete on his throat. "What about my other grandparents? You know the ones I never met?" The machete pressed tighter against his neck. He stuttered and gasped, as the scar on his face begged to enlarge. "You have something to say?"

He lay on his back with hands clenched and his free leg was raised, trying to squirm out of the trap. He looked pathetic, and he sweat like a whore in church. "I was paid. I worked for the government." His voice cracked, and the mercenary saw his defeat. His pinky finger was quickly removed with one quick snap of the blade. He howled and then continued. "They are all dead, but it was

Wilson behind it." I stepped off his chest and tossed him his finger. "Thanks, you can have this back." He threw it at me, but just like Ted Williams hit baseballs, I swung and hit his chopped finger deep into the grassland.

"Why my dad? Government wanted him dead, too?" The blade of the machete rested nicely on the scar on his cheek. "I can split this open again."

"No. Got hired by Zeke. He deserved the whiskey business since your father didn't want it. Zeke figured if he killed Bo, he'd get the business."

"He figured wrong, didn't he? Now take off your shoes." He kicked off his muddy boots and his trapped big toe flew off. "I want to let you go, cause I ain't gonna kill you." I stepped off his chest, but my foot made a slight circle on his torso. I pressed my 118 pounds on him, all my weight with my right foot and stepped off his screaming, weak bleeding body. "I have to check on my brother and uncle." Before I left the wounded and beaten assassin, I cleared all the phlegm from my throat, and deposited the goo on the scar which sliced up his face.

I walked up and Tommy had Uncle Zeke in handcuffs and stuck in a trap also. Tomas flashed his charming smile and said, "This was too easy. Dat man ain't smart enough."

"What are we going to do with him?"

"Frame him for that." He pointed to my outdoor torture chamber and the old man who lay in the tall grass, slowly bleeding, waiting to be devoured by an alligator.

"Yeah, I need to wash this stuff off of me." I went to the river and dunked the machete into the water of the Sabine, submerged myself, washing the blood off of my body and headed up toward where Tommy and Uncle Zeke waited. Tommy took off the hand cuffs, and I handed Zeke the machete and said, "Hold this." We left the Barnum land and headed to Caddo. We called the Sabine Parish sheriff's office from there. I never doubted we had the killer. Not sure about the former FBI agent who had more experience with crime solving.

Epilogue

Cecil Barnum was buried three days after Early Greene was devoured by alligators and drug into the Sabine River. The lackluster sheriff's department of Sabine Parrish never found the body, so Uncle Zeke was not convicted of his murder. He was charged and convicted of the murders of my father and grandfather and spent the rest of his life in Angola. Rumor had it he tried to escape and drowned in the Mississippi River.

Tomas Barnum worked at making Grandpa's whiskey legal and selling it in liquor stores across the country. He set up a distillery in Monroe and became a successful businessman. Tommy married a younger, black blues singer, and they had two kids. Of course, the oldest was a girl who was a terror from the start. She was my favorite and had the darkest complexion. The boy, Merle, the lightest Barnum I had seen in person or in photographs. He was proper, but even as a three-year-old, he distanced himself from the family and family traditions a bit. I couldn't see him as a radical activist.

When I visited Mami for the last time, I did it the old-fashioned way. I hopped the freight train that took me right by the state prison. I jumped off, guitar in hand, and took a tumble down the hill. I rolled in the tall wet grass, still covered by the morning dew. I got up smiling and did not see her. I camped out and wrote some folk songs and sang some of the spirituals that the Civil Rights movement folks used as anthems. I sang in the forest to the birds, squirrels, rabbits, and deer and hoped no one else was listening.

Soon I heard some people singing to the spirituals. They sounded like a church choir as they shouted out to the same rhythm I played and sang. We made good music, with me hidden in the forest and them ladies caged up behind the prison fence. Slowly, I left the forest, still strumming my E's and G's and singing praises to the almighty, who God willing, would free the people. I stood by the fence where Miriam and Mami escaped. It was my usual place to meet Mami, but she weren't there.

I kept singing and rousing up the convicts until they beat on the fence, trying to knock it down. Twenty or thirty of them pushed, just like the chain gangs of the twenties driving that steel rail down. They had the call and response, and the fence shook. I knew it was going down. The wire fence, with the razor loops on top came crashing. Alarms sounded while the prisoners followed me to the train. I quit performing and made a beeline for the railroad track. Looking around, I noticed the smoke from the westbound sky and the sounds of the freight train increased. In two shakes of a pigtail, I hopped on a vacant car as most of the newly freed black women captives made their escape to the Texas forest. The quickest ex-inmates hopped on the car with me. I played my spirituals again as the mini choir sang, while the train methodically chugged toward Louisiana.

The prisoners stayed with me, danced, prayed, and sang, "Free at last, free at last," and none of them joined me rolling down the hill once we crossed the Sabine. I got in my 1958 Chevy pick-up and headed back to Caddo where I now made my home. I sat on the dock and listened to my friends the bullfrogs, muskrats, gators, cicadas, and owls, the only creatures that would speak with me. My eyes watered with each croak of the bull frog and soon the tears flooded my face, like a dam burst. I've fought for things for so long now. Felt like it had been a lifetime, which it probably was. Mami and Papi took me around the streets when I was still in the womb and now, I sat alone in my house. There was a time I would only want it this way, but now, at the age of thirty-four, I felt loneliness instead of solitude.

I grabbed my guitar and started the shuffle. I should write some blues, since it was better than crying myself to sleep again, but the words didn't come. All I had was the shuffle, that damn replicating shuffle that I could play when I was eight. I set down Daddy's guitar and found a cheap one I no longer played and made a commitment not to play it again. It crashed against the wall as the neck split from the body and the strings snapped with a loud twang. I kicked and cursed my daddy. "Why couldn't I be a normal girl? Why did you make me want to change the world? Why, Daddy, why?"

Everyone from my life was gone. Miriam took off after Grandpa's funeral. Tommy barely called or wrote. He was much too busy with our business and his family. I didn't talk to the SLC folks anymore. I did burn bridges with them in the Topeka case. Burned bridges, prison, death and more death was my life. I never knew what happened to Mami, and the heartless soul I had become didn't care. I needed to make changes. Next morning, I decided to take a vacation and head down to Lafayette.

My favorite times as a kid was playing the Zydeco with Miriam, my boy crush, and Papi. I grabbed the remaining guitars that were spared the Sara-inflicted mutilation and headed south.

The music craze was Swamp Pop and Lafayette was the center and just over 200 miles away. The drive was beautiful, but all I thought about was being lonesome. I didn't really want or need a man in my life, but my clock was ticking. I wanted another Barnum to carry on this screwed-up legacy. Daddy once said no man is good enough for you, but I was out to prove him wrong, and I did.

I met him in Lafayette before one of these Swamp Pop shows. His name was Sammy Fontenot, when he played his brand of zydeco and Sam Fountain and the Mudbugs, when performing the brand of music making Lafayette more than a regional spec on the map. I dressed in overalls with no shirt, just the proper undergarments, and wore one an old straw hat of my daddy's. My harmonica nestled in the top pockets of my overalls, and I carried my trusty old Regal guitar. I set up shop on the street corner downtown and kicked off my shoes, where I was the most comfortable.

I strummed in rhythm, the rhythms Papi and Miriam played together, and I wailed some vintage tunes as well as a couple Daddy wrote. Pedestrians dropped anything from two bits to singles bills in my guitar case. Then this well-dressed man in a Zoot suit stood above me. He was medium height, looked Creole since he was a light-skinned black man, and wore a red and black hat. The suit was red, and he wore black pants and a black tie, with his red shirt.

He was a fine-looking man, and my guitar playing, and my heart skipped a beat. I kept playing and tried to be oblivious to this older man. He kept listening to me play. When I took my gaze off the

Regal, I looked directly at his eyes, even though they were covered with his dark sunglasses, and it appeared he was gleaming at me. I quickly turned away, trying not to miss the beat or a note, and kept on playing until I finished the song. He didn't applaud but stared at me, like he knew me from somewhere. He reached for his yellow belt and took off his money clip. I watched him count out five twenties.

"This for joining the Mudbugs," and then he dropped a C-note into my guitar case, "and this is for a street musician. I'm Sammy Fontenot, from Houma. You probably know me as Sam Fountain."

"I like you better as Sammy Fontenot. I'm not crazy about all that radio stuff you guys play. Sometimes, I get sick of listening to it. I like the dirty, greasy, bluesy stuff you play better." The ends of my mouth curled in a little smile. My eyes brightened, too.

"You've heard the good stuff then?"

"Yeah, I got records, plus I've seen you in Natchitoches and Baton Rouge a few years ago. Saw you up in Shreveport last month. I just wish folks playing lala would stick to it. Stop the Swamp Pop."

"You know it's for the money."

"Yeah, well music should be from the heart, not for the bank account."

"That's easy to say from a white woman."

"I ain't a white woman. Well, maybe about this part white." I held my thumb and index finger about two inches apart and decreased the size of the space between them. "Well, maybe this much white," as the gap in my digits increased, and then I shrunk them again. I was fascinated by this man.

"We playing a show tonight and we gotta rehearse. Head over to Breaux Bridge. That gigs tonight at La Poussiere."

"How do I get there?"

He just smiled, turned his head and like a Count, and pointed to a 1955 Cadillac. I struggled to get to my feet, probably cause my knees were knocking, so he reached out his hand and helped this lady up. The guitar went into the case, and I was fittingly about to become a Mudbug. Sammy held the Caddy door open for me, and I smiled the most flirtatious smile I ever given a man, which ain't saying much. His dark sunglasses stared right at me, and I knew this man would be my donor. We got to Breaux Bridge quicker than a hot knife through butter as Mr. Fontenot weaved that Caddy through the sparse traffic.

"I used to run whiskey down there on the peninsula for my daddy. Made me some good money."

"My daddy used to run when he was a kid. His daddy made the best damn whiskey. My brother makes the stuff legal now. We call it Grandpa's Hill Whiskey."

"You don't say. I got me a bottle of that stuff. It's my favorite whiskey. Like it better than that Tennessee crap. You want some?"

"I don't drink. Not even beer or wine. I want to stay in control."

"A couple of good ol snorts helps me unwind before and after a show. Well goddamn, we are here. Let me help you with your stuff." I carried my guitar, and he grabbed my bag, which weren't that heavy, but Sammy showed true signs of a gentleman, (or a ladies' man), but I didn't care. He wasn't going to be my husband, just a lover, and the man who will give me my child.

We went into the beautiful hall. "I ain't never played in a place like this. I only played in some juke joints up in Caddo and my daddy's ol' place off the Sabine."

He took off his dark shades, then put them back, but they were setting on the bridge of his nose and tilted. I noticed his beautiful dark eyes looking at me religiously. "Your daddy ran a place on the Sabine? You that little teenage girl who sang and played guitar? Well everyone had the hots for you girl! Damn, girl, let's start practicing."

"Practicing what?" I asked him seductively. I batted my eyes, twisting my long, dark hair and my lips got real pouty. I even licked them my with tongue circling them a few times. I hoped I was doing it right. He took my hand and led us back to the dressing room where we could be alone.

He placed his wide lips upon my waiting and soft lips and gave me the kiss I've waited for my entire life. The commie folk singer that I dated for a few months, kisses weren't doodly squat compared to Sam Fontenot. We kissed standing up for an eternity, as our tongues explored each other's mouths like they were lost in a deep cavern. His wandering hands grabbed my butt and worked their way up to my breasts. I moaned, and my body ached for him. I needed that man desperately to fill the void in me that has been my empty love life.

When we finished, I leaned over and kissed him deep and soulful on those magic lips of his and whispered ever in his ear. "We need to do this more often."

He picked himself up, and then carried me to his private dressing room where we laid down on a bed and held each other close, slowly kissing and cuddling. "That was just rehearsal girl. Can't wait for the performance."

"After the show, Sammy?"

"Yeah, baby, foreplay will be the show. The real performance will follow the gig."

The rest of the band soon came backstage to join us rehearsing music. There were a lot of folks who needed introduction. Ain't going to name them here, but there was another guitarist, the drummer, the saxophone man, a stand-up bass player, the accordionist, and of course, a fiddler. The fiddler was an older white man with a cross shaped scar across his left cheek. The band was mixed with Creole from down South and a couple of white guys: the fiddler and bass player. They eyed me over, not sure what to think of their new girl singer and guitarist. My eyes looked at them, moving from one creepy guy to the other. Extra attention was put on the fiddle player, since there wasn't much trust in my blood for fiddle players with scars across their cheeks.

Sammy came and put his arm around me. "Now guys make Sara feel welcome. This girl got some soul and blues in her blood. She can wail on dat guitar, and she got a voice that can shut up a bull frog, and Ol Sammy got himself a hankering for her. So, you Mudbugs better make her feel welcome. Now you and me, we going to do harmonies and some duets."

"I ain't never played on a band before except Daddy's back on the Sabine."

"Follow my leads. You sing after I do, just repeat the words."

It was time for the foreplay, the prelude leading up to Sammy Fontenot's second performance of the evening. My knees and legs shook, like I was a juking away, but that was before we kicked into the music. I sweat away like a whore at church, and kind of felt that way too. I'm still not sure if I was here for the music or to get a sperm donor, and that man was definitely Sammy Fontenot. I knew if I we kept fooling around, one time I'd get lucky and that man would impregnate me. That was what I was after.

Grandpa had Daddy and Papi had Tommy and me and now Tommy had his kids. I hadn't got nothing right now, no one to carry on my tradition. I had no legacy to call my own. Guess some of my lawyering, the boycott, and the other projects I was involved in to give us minorities in the South and the rest of the country rights can be my legacy. But I really needed someone to carry on the tradition. I noticed Barnum's don't live too long.

Perspiration moistened my forehead, the curtain slowly raised, and we stood in front of a crowd estimated to be about 500 people. Daddy's juke joint held about 50 or 60, but if you wanted to shake it around a lot, maybe 40 people could get in at the same time. I stared at these folks that came to see us play. Suddenly, like I got Jesus or got hit by a cool wind, my lips parted, and a confident smile came on my face. It didn't hurt that Sam was shaking and dancing in his Red Zoot suit, staring at me. We kicked off the first song, and it was an old Cajun waltz played in 6/8 time. As I strummed, I stared deeply into Mr. Fontenot's dark shades, wishing I could see his beautiful eyes. Waiting patiently for the harmonies and duets so I could share the microphone with him and get my moist and parting lips close to his delicious lips, only to torture the man.

This went on for two sets, one set for Sammy and Mudbugs, and the other for just Sam Fontenot, where we would liven up the place and knock off the pop crap and play the bluesy lala styled zydeco, this swamp lady was accustomed to. When the radio friendly songs ended, the crowd dispersed a little and it was time for fun. As a band they let it fly, and this girl loved to let it fly, I jammed on stage looking at the potential father of my unmade child with love and lust. Yeah this was foreplay, and I loved it. Back in Sammy's hotel room after the show, I cherished every moments.

We toured together for six months, from Louisiana to New York. Except for living in Nebraska, I had never been out of the South before so traveling to these big East Coast cities was a culture shock for me. Those city slickers thought this girl was a bumpkin cause all

I did was look up at the tall building, amazed by their height and girth. I was in my overalls, and nothing else, and saw people's pointing and laughing at me. Da hell with them I was playing at the Apollo.

By the time the band got to the East Coast, the Mudbugs were coming apart. Thinking some fancy French chef was going to chop us up and put us in an Etouffee. The saxophonist quit the band down in Richmond. The accordionist quit in Raleigh, but we replaced him with a lady who the bass player took a fancy to, even though they were both married. Sammy and I were still going strong, even though we were both exhausted. I had to drag his butt up every day, but he always got up. Sometimes he hacked up the weirdest color phlegm I ever saw, but he always performed, on stage and off.

The next gig after the Apollo was the Newport Folk Festival up in Rhode Island. Lots of people and lots of bands were going to be there. It was a folk revival happening up in the Northeast, but to me, it was the music I grew up with. Somewhere I got out of touch with what was going on music wise, since Jerry Lee and Elvis weren't my thing, and neither was swing. Well the morning of the festival, I puked right after I awoke. Before I let it go, I looked at myself in the mirror and there was a radiant glow on my face, and I knew my little legacy was inside me. I wasn't sure if I should tell Sammy or not, so I waited. Just then, he came crawling into the bathroom. Stepping back a few steps toward the hotel sink, I watched him as he slowly put his head above the toilet and let go. Blood spewed from his mouth with his vomit. This continued for a couple of more times. I helped him up, but he sat on the toilet.

"Sara, honey", he said panting. The poor man was pale and looked like the devil snuck inside our room. He wiped his eyes and mouth with a damp wash cloth. "Baby, I'm not going to make it. I can't play the show tonight. Think this cancer finally caught up with me. Not even sure I'll make it through the night. You'll have to do the show. You know all the parts anyway."

"Can't we cancel?"

"Sammy Fontenot has never cancelled a show in his life. I always said I would only miss a show if I'm dead. That's probably going to happen now, but we gotta contract. Play on."

"Baby, I got something to tell you, too. I'm going to be a momma." His eyes brightened for a minute, just like he had a flashlight, and then he smiled. Then those beautiful eyes closed for the last time and I heard a sigh, and a long deep breath. I tried to help him, but there no breath. His chest was soon covered with my tears as my dam burst, and they could not control the deluge. I called an ambulance and gathered the band up. Sammy Fontenot was pronounced dead at the age of 42. An autopsy said he had lung, liver, colon, and pancreatic cancer. He never told me. I suspected something but was too wrapped up in my aspiration.

Sammy wanted us to play, and we did. I was now center stage, and it was heartbreaking, painful, and emotional. It made for some awesome music, and we were invited back to next year's show.

It was a long eight-month tour, but the three days after the tour seemed to last longer than the previous months. Preparing for the funeral, making arrangements, talking to family, and trying to be nice to his friends, family, and all the fans wore this girl out. I didn't know his family, I was only acquaintances with the band, and we fired half of them during the tour. The only folks who I felt comfortable with, surprisingly, were the fans that showed up in Houma for the viewing and the ceremony. They by far, outweighed his friends and family. His family didn't know me, and his friends down here in Houma figured I was responsible.

"Girl, what kind of drugs were you giving him?"

"Girl, what was you poisoning little Sammy for?"

"Who the fuck are you? Take your sorry ass back where you came from."

Yes, the comments of those mourning a loved one. I found my Chevy and fired it up and was on my way to Monroe to visit my brother. I realized once again, I had no one. It was late at night when I arrived at his plantation-style home. The home was a large, modern home, recently built. It was a four-bedroom mansion off the water of Monroe's version of Black Bayou. Tomas greeted me at the door. He took one look down at the tightened sun dress, and he smiled a smile that must have melted his wife's resistance. He had the smile of a movie star, but it was a trusting smile.

"Welcome to parenthood. Where's the father?"

"Don't you mean who's the father?"

"You were never a whore. I know you know who the father is."

"Have you ever heard of Sammy Fontenot of Sammy and the Mudbugs?"

"No way!"

"I was on the road with him the last eight months. I saw him take his last breath. Cancer got him, too. He played to the end and had game until the end."

Tomas hugged me. I was never a hugging person, but sometimes the little guy gave me what I needed. Small tears soon became puddles on his shoulder. It felt good to cry.

"I'll be with you for the baby, big sis." He held me tighter.

"You're all I got, little bro."

"No, you don't. You have more than you know. Tell you what I'm gonna do. You can crash here tonight. I have another surprise."

It was Miriam. "Girl you gotta bun in the oven I see? Sam Fontenot's the dad?"

"Well yeah, but he died before last year's festival. I got invited back but I need a band."

"I hadn't played in years, but that dirty blues singer is playing. He don't like me coming with on his shows, but I gonna show his ass up."

"Which guitar do ya want? Stella or the Regal?"

"I always liked Stella. It brings the swamp out. "I whipped my switchblade out, and the blade snapped out like it was shot out of cannon. Miriam smiled at me almost like we were long lost lovers. "Here's your slide."

She took the switch handle first and followed my lead. It seemed like we were back in 1944, and Miriam Landry and I rode the next Greyhound bus, away from integration, away from shared toilets, and back to Jim Crow and segregated Louisiana. "I'm so happy to home Sara. Dat mean ol' man gonna be mad at me, but he got nurses there in rehab he can abuse."

February 19, 1958, the great-grandson to late Cecil Barnum, the grandson of the late Bo Barnum, and the son of the late Sam Fontenot was born. Tommy and Miriam were in the hospital to take care of me. I named him Roberto Thomas Barnum, and I knew right away he would change the world.

That summer Miriam and I played at the Newport Folk Festival. In the background, fancy sailboats and yachts anchored in the harbor, and it was the two of us, her on the Stella, and me on my Regal. Little Berto was in back with Tommy and his family. Our set was about thirty minutes long, but we were able to sneak in eight songs. We ran a little long, and we got good ovations, but that is not the story. The story came from the legendary bluegrass band that played early evening. Earl announced it as the sun set over the harbor. "This is a story about an old banjer player who fought prejudice with this." He held that five string up, so all the kids could see.

Lester continued, "He helped battle racism with this here guitar." He held that Martin D28 up high, twirled it around before his partner and him cranked a new tune out.

The Ballad of Bo Barnum

Bo Barnum came from Texarkana,
It was the Arkansas Side,
When his family needed the money
He'd get in the jalopy and go for a ride.

Took the hooch down to Coushatta,
And sometimes down to the Pontchartrain.
Most of the runs were to El Dorado
And that is where he met Early Greene.

Hopped a freight and went to Omaha,
Got a job doing real man work.
Shoveling coal, while sleeping in a rail car,

But Bo, met himself a girl.

Got married and had two kids,
So, he got a job, driving a truck,
Delivering food to the people in town,
And that's when it all went down.

He moved down South where the Gators grow.
Right on the edge of a dark bayou.
But he built a jive to play zydeco.
People came from all over, for his zydeco.

Bo Barnum died in Louisiana,
Or was it Texas I don't know.
But Bo Barnum came from Texarkana
Yes, it was the Arkansas side.

I looked at Tommy, and he had that movie star smile. I knew he was responsible. Then I looked at my little Berto. He smiled, laughed, and cooed, like a happy baby should. He must have known.

Tommy clued me in. "This man came looking for a trail for an old folksinger who used to live around here. Also, they looked for a fiddle player. Told me those guys use to run together back in the 20s. Gifted musicians, both of them. I told them to follow me. I can help you with the banjo player, and we got in the car and headed to your place. Got the old recordings and played them. 'What's his name,' they asked me, and I told them, 'Bo Barnum, but I knew him as Pa. Sara Barnum, my sister is playing at the Newport Folk Festival.'"

Mr. Lomax smiled and rerecorded Pa's 78s and put them onto two 33s. The man made three copies, one for me, and one for you, and one for him to take back to DC. "I hope you enjoy them."

Next up was the old but famous blues singer also known as Miriam's former lover. He led off with a song called "The Bo Barnum Blues" as the harbor lights had overtaken the sunset.

Bo Barnum was the man, who fell in love with that Mexican girl.
Said Bo Barnum fell in love with a Mexican girl.
That sweet little thing was his world.

Bo Barnum was there when her parents were found shot dead.
He was there when her ma and pa, were shot to death.
Nowhere to go, they were soon wed.
He married the pretty girl and they had a daughter and son,
I said he married that girl, and they had a daughter and son
Their life was always on the run.

They watched as that black man, swinging from a tree
They watched a Mexican man swinging from a tree.
Justice they felt could never be free.

They moved to Louisiana, by the banks of the Sabine.
They lived in Louisiana on the banks of the Sabine.
His daughter watched him fall off the train.

Not in the papers or radio, didn't even make the news,
Not in the papers or radio, it didn't even make the news.
Keep fighting people, The Bo Barnum Blues.

I was crying, Tommy rubbed his eyes, and my Berto, he kept cooing in rhythm.

Also, by Rob Cooke Sara's Swamp Blues and The Lost Song of Miriam Landry.

Follow Rob Cooke on Facebook.

https://www.facebook.com/Rob-Cooke-661803964000938/

And on Twitter.

https://twitter.com/BoBarnum1

Lyrics by Rob Cooke.

Cornbread, Crawfish or Me

copyright 2017

Springtime in Louisiana
A Lot better than Alabama
At least that's what I've seen
Cornbread is Sweeter
Crawfish are boiling
And this lady is waiting on the banks of the Sabine

Oh Yankee Man keep rolling
Oh Cowboy keep on a strolling
Let me grab that Creole man,
with the banjo in his hand
and two step the night away.
Cornbread, Crawfish or Me
Cornbread, Crawfish or Me
You don't have to choose,
You can have all three,
Cornbread, Crawfish and Me.

The accordion is a rocking,
The guitar is chopping,
and the ladies are prettier than me.
The music much sweeter,
The night getting hotter,
Come love on me down on the banks of the Sabine

Oh Yankee Man keep rolling
Oh Cowboy keep on a strolling
Let me grab that Creole man,
with the banjo in his hand
and two step the night away.

Cornbread, Crawfish or Me
Cornbread, Crawfish or Me
You don't have to choose,
You can have all three,
Cornbread, Crawfish and Me

Jonesboro Arkansas.

Copyright 2018
It all went down in the middle of the town of Jonesboro, Arkansas.
There was the man, guitar in hand, but blowing a harmonica.
Til was driving, I was riding in Jonesboro, Arkansas.

I climbed in the back, or her new Cadillac,
in Jonesboro, Arkansas
In hopped the man, with guitar in hand,
But blowing that harmonica"

We were on the run, down Highway 1
Leaving Jonesboro, Arkansas,
Then Til had a plan, with that brown skinned man,
blowing that harmonica,
Until he looked to the back, of her new cadillac,
and liked what he saw
That little brown skinned girl, became his world
South of Jonesboro, Arkansas.

I was on the run, on Highway 1
escaping from the law.
Til was dead, and so was the man,
that use to play the harmonica,

I had to run, but I had no gun,
took the ferry to Arkansas,
with nowhere to hide, and no one on my side,
just had his harmonica
I went on the run, up Highway 1
to Jonesboro, Arkansas

Take Your Hands Off My Mojo.
Copyright 2019

Don't you go messing with my mojo,
Don't touch you above my knee,
Don't be messing with my mojo,
And keep your hands of my gris-gris."

"I don't want your mojo,
It's not your mojo that I want
"I'm not after your mojo,
Mwen vle fe seks avek ou."

"Baby don't mess with my mojo
You touched me above the knee
Dat's messing up my mojo

And don't mess with my gris gris.
Baby don't you mess with my mojo
You know I had plenty of dat.
Oh baby, don't be messing with my mojo,
Eske ou vle danse
"What if I'm that man
That you're supposed to see

What if that little red mojo bag
That you call gris gris
Now red is the color of love
Maybe we is supposed to be
This comes from the Lord above,
And that bag you call gris-gris."

"Baby you mess with my mojo
Touch me above my knee
Baby you can have my mojo
Thanks to my gris gris.